DIVIDED ROADS

By

Ned Mansour

© 2001 by Ned Mansour. All rights reserved.

No part of this book may be reproduced, stored in a retrieval system, or transmitted by any means, electronic, mechanical, photocopying, recording, or otherwise, without written permission from the author.

ISBN: 0-7596-5287-2

This book is printed on acid free paper.

1stBooks – rev. 04/19/02

"Many people will walk in and out of our lives.

But only true friends will leave footprints in your hearts.

To handle others, use your heart."

                                              Elenor Roosevelt

"When you come to a fork in the road, take it!"

                                              Yogi Berra

FORWARD

This project began as a simple magazine article about the world of multinational mergers and acquisitions. During the course of my early research, Peter Franklin's name often surfaced as the "man" to talk with on this subject.

After repeated unsuccessful attempts to speak with him, I finally secured a half-hour "audience" with the infamous Mr. Franklin in February 1999. I must confess that I was only able to penetrate his calendar after I mentioned to his assistant that Pete would be the focal point of the article. Instead of talking about business exploits as I had expected, Pete digressed to a pressing personal topic. A short time later, I was introduced to Rocky.

My first task was to convince these two cynical characters to allow me to record their thoughts and observations. But Rocky quickly saw the merits of my proposed approach. I suspect that Pete wouldn't have agreed if Rocky had not issued a challenge. To be specific, Rocky openly referred to Pete as "chicken" after he first declined. In the interest of obtaining frank and candid comments, I agreed not to disclose Rocky's comments to Pete and vice versa before publication of this book.

The end result was far more interesting than I could have ever imagined. You will soon understand why I dropped the dry topic of mergers and acquisitions in favor of the Pete and Rocky saga.

You usually expect to see an author's acknowledgements and comments at the beginning of a book. I have, however, included them at the end because of my concern that they might give you unavoidable hints about the story you are about to read. Nevertheless, one acknowledgement is appropriate at the beginning. Thank you Pete and Rocky for being yourselves.

Ned Mansour

CHAPTER 1

INTRODUCTION BY PETER

At first, the idea of describing myself to a complete stranger felt awkward. Ned, however, suggested that in order for me to be as candid as possible, I should pretend that I am speaking with a therapist.

Actually, this will be an interesting exercise because the most difficult part for me will be to remain objective. My family claims that I have a tendency to stretch the truth, particularly when talking about myself.

First of all, my full name is Peter James Franklin, Jr. and I was born on April 1, 1946 in New York City, the eldest son of Peter Sr. and Nancy.

All of my family members, business associates and close friends call me Pete, except for my mother, who still insists on calling me "Skip."

In the interest of full disclosure, you should know that people who sit opposite me in business dealings sometimes call me horrible names.

I say horrible, but I readily admit that in most instances, the name-calling is probably justified.

Recently, while sitting in a stall in the men's room of our offices, an adversary from a competing investment banking firm called me three things in one sentence. I won't repeat what he said, but you can use your imagination; in fact, they are the kind of things you would say to someone who cuts you off while driving.

This guy didn't know I was in the stall; I actually lifted my feet to remain concealed, hoping to hear him and his client discussing their negotiating tactics. Instead, I heard a mouthful about myself. So, his labels of me were more than fitting. I can be a real jerk at times.

I could write an entire paper about the various "tags" that have been attached to me, not only in my business career, but sometimes in my personal life as well. Some of the labels have been so exotic that I have had to use a dictionary to decipher their meaning. One guy was so mad at me recently that he called me an "unscrupulous Hessian." I couldn't recall what "Hessian" meant, but I certainly knew it was by no means a flattering term. So, without saying a word, I immediately exited the conference room, went to my office and returned with a dictionary. After reading the meaning of "Hessian", I told him that he was very accurate in his description; I am a conscienceless mercenary.

When my opposition gets really pissed during negotiations, I know I'm making an impact. This is when I really shine. I enjoy putting people on their heels.

The worst part is when I negotiate international transactions and am called something in a foreign language. Without an interpreter, I have to make an educated guess, but I know that whatever is said can't possibly be complimentary.

Anyway, enough about names. Please feel free to call me Pete, unless I do something that irritates you, in which case you have a blank canvas on which to paint me in any manner that you may desire.

I suspect that you are already beginning to dislike me. That's really not entirely fair since I have just started giving you my background. You should at least give me a reasonable chance.

Actually, my clients love me because I produce positive results for them. This is not an exaggeration; otherwise I wouldn't be in such demand.

I seem to recall that I was once a very decent person; at least that is what my wife often says. I didn't become an asshole overnight. It took nearly three decades of hard work and dedication to acquire this much attitude.

Let's return to my background.

My two sisters, Maggie and Amy, arrived evenly spread apart, two and four years after my birth.

When I was six years old, my parents decided to move to a new house near Darien, Connecticut, but my father maintained a small apartment in the city since he often worked long hours. Occasionally, he would be missing for weeks at a time while engaged in major projects as a senior corporate partner in a major New York law firm. In fact, there were times when he would not even join us for Thanksgiving and Christmas vacations.

Forget about summer vacations; I can only remember him joining us for three of them and one of those didn't count because he spent most of the time visiting an important client who lived in the area we were vacationing.

As far as I could tell in my youth, my parents had a civil relationship, but they never exhibited any affection. Sometimes I wonder how the three of us were conceived. I am told that I look very much like my father, so we know it wasn't the mailman or milkman in my case. However, I think that Maggie looks a bit like the tennis teacher and Amy like the handyman who often worked around our house.

Just kidding – I'm concerned that this description may bore you if I don't spice it up here and there. I should alert you that my family hates my sick sense of humor.

Despite my father's constant absence, I have good memories of my boyhood home, which is still Mother's residence. It is a colonial style house, with four bedrooms and three baths. I had my own room and Maggie and Amy shared their bedroom. The house has 11 rooms, plus a full basement, and sits on over an acre of wooded land. It was a great place to grow up and I had a blast playing with my friends in our yard.

Anyway, Father was in charge of bringing home the money and Mother was responsible for raising the three us. Mom also took care of a menagerie of pets, including rats, birds, hamsters, two cats and three dogs, including Otto, my German shepherd. He was my best pal from the time I was six until I reached my junior year of high school. Just so you don't think I have always been heartless, you should know that one of the lowest moments in my early life was the day Otto died.

I was always a top student in high school with an overall grade average in the low "A" range. By today's standards, this would have equated to a 3.8 grade point average.

Even though I did well in mundane subjects, I seemed to gravitate more towards the arts, whether visual or theatrical. I can't really explain why, but I always felt comfortable on stage during school productions.

While Father rarely became involved in our day-to-day lives, he was always concerned about our academic progress and sports activities. He didn't attend any of our games or other events – he simply wanted to know our grades and whether we won a particular competitive event.

I was expected to excel in sports, particularly football and baseball, like my father, who was a three-sport star. Unfortunately for both of us, I was pretty much a bungler when it came to sports.

On one unforgettable occasion, my father somehow found out that my high school baseball team was competing for the league title. I think Mom told him. Anyway, he arrived unexpectedly and sat behind our dugout. He didn't say a word to me and I wouldn't have noticed he was there, but my friend pointed him out to me.

Prior to the game, our coach announced that our regular right fielder had been kicked off the team because his grades were below the minimum. The other reserve outfielder was out for the season with a broken leg. So, without having to say a word, the coach looked in my direction, as did the rest of the team. I am sure they collectively thought that the season would surely end with a loss.

In my defense, you should know that I was being pressed into duty after either warming the bench or serving as the first base coach for the better part of the prior 22 games. You can't expect a third-stringer to be competitive in a big game after collecting splinters in his ass all season.

Had they asked me to participate in a spitting contest, I am confident I would have successfully delivered. I had so much practice spitting in the dugout during that season that I could hit a small object five feet away.

Unlike other players who sat on the bench, I actually enjoyed the role. I even became a decently proficient first base coach, giving signs to our batters and telling our runners when to advance to second base.

The truth be known, however, I'm probably one of the few people who has been hurt while coaching first base. During an earlier game that season, I was standing in the coaching box while the opposing team was taking infield practice. Instead of watching the practice session, I was playfully clowning around trying to attract the attention of a girl I knew who was sitting in the stands. The shortstop's throw went over the first baseman's head and the ball hit me right in the nuts. I saw stars – it literally took my breath away. That was a truly embarrassing moment – to top it off, it seemed that everyone in school heard about the incident. I was surprised that it wasn't a headline in the school paper.

As you can tell, I never enjoyed playing baseball, but I had to play because Father expected it of me. I was terrible at it, but since I was a senior and our coach carried as many players as he could, I made the team. I frankly hoped that I would never have to play.

Sometimes, when we were winning by 10 or more runs, I would be sent to right field in the late innings. Rarely was the ball hit in my direction. I only batted six times all year, never getting a hit. In fact, I never hit the ball, not even a foul ball.

In the fourth inning of the championship game, the opposing team had the bases loaded, with two outs. A fly ball was hit in my direction in right field – I only needed to move a few feet to get under this ball and make a routine catch for the third out. However, something happened which to this day still bothers me – simply stated, I dropped the ball, both literally and figuratively. Three runs scored and we ended up losing the game by one run. Some of my teammates tried to console me, but it was to no avail. I had screwed up and let my team and myself down.

That was the last time I played baseball and it also marked the final time Father attended any athletic event for my sisters or me. After I dropped the ball and went into the dugout with tears in my eyes, I looked towards the stands to see my father. I know he was there when I misplayed the fly, but he had already returned to the city by the end of the inning. To his credit, he never mentioned that game to me.

Not only did Father miss most of our sporting events, he also managed to be inaccessible during my theatrical and musical performances. In addition to performing in school plays, I very much enjoyed playing the piano as part of the school jazz band. This was my real passion, but I could never make this admission to father. He always expected me to be a superior student, a super athlete and eventually, a successful attorney.

Even though Mother, and sometimes my grandparents, attended my performances, Father missed virtually every one. One exception was our high school production of "***Oklahoma***" , in which I had a leading role. The previous evening, I overheard Mother shouting at Father during a telephone conversation – she was castigating him for missing all of our past performances. This conversation must have struck a cord with him because he unexpectedly showed up for the play. After the performance, he actually seemed to relish the favorable comments that were made about me by teachers and parents.

During my senior year of high school, when the time came to apply for colleges, I decided on my preferred schools and waited until one Saturday afternoon to approach Father. I really wasn't sure whether I needed his blessing, but I decided to play it safe by seeking his approval.

I'll never forget the way he quietly looked at the list and nodded occasionally. Finally after a pregnant silence, he asked the question which I had anticipated – namely, whether I had considered applying to his alma mater, Princeton University. Even though I had prepared for weeks to give him a cogent response for electing not to apply, I "choked" big-time and made an inane comment, which was not at all persuasive.

The truth be told, I simply did not want to follow in Father's footsteps. His interests were far different from mine. While he may have enjoyed attending the theatre once or twice each year, no doubt he would have thought I was crazy if I majored in something like drama or theatre arts.

I'm sure he would have said something like: "How do you expect to earn a living with that kind of degree - as a high school drama teacher?"

Please understand that Father was an honorable man. He was a well-respected attorney and held in high esteem by those who worked with and for him. As a father, he never raised his voice or touched any of us in a violent manner. But, he was certainly stern, and treated us like junior associates in his firm. By this I mean, there was no warmth- just brief and unemotional conversations. Actually, conversations suggest a two-way dialogue – it was typically more of a monologue in which he did the talking.

Even when he was sitting around the house on weekends, Father never seemed relaxed. He was always formal - both in his nature and in the manner of his dress. At mealtimes, everything had to be proper, starting with the placement of the silverware and napkins. But when he wasn't around, dinner was a free-for-all, with constant badgering between the three kids.

Father always intimidated Maggie and I while we were growing up, even if he said nothing at all to us. We acted differently just being in his presence. However, for some reason, he was never a threat to Mom or Amy. Mom basically ignored him and Amy was always a free spirit; she didn't seem to ever care about getting his approval. Perhaps it was because he was hardly around while she was growing up.

I suppose I could have mustered the courage to tell Father that my real interests were in the theatre and arts, but I felt that I would be letting him down by not following his direction. I will never know whether he would have accepted another career choice had I been adamant about my desires. In all fairness, I never asked him, so I really can't blame him.

In the end, I applied to Princeton and joined my father for a personal tour of the campus followed by a private meeting with the President of the University. I hated to admit it, but the tour was truly impressive and yet I was still focused on other schools because I didn't want to be my father.

By the time I received my acceptance from Princeton, I (we) had already determined it was the first choice. In retrospect, I have no regrets about this decision because I immensely enjoyed my undergraduate years, during which I majored in history and minored in theatre arts. I also joined a fraternity and established lifelong relationships with some of my "brothers".

After graduating from Princeton, I was again expected to follow my father's trail by attending Columbia University Law School. This time I confronted Father and told him I had absolutely no desire to attend law school. After working at his law firm for two summers while in college, I knew that the legal profession wouldn't be my career choice.

I suspect that a psychologist would say that my decision against pursuing a legal career was my own way of finally rebelling against Father. Not so, I just couldn't stand the work, particularly the litigation side. There is so much wasted time preparing papers that eventually prove to be meaningless. I wanted to do something more constructive with my life.

Father first suggested that I consider specializing in corporate or tax law, but I couldn't possibly imagine doing this kind of work all of my life.

To my surprise, after a while, Father eventually accepted my decision to seek an MBA at New York University. I have a feeling that Mother put the squeeze on him to let me do what I wanted. Also, I think he assumed I would come to my senses and seek a law degree after I earned an MBA.

After graduating from NYU, I worked for two years in the bond-trading department of a major investment-banking firm, which happened to be a major client of Father's law firm. However, I have always told myself that I earned the position on my own. The fact that he called the chairman of the bank didn't necessarily mean that the job was automatically mine.

Whenever Father asked about my job, I told him it was exciting work and I therefore had no desire to enter law school. In truth, however, I was bored to death.

I was then approached about a position with a mid-size banking firm specializing in corporate matters. I was recruited to become a mergers and acquisitions specialist and I accepted the offer in a heartbeat.

It was probably the smartest decision I ever made during my business career. I loved the work, particularly the excitement of putting mega-sized deals together. But most of all, I enjoyed the recognition and the big bucks. I felt like a real hotshot.

During the early years at the firm, I was truly the fair-haired boy. It was apparent that I was destined to become a partner earlier than my peers. Actually, very few members of my "starting class" became partners – only three of the original 19 associates earned this honor. Sadly, my closest friend didn't make the cut after practicing with the firm for eight years – he was justifiably bitter, feeling he should have been told much earlier that his chances for partnership were slim at best.

I was literally a madman during those early years, working more hours than any other associate – like my father, I had precious little personal time. Unfortunately, I thought that my lifestyle would improve when I became a partner, but this wasn't the case, at least not for me. In fact, I became even more absorbed in my career.

On those rare occasions when I attended social events, they were typically firm or client-related. One evening, I attended a cocktail party hosted by our firm's office manager, who was celebrating two memorable events, his 25th anniversary with the firm and the college graduation of his only child, Katherine.

I was immediately attracted to her, but she didn't seem to have any interest in me. Every time I tried to speak with her, she immediately spotted someone else she knew at the far end of the room. There was no question that she was blowing me off.

I didn't think I would ever see Kathy again, but much to my surprise, her parents invited me to join them and Kathy for a Sunday dinner at their house. I think her parents had said good things about me; otherwise, I doubt she would have agreed to reconsider me. Unlike me, she respected her father and they had an incredibly close relationship.

I must admit I was somewhat conceited in those days and I am sure this was a major turn off for Kathy. This is not to suggest that I am less arrogant now; trust me, I am not. However, in the past, I had nothing concrete to back up my inflated ego; now, I do.

In any event, I toned down my conceit and acted fairly normal with Kathy. I quickly realized that unlike other women I had dated, the successful banker attitude was a negative with Kathy. Anyway, we started seeing each other on a regular basis. Thankfully, Kathy was familiar with the stressful life of an investment banker and she didn't seem to expect me to have much free time.

But somehow, between my hectic schedule and Kathy's as a teacher, we managed to have a few free weekends together. These were truly the best of times for us.

The difference between then and now is that I used to listen to Kathy, but unfortunately I no longer do; consequently, she gave up long ago her futile attempt to focus me on priorities. In the past, she helped me maintain a sense of balance and even though I was never a full-time husband or dad, at least I spent more time at home in the early years.

We were married when I was 29 and Kathy 23. She stopped teaching two years after our marriage when she became pregnant with Josh. Jennie arrived eighteen months after Josh.

I focused on Kathy, Josh and Jennie during the first five or so years, but then, I became more like my father, meaning I had little free time for my family. As for Kathy, she became like my mother, which for all intents and purposes meant that she was essentially raising the children as a single mom.

To this day, I really can't understand how I turned out to be like my father. In my teenage and college years, I had promised myself that my family would never take a back seat to my career. I suppose it is akin to an abused son who turns out to be an abusive father – even though he vowed never to let himself become like his father.

Since I was absent from home so much of the time, Kathy needed an outlet. So, in 1988, I surprised her on our anniversary with a "second honeymoon" trip to a delightful bed and breakfast in Connecticut. I must confess, the idea wasn't original – a senior partner in our firm saw me constantly working nights and weekends and he was concerned that my workaholic nature would eventually destroy my marriage. He told me that at one time, his marriage was on the rocks. He took a similar weekend away and ended up buying a small beach house, which was often occupied by his wife and children during his long absences.

In hindsight, this was poor advice, since the only real solution was to spend more quality time with Kathy and the children. But, I went for the easy fix.

Sure enough, during our get-away weekend, I convinced Kathy to go with me to a local real estate office "just for fun." She showed little interest as we toured a few cottages, so I scrapped the idea and didn't bring it up again.

Six months later, Kathy treated her mother to a weekend stay at the same bed and breakfast. What I didn't know was that I had planted the seed about a getaway cottage in Kathy's mind. Behind my back, she had scheduled a meeting with that same real estate agent and asked her mother to join in this conspiracy.

Kathy fell in love with a two-story, farm-style house in a small community near Danbury. It was built in 1948, but completely renovated eight years ago with new fixtures and appliances. The most enticing feature was its waterfront location on a lovely, tranquil lake. Its current owners called their home, "The Nest".

Kathy was so excited when she returned to the city that she could barely contain herself. She called me at the office and she made a date for dinner that evening to discuss "something important".

I must admit I was more than a little apprehensive when I received the call – I was convinced that she was about to give me some kind of ultimatum about our relationship or worse yet, that she was filing for divorce. I couldn't function effectively for the remainder of that day.

I was so relieved at dinner when she gave me the news – she had placed a small deposit on the "Nest". She was nervous about telling me about her spontaneous action, even though the deposit was refundable.

The following Saturday, we went to the Nest. I gave her my blessing, but it really wasn't necessary. I would have approved of the place, sight unseen, since I had not seen Kathy this excited since the birth of our children.

The Nest became Kathy's project – she couldn't wait to go on the weekends to complete the interior redesign. She was incredibly proud of her accomplishments, and rightly so. The Nest was totally transformed from a dark and sterile interior to a colorful, cozy country-themed lake cottage – it looked like it came from the pages of an interior decorators' magazine.

Kathy usually took the kids to the Nest for the better part of the summer until Josh was 17, at which time he preferred to stay in New York with his friends. Now that the kids are away, Kathy still uses the Nest, sometimes alone and other times with her mother or friends.

It's been two years since I've seen the Nest, though each year I tell Kathy that I am determined to schedule a few long weekends and vacations at the lake. I had every intention of doing so last year and even arranged to have the Nest set up with a computer, fax machine and second phone line. However, time slipped away from me.

As a result of my devotion to the firm and its clients, my career flourished. At the ripe old age of 37, I was promoted to head the mergers and acquisitions group. This advancement presented some political problems for me within the firm because I nudged out some of the senior partners, but it didn't bother me for one second. I truly relished the role in those early years.

While I faced many trying and stressful deals during my career, the most difficult was the time I went head-to-head against my father. He represented a company that had been his client for more than twenty-five years. The company I represented went after my father's client in a hostile takeover.

At first, I was most enthusiastic about going to war with the target that was represented by Father and his firm. At the beginning of the project, it was as if I was a field commander of a tank unit that was about to perform a "blitzkrieg" offensive against the target company and therefore against my father's firm. We truly took them by surprise, mounting such an effective campaign, both in terms of publicity and legal maneuvering, that they eventually came to the table with little bargaining power.

What I hadn't anticipated after completion of the deal was my feelings towards Father. I should have been gloating with success, but I couldn't savor the moment. Father was nearly 62 years old at the time and looked totally worn out. As an outside observer, I felt that he could have taken a different tactical direction, which undoubtedly would have lead to painful litigation. In the end, I suspect his client could have won if litigation had been pursued.

However, Father seemed to be a defeated man, one who no longer wished to wage a battle. So, he convinced his client to surrender, which was probably the right thing to do in the best interests of his client's shareholders.

What continues to surprise me is that Father's client had not adopted a single anti-takeover measure that could easily have prevented our guys from successfully mounting the hostile effort. Perhaps Father recommended protective measures, but for some reason these actions were not adopted by the client's board of directors. I never asked him about it and I doubt he would have answered me anyway since he would have invoked the attorney-client privilege.

Rather than celebrating with my team after the merger was publicly announced, I remember going to my office, closing the door and feeling terribly saddened for my father.

Shortly after this deal, I met Father at our family home one weekend. For the first time in our lives, he suggested that we take a walk together.

During our one-hour stroll around the neighborhood, he told me that he had decided to retire. He felt that he had done his client a disservice in this particular transaction because he could no longer keep up with the young guys like myself. It was at this point that he said something that I thought I would never hear from him – he was proud of me, not only my business accomplishments, but more importantly, as a person.

This conversation, which consisted primarily of my father talking in a stream of consciousness, left me totally speechless. As we walked back to the house, neither one of us said anything. I still felt sad for him.

Here was a man whose only real passion was his work. Now, he realized it was soon to end and he was not prepared for the next chapter of his life.

From a selfish standpoint, I wished he had said he was proud of me when I brought home a report card or after those few times that he saw me perform in a high school or college theatrical production.

The real irony is that he was proud of me at a time in my life when I was the least proud of myself. A hired gun that doesn't care who he cripples by his tactics and a piss poor husband and father.

Within two weeks, Father announced his retirement to the partners in the firm. Despite the significant contributions that my father made in developing the firm's corporate business, the younger partners who sat on the firm's Executive Committee apparently did not appreciate my father's history with the firm. As a result, he was not treated in the regal manner he so richly deserved, either financially or with a gala retirement affair. Instead, there was a small dinner in his honor that was hosted by the firm – quiet and sedate, with little fanfare except from his senior colleagues, in particular, those who had pre-dated him in retirement.

Whether it was the unexpected nature of his retirement or the unceremonious sendoff by his firm, my father was initially a broken man. Whenever I called to check on him, my mother would say that he was spending time in his study reviewing correspondence, reading or napping.

I tried to encourage him to return to golf and even purchased a new set of clubs for him; but aside from a few lessons with the club pro, he rarely picked up the clubs.

For some unknown reason, after the first year of retirement, Father seemed to regain some of his spark. Perhaps it was his competitive spirit that led him to crawl out of his deep funk. He started to talk to Mother about a lengthy cruise in the Mediterranean and he volunteered his time at a legal clinic that assists senior citizens.

Sadly, just as he was finally beginning to enjoy his free time, he passed away from a heart attack while taking his afternoon nap.

Thankfully, unlike a number of his friends who lingered with various cancers and other diseases, Father didn't suffer. On the other hand, he had not truly enjoyed himself in decades.

A number of years before Father's death, I asked Kathy whether she thought it would be more difficult for my mother or father to lose their spouse. Kathy concluded, and I agreed, that Father would be totally lost without my mother, particularly during his retirement. Mother was strong and could manage without him, just as she had for all of their married life.

While my mother very much missed her mate of 40 years, she was able to continue with her activities and actually became more involved in charitable events after Father's death. I have to give Mother credit, she has always maintained a positive attitude and her giving nature despite Father's lack of emotional support.

I will always remember and cherish the few minutes we had on our walk on that quiet and sunny Saturday afternoon. I only wish we had done it many years earlier. I regret that I didn't make more of an effort to do so.

After my father's death, I realized that like him, I had very few outside pursuits. I had once played a fair bit of golf during my high school summer vacations. My father belonged to a private golf club and I was the only family member who used the course with any frequency. One summer, Father arranged for me to work at the course as a caddy and as a result, I lowered my handicap to a respectable twelve.

I still manage to play golf once or twice each month when the weather permits. My mother maintained the golf club membership after Father's death in order to maintain her close relationship with long-time friends.

Other than my family, the only interests that can be described as real passions for me are the theatre and movies. I try to see as many Broadway shows as possible and frequently go to the movies on weekend evenings. I also read a fair amount, but nothing is more relaxing for me than watching a play or movie. I completely escape when sitting in a theatre.

As you can easily see by now, as far as my family life is concerned, I haven't been a good husband or father. However, unlike many of my business associates, at least I have always been faithful to Kathy. Other guys pretend to be great husbands and fathers, but screw around on the side all the time.

Don't get me wrong; I'm not saying that being a successful businessman or professional necessarily comes with a lousy family life. On the contrary, I have seen many people who can effectively balance their lives and succeed in both areas, but I never really tried. Although I have always said that my family comes first, I never effectively practiced this philosophy.

The funny thing is that when I am at the office, I bark orders and all of the associates and assistants jump to satisfy my commands. At home, the exact opposite happens. Whenever I have a strong point of view about something related to the household, Kathy pretty much ignores me.

Josh is my real nemesis. He and I are polar opposites; he is funny, lighthearted and a real sports nut. He is an awful student, but excels in football and baseball. Josh was named homecoming king; three girls rejected me for the senior prom before the girl next door accepted my invitation. Josh is an absolutely delightful kid, but we drive each other crazy. Unfortunately, we are very similar in one respect; we are both very stubborn.

In order to describe my relationship with Josh, it may be best to use one of his phrases; *it sucks, big time.*

Jennie, like Kathy, basically blows me off. She is very much like Amy was with our father; Jennie doesn't care what I have to say. However, she will always be my little sweetheart and I can never really get mad at her.

I don't even think that Kathy's dog likes me. She greets everyone with a wagging tail, but tends to bark or growl at me.

Look, I'm not asking for any sympathy from you.

I know exactly what you may be thinking; this guy has it all, why the hell should he be so unhappy? Many of you probably wish you could trade places with me. Well, I would feel the same.

Here I have a high paying job; I am at the top of my game from a business standpoint; I own two homes; I have enough money so I can quit today and live comfortably for the rest of my life; a healthy family; an unbelievably loving and supportive wife; and at least one of my two kids seems to like me, or at least that's what she claims.

I had choices to make in life and sadly, I took the path that lead to business success at the expense of everything else, including my own best interests. Consequently, I have no one to blame but myself.

I see that I have gone on far too long with this introduction, which is uncharacteristic of me. I have given you far more personal details about myself than I ordinarily share with anyone, let alone a complete stranger. I am usually somewhat aloof and unemotional, but I have just revealed a side of myself that most people, including my family members and close friends, have not seen.

CHAPTER 2

INTRODUCTION BY ROCKY

My instructions from Ned were to simply be myself and as creative as possible. There are no rules about how I should describe myself.

With these unhelpful suggestions, I decided to pretend that I am an important person and you will be authoring my memoirs. As this is our first meeting, I will now give you a briefing about my family members and myself.

My full name is Andrew Michael Brooks and I was born in New York City on July 16, 1985. I have lived in the same apartment in the upper West side of the city since my third day of life.

During my early years, my family called me "Andy", but since I'm a big movie and television nut, that name always reminded me of Mickey Rooney in the old "***Andy Hardy***" movies or Andy Griffith in his old television show. I mean no disrespect to anyone, but I really didn't like being called Andy.

When I was seven years old, I saw my first "***Rocky***" movie starring Sylvester Stallone. I decided immediately after that movie I should be called "Rocky" instead of Andy and I made this known to my family and friends.

Whenever someone asked me, "why Rocky?" I would respond with a long answer about Rocky's winning spirit despite the odds that were stacked against him, but now, my standard response is –" it was either Rocky or Rambo – I chose Rocky because it fits me best."

I am the second child of Michael and Evelyn Brooks. My older sister, Laura, was born four years before me. It would have been better for everyone if my parents stopped with Laura.

I had a bit of an unusual childhood since my parents found out shortly after I was born that I have an incurable disease that will prematurely take my life.

As my dad tells me, I had few symptoms at that time and when my mother became ill, she was diagnosed with the disease. The doctors then conducted tests on me and found out that it had been transmitted to me.

As a result, I was pretty pampered during my childhood. I don't mean I was spoiled – far from it, but I was prevented from participating in sports and other such activities.

This was not due to my physical limitations, but rather to a sense of parental concern that these activities would sap my strength. I really don't know if it would have made any difference because a doctor told my parents that physical conditioning would actually improve my resistance level.

It really doesn't matter, because I don't remember missing playing outside with the other kids. From the time I was five, I basically grew up enjoying indoor activities, consisting of television, watching movies, playing video games and learning computer programs.

When I was nine, my mother's condition became worse and she weakened very rapidly. It was an ugly time and I prefer not to discuss that period with you or anyone else. Mom passed away shortly after her 39th birthday and life has not been the same since for Laura, Dad or me.

The next couple of years were brutal for my family. Dad became very quiet and reclusive. Consequently, I became the same way. It was fairly quiet around our apartment after Mom's death, with Dad usually reading books, Laura studying and me holed up in my room with my computer, television and video games.

School became unbearable after the kids found out about my disease. I didn't have problems with most of the kids on a one-on-one basis, but when they got together, they seemed to feed off each other to see who could inflict the most punishment. No one physically hurt me, but the words were sometimes more painful than a punch in the stomach.

When I was about to enter the sixth grade, I asked Dad whether I could be educated at home, through tutors and computer programs. He agreed on a trial basis because he had heard about my problems at school through Laura and school officials.

The experiment proved successful, and, in fact, I think I excelled more through home education than I would have in school. The program worked so well because I was determined not to return to school.

Consequently, I maintain a rigid schedule, meaning school-related activities from nine until noon, followed by tutoring three afternoons each week, either by college students or teachers.

Laura suffered far more with Mom's death because she was older and very close to her. They did everything together; maybe because they always knew that their time together would be short. So, while many of her friends couldn't stand their mothers, Laura loved Mom and confided in her as much as possible. They were truly best friends.

Unlike Laura, I didn't go through professional counseling after Mom's death. I probably should have, but it really didn't seem necessary. I have no idea if Dad ever even talked to a therapist; if he didn't, I wish he had. He probably could have used the help as much as Laura. He never coped well after her death; he often broke down whenever something about her surfaced. This was understandable at the beginning, but he still does it today.

What made it harder for Laura was the fact that she essentially became the "woman" of the house when she was only 13. She wasn't prepared to for the strain of Mother's death and becoming the guardian for Dad and me.

Despite all of the hardships, Laura managed to graduate from high school with honors and she is now studying psychology at Cornell University on an academic scholarship.

I know she had mixed emotions about leaving home. On the one hand, college life would actually be easier for her than everything she had to do at home. On the other hand, we were always a close family, but after Mom's death, we really bonded.

As far as my dad is concerned, he has been employed in the finance department of a major insurance company for the past 19 years. He seems happy with his job and although he has received a number of promotions during his career, he is content with his current level; Dad has no aspirations about joining the ranks of senior management. He likes to remain "below the radar screen", whatever that means in the corporate world.

I suspect Dad will eventually retire early and move away from the city for a quiet and peaceful life where he can get lost in his books. He would retire today if possible, but financially, he can't. The other big problem is medical insurance for me.

Now, back to me.

As I said earlier, I spend a lot of time each day on school stuff. I understand from my tutors that I will soon be ready to take advanced placement type studies in a number of subjects, but honestly, this really doesn't matter to me because college, for me, is not a reality.

I can't honestly say that I like any of my school subjects, but I seem to excel in English, history and geography courses. I find math and science challenging, but there is no question that my attention span is noticeably shorter on these subjects.

The remainder of my day is typically filled with personal reading, mostly mystery books, writing short stories, watching movies and messing around on my computer.

Dad and Laura constantly encourage me to get outside more and as she says, to actually experience life as opposed to "living" through books, television and the Internet. Despite my outwardly happy exterior, I think they believe that I'm depressed.

Well, I'm not depressed. Sure, I sometimes think about my disease, but since it doesn't really affect me much, I have come to the conclusion that I should have as much fun as possible. After all, I really have nothing to lose.

My Dad rarely gets upset with me, but when he does, he typically explodes. Usually, he does so with good reason and most often, it occurs when one of my practical jokes gets me in trouble. I admit that I have an unusual sense of humor.

I don't mean that I hurt people. On the contrary, I think of myself as a protector of others and when someone receives what I consider to be unfair treatment, I find a creative way to "deal with" the wrongdoer.

For example, last week, Laura had been browsing the shelves in a nearby bookstore, which is part of a national chain of stores. As she often does, Laura sat down to read a particular book. She can usually tell whether she will like a book after reading the first few pages. She had finished two pages when she noticed the store manager standing next to her. Even though she is a regular customer of the store, he treated Laura in a rude manner and instructed her leave the store. He yelled something like, "This isn't a public library." After she tried to explain, a security person was called to escort her from the store in front of a bunch of customers. She came home in tears.

I called the store and told them I wanted to send a favorable letter about the store manager to the president of the company. After I got both the manager and president's names and the company's address, I sent an anonymous letter to the president saying that I had witnessed the manager evicting an elderly woman from the store who was quietly reading an Amish recipe book.

Now I know the manager may have thought that he was doing his job by kicking Laura out. I also realize that he may have a family and kids to feed, but there is no reason to treat anyone, let alone Laura, in such an indecent manner in front of other people. By sending the letter, I thought that I was actually helping his career – he needed a lesson in good manners to succeed in the retail business.

Another thing that seems to get me in trouble is when I have my computer, television and stereo on at the same time. Somehow, I can focus on the computer and whatever show or movie I am watching and still enjoy listening to the mellow sound of Mel Torme or classic rock and roll.

Even though I have been on an airplane only twice in my life and have visited just three other states, I feel like I know the world through my computer, books and television. Whenever something happens in the news that interests me, I research the subject with my computer, often reading newspapers from various places around the world through the Internet.

This past week, I heard about a bank robbery in a small seaside community in Northern California during which the robber took a number of employees hostage. Since this particular community was unfamiliar to me, I looked up everything I could about that area through the Internet and got information about the population, attractions, crime rate, economy, climate and even housing prices.

The Internet has enabled me to learn about the world without ever leaving my cozy little room. I used to chat with people on the Internet, but after running across a bunch of crazies, I stopped.

Three other things that you should probably know about me – first, I have been told that I have a "gift" . This information surfaced when I visited an astrologer with my mother a couple of years before she died. I actually think this lady was more of a fortuneteller than a true astrologer because she also read peoples' palms and often relied on tarot cards to confirm her initial findings.

Mom visited her at the suggestion of her aunt who believed in such people. I went along for the ride because I thought it would be a kick to see one of these people in action. The purpose of the visit was to determine whether Mom should undergo an experimental medical procedure.

While we were there, this woman continued to look at me throughout Mom's session. She was real creepy and spoke with a phony accent in order to make herself appear to be more mysterious, but she probably grew up in the Bronx.

Anyway, after she finished with Mom, she asked whether I wanted my fortune told. Since we had some time to kill before meeting Dad and Laura for dinner, Mom agreed, but only for half price.

This woman read my palm and shuffled some tarot cards around. She constantly made odd movements and noises that I can't even begin to describe because they were so bizarre. It was actually kind of humorous – like an old movie. I expected spirits to appear and the table to start moving.

I have to give the fortuneteller credit, however, because she immediately knew my astrological sign without any prompting from Mom or me. She also said that I had the same affliction as Mom, even though she was never told the nature of the medical condition. She also correctly said that I was named after my granddad. This could all have been pure dumb luck on her part, but she since was right on the money up to this point, Mom and I became all the more attentive.

Then came the real revelation– she told us that I possess a special "quality" , as she called it, a "gift" . She said that people, even strangers, would tell me their problems, ideas or thoughts - things they wouldn't feel comfortable sharing with others, even those closest to them. She also said that I have the ability to help others. She didn't mean a faith healer – I could just see myself like those people on cable television with funny hair who touch people on their head and make them fall to the ground. What she said to Mom was that I would help people resolve personal problems or at least I would give them a sense of direction so they could heal themselves.

Even though I still have doubts about her, it is true that friends and family members often share private issues and thoughts with me. They are not really asking for any advice from me, they just want to unload on someone. Sometimes, I really don't care to listen to this stuff because it can get embarrassing, like the time that my grandmother told me about her affection for an elderly man in her convalescent home. I thought this was a pretty sick subject to discuss with your grandmother, but I was patient with her because no one else paid attention to her.

But you know, this "gift" is really nothing more than an ability to connect with people. When a person is alone for long periods at a time like me, you tend to take more of an interest in others. As a result, you become a better listener.

I guess if I was with people all day, it would be a different story, but I enjoy talking to people and I actually do better with adults than kids my age.

In addition to paying attention to people and focusing on whatever they may be saying, I don't hesitate to ask questions that decent people may consider to be far too personal. I really don't care what people may think – I ask whatever is on my mind.

Dad is often surprised and embarrassed by what I ask other people. I know I have gone too far with my questions when I get the "evil glare" from Dad – which I probably deserve. But on the other hand, it's frustrating when I know that someone is about to bust loose with emotion and needs only a little nudge to open up.

Recently, we had an unexpected visit from Uncle Marty, who is Dad's younger brother from Ohio. Now, it doesn't take a rocket scientist to figure out that Marty was facing some sort of problem when he came to see us. For example, he never travels alone, but this time, he didn't bring any family members with him.

Even though all indications suggested that Marty wanted to open up to Dad, they somehow avoided a heart-to-heart talk for three days. They watched the football playoffs on television for an entire day and rarely said a word to each other, other than when there was a significant play or bad call from a referee.

Finally, I couldn't stand to watch the shadow boxing between Dad and Marty any longer. So, when Marty and I were alone, I bluntly asked him – "Are you having personal problems at home or work?"

After dodging my question for a while, he finally told me everything. I just listened. Yes, there were problems between him and his wife and he needed to take time away from home to think. Since he didn't have enough money for a real vacation, he found a cheap airfare on the Internet and had decided to camp out with his older brother for a while. He knew Dad wouldn't bug him about the visit, but he hadn't considered that I would drive him crazy with my questions.

After talking for a while, Marty decided that he would try to patch up his differences with his wife. He said he realized that he needed to become more mature and settle down for the sake of his family. He would have to make a big sacrifice; no more than one night each week with the "guys."

He was now averaging three per week with the boys, so this would be a major compromise. I know I shouldn't say this about my uncle, but what an absolute jerk – ignoring his family three nights each week to play poker, watch games and drink with his buddies.

Now, couldn't my Dad simply have asked Marty if there was some reason why he was traveling without his family? Or, couldn't Marty have asked his older brother to listen to his problems? Anyway, all it takes is the simple act of connecting and showing interest in people –this doesn't mean you need a magical gift or power.

The second thing you should know about me is that I keep a secret "list" . No one has ever seen this list and other than Laura, no one knows of its existence.

It's not what you are thinking– this is not a "hit" list of targets for my practical jokes or retaliation for wrongdoing. It's what I label on my computer index as my "Regret List." Unlike other people who discuss past regrets, my list speaks to the future. It is a list of things I wish I could do and places I wish I could see before I pass on to join Mom. In other words, when I am literally on my deathbed, I will look at the remaining items on this list and say that these are the things I missed doing before I walk down that famous tunnel with a light at the other end.

The reason I have never discussed this list with Dad is because he already thinks I'm far too absorbed in my thoughts of death. At times, he lectures me about fighting rather than resigning myself to an early demise. But I figure it this way: If I happen to live longer than expected, this would be absolutely great – but if I don't, I'm emotionally prepared for the worst. It's a lot easier to accept the fact that it will happen sooner than later.

As I told Dad when this subject last came up: "Why should I chase rainbows?" I prefer to be a realist about my future.

This is why I never bother to read positive articles about medical advances that are made in attacking my condition. I figure that I have a very knowledgeable doctor who specializes in this particular area of medicine and often lectures on the subject at medical conferences. He should be familiar with any new findings on my condition, not me.

But in actuality, the real reason I don't bother to read these articles is because I prefer not to get my hopes up about a possible treatment. I must assume that I belong to a large group of people who will perish before a cure is found. At least I am in good company.

The third thing about me you should be aware of is that I love to gamble. Of course, there are the Vegas-type games I play on my computer, ranging from all sorts of card games, to roulette and craps. But my favorite games are poker and blackjack – I have a system for each that works far more often than not. I know I could make a killing at blackjack if I was old enough to play in Vegas.

I have kidded with Dad that he should take his retirement fund to Vegas or Atlantic City and use my system to double his money. As I tell him: "If I'm wrong and we lose all of the money, what's the worst thing that will happen? Big deal, you'll just have to work for the rest of your life."

My dad and I often make bets with each other and not just on sports events - on virtually anything. For example, yesterday, when we ordered takeout Chinese, we bet on the time it would arrive. We bet a dollar on whether Laura would call from college last Saturday (she did, and I won) and this past Sunday, we bet on whether we would get our newspaper delivery before eight in the morning. As usual, it was late.

I have now taken my gambling "bug" to a higher level. First, with Dad's permission, I opened a joint account with him for my Internet stock trading.

When my grandmother died, she left her estate to Dad, Laura and myself, to be divided equally. After all of her remaining expenses were paid from the estate, we each received about $32,000.

I used $5,000 to start the Internet stock trading account. I have increased the value of this account to $7,700, but I must admit that my stock picks are not based on skill. I just get a gut feeling about certain companies that I hear about in the news.

Dad suggested that I invest the rest of the money in something safe so that I can use it for my college education. Since the odds are at least 100 to 1 against attending college, I prefer to enjoy using the money on things that interest me as of today. It's awfully hard for me to project beyond the next few months of my life.

As I said before, I enjoy betting – so Dad doesn't know that I also started an offshore betting account through the Internet. I originally placed $1,000 into this account, but I am thrifty because I never bet more than $20 a day. I'm not really a compulsive gambler – I just do it to break the monotony of my otherwise boring life.

Overall, despite my medical condition and the loss of Mother at an early age, I truly feel that I have a decent life, at least far better than most people, and I want to enjoy the remainder of it as much as possible.

Don't misunderstand me, however – I am by no means saying I am happy about my condition and the bleak prospects for the future. I wish I could plan for a bright career (I would love to be a writer since I seem to have a knack for composition) as well as having a family with at least three kids. However, I'm "content" with my life and appreciate the fact that it may be relatively short.

So, I assume every day when I wake up that I may have only six months to live. Hopefully, I will be dead (pardon the pun) wrong; but if not, then I'm prepared to quietly go to the next life with grace. Maybe I will be more fortunate the next time around – like maybe I'll become a world class tennis player and have all of the pretty young women idolizing me. Actually, I would just settle for a normal childhood – one in which I could get dirty like the other kids and drive my mother crazy for leaving dirty clothes all around the house.

Before her death, Mom told me to always look at the positive side of life, but quite honestly, other than my family, there is no bright side. I know this sounds morbid, but it is exactly how I feel. However, trust me, you will never see me down, especially around my father or sister. They will have enough burdens after I am gone so I try to make things as pleasant as possible for them while I am still with them.

That reminds me, I have been driving Dad crazy for the past couple of nights by calling him while he is peacefully reading and pretending to be a foreign person. I have used Italian and Spanish accents. Tonight, the call will be from a Japanese businessman who will ask whether he has reached Ito Enterprises. It is hilarious to hear Dad trying to patiently tell these callers that they have the wrong number. Most people would immediately hang up, but Dad, being ever so helpful, tries to help the foreign caller.

I have to admit that I played a cruel joke on Laura last month. I wrote her a note identifying myself as a guy in her History lecture class, which has over 300 students. I said that I have admired her all semester and would love to meet her, but I don't have the courage to approach her. I vaguely described myself as a six-footer, with black hair and an athletic background. I poured it on by saying that my major is European History and my goal is to earn a doctorate so I can teach at the college level. The note was signed "Romeo."

I made a big mistake by asking Laura a week later about her "love" life. When she didn't say anything about the letter, I let it pass. Later in the conversation, I mentioned that I had just finished reading "***Romeo and Juliet.***" We continued to talk and then all of a sudden, she was silent – the next comment she made was, "you sneaky little shit." Then Laura went off and used language I didn't think she knew. I was actually proud of her because she can work herself up and become belligerent if pushed too hard.

Laura usually doesn't tell Dad when I have done something inappropriate. She doesn't hold back because of her affection for me, but she knows that she lives in a glass house and she should never throw any stones. But not this time; when Dad called her the following weekend, she casually mentioned that I had sent her this love note.

Dad flipped out and I must confess that he was absolutely right. In this day and age, there are sicko people everywhere and Laura could have been a target of one of these people. My punishment for this grave offense was steep because I had to pay Laura a "fine" of $100.

Laura later told me that she was actually flattered by Romeo's note. At the beginning and again after each lecture, she looked around the hall to identify Romeo. She smiled at the six-foot athletic guys with black hair. Now, she is embarrassed to see them because they must think she is a big flirt. I have to admit it would have been funny to see Laura flashing her big smile and giving the "eye" to all these guys.

Since I have this so-called "gift", I know what you may be thinking after reading about my background and especially the pranks I recently played on Dad and Laura. You're probably saying to yourself, "This kid should get a life." I couldn't agree more with your conclusion. However, after you read this entire story, carefully think about whether you know of any healthy and well-adjusted kids of my age who would trade their lives with mine. I suspect you will determine that this is very unlikely.

So, without being pissy, my comment to you is, "Don't even think about criticizing me unless you are facing my exact situation."

I'm sorry; I don't even know you and here I am already engaging you in a philosophical debate. I apologize, but my condition and the way I live is obviously an emotional issue with me. This is the reason that I do everything possible to avoid discussing this subject; not just for myself, but more for Dad and Laura's sake.

CHAPTER 3

"THE RELUCTANT HERO"

BY PETER

March 9, 1999 – New York City

We had been negotiating for the better part of three days, virtually living in the 46th floor conference room of our firm's offices.

Two major corporations were about to merge with billions of dollars involved, but as usual, we were down to a few relatively minor points. These issues will ultimately prove to be meaningless, but are nonetheless important to some lawyers.

Unfortunately, the lead attorney representing the other party seemed determined to prove his worth to the client by remaining stubborn on a couple of issues that should have been resolved yesterday. I suppose that since he was a young partner in his firm, he wanted to demonstrate that he can stand his ground against the big boys, meaning my investment banking firm and the major law firm representing our client.

The executive of the corporation for the other side simply didn't have the balls to tell his attorney to stop pushing on these points. He seemed scared to death that if something should go wrong, his tyrannical chairman would chop off his head or some other part of his anatomy. So, he sat back for hours and let his attorney pontificate about why the issues were "deal breakers" from their standpoint.

What bullshit! Everyone around the table knew that the deal would not blow up because of these remote issues. After all, our proposals for handling these matters are standard approaches, but for whatever reason, perhaps due to the inexperience of the lawyer on the other side, they had not been accepted.

When I noted it was already 7:40 in the evening, I suggested that we take a 15-minute break.

I had promised Kathy before I left the house that I would join her tonight at a fundraising dinner for a medical foundation she has supported for many years. Since I missed the last two dinners for this foundation, I could ill afford to stand Kathy up again, particularly after making a firm promise to her this morning.

In anticipation of another long day of negotiation, I fortunately brought my tuxedo this morning so I could get out of the office quickly, should I be delayed.

During the timeout, I knew I had to break the deadlock in this negotiating game so I could join Kathy, even though there was no question I would be terribly late for the dinner.

When the other side left to use another room for their conference, I recommended a series of compromises to our client's representative; I had employed these proposals in several past deals to resolve the same nagging issues. I didn't think my client would be placed at any meaningful risk through the compromises. In this way, the arrogant ass representing the opposing party could claim victory and we could finally put the final details to bed.

I always try to keep emotion out of my dealings, but sometimes, I run across a person I just can't stand. The worst guys to deal with are the "professionals" who think they know what they're doing, but actually don't have a clue. They are typically the most unreasonable in negotiations because they always think that I'm trying to take advantage of them or their client.

This is exactly what we were dealing with in this negotiation, a guy who didn't trust any one on our side. He was terribly insecure and thought we were about to screw him. When we made proposals, he jumped to the conclusion that we were making an underhanded maneuver.

There was no way I could stay around any longer for this marathon session, partly due to my frustration, but mostly because of my commitment to Kathy.

To the surprise of my client's representative, I told him I had to leave for a critical engagement that could not be rescheduled. I said he was in the capable hands with my senior associate, Chris (Christopher Chance hates to be called Chris, which is why I do so as often as possible, particularly in front of a group of people).

I could see that my client was genuinely concerned, so I told him I would call after 10 this evening to get updated on their progress. I also offered to return to the office after my engagement should it be necessary. I said I would be away for no more than three hours.

Chris seemed delighted that I was leaving, particularly since I had given him a road map for concluding the final sticky issues. He could then tell his fellow associates and my partners in the firm that he salvaged a multi-billion dollar merger before it went down in flames.

I couldn't blame Chris because I would have done exactly the same thing under these circumstances. In fact, I remember a similar situation in my younger years when a senior partner became so drunk during dinner that he could no longer effectively function. At one point during the negotiations, I turned to see the partner sleeping, with his head resting on the conference room table.

I concluded that transaction without any of the partner's help. Naturally, he told other partners he had given me all of the needed pointers to get the deal done and that it was his intention to give me confidence by leaving me alone with a bunch of sharks.

This evening, after our game plan was decided, we returned to the conference room. I first told the other side I would be leaving for the evening. This obviously startled the opposition, particularly the corporate executive who thought I was leaving because of my disgust with his attorney. He could probably visualize a career-ending move for not taking a more active role in controlling his attorney. The opposing attorney also seemed concerned about my departure. He started to object, but I rudely interrupted him before he got rolling with another of his lengthy and meaningless speeches.

After explaining that I couldn't cancel my other engagement, there was a sense of relief on the other side. They became even more relaxed when I said we were prepared to propose compromises to resolve the remaining issues.

I left the meeting in the capable hands of Chris, who immediately assumed my position at the head of the long conference table. He was in his glory.

The opposing attorney was also enjoying the moment because he felt that he had prevailed. I'm certain that he and Chris enjoyed their time together during my absence. They became the co-kings of the 46th floor conference room.

After my exit, I rushed to my office on the floor below the conference room, closed the door and changed into my formal attire as quickly as possible. By the time I was in a cab, it was already 8:30. Despite heavy traffic, I knew that with any luck, I could reach the dinner shortly after nine.

The promise of a $20 tip to the driver resulted in a wild ride through side streets that I didn't recognize. At one point, I was sure we were going to plow into a garbage truck, but we escaped and arrived at the hotel at 9:15.

I went through the lobby in a semi-jog, checked in my coat and casually strolled into the ballroom. I was hoping people would think that I had been visiting the restroom.

I spotted Kathy at a table near the stage with a vacant seat to her right. I noted that the other guests at the table were already enjoying their dessert.

The reaction by Kathy was so cold that others at our table had to have felt the chill. I know that a friend of Kathy's, who sat at the other side of the table, must have taken delight in Kathy's hostile greeting. This woman never liked me, perhaps because she knew I felt the same about her.

Kathy didn't respond after I quietly greeted her. She simply picked up the dinner program that was lying on my chair and placed it on the table.

The president of the foundation, Dr. Max Willingham (better known as "Dr. Max" to those close to the foundation) was on stage thanking the attendees for helping the charity. He then showed a video demonstrating the foundation's activities in helping children receive medical attention.

The video focused primarily on the foundation's pet project of sending volunteer doctors to underdeveloped countries to provide medical treatment to needy children. This past year, doctors had directed their attention to underprivileged children in Peruvian villages.

Dr. Max identified those who had made significant contributions to the foundation during the past year. After introducing the foundation's board members, he escorted a young man named Rocky to the stage. I first suspected that Rocky was a pre-teen given his slight build, but after he spoke, it became obvious that he was older.

From what I could gather from Dr. Max, Rocky was inflicted with a potentially life-threatening disease. The foundation had helped Rocky and his family in the past in seeking appropriate medical attention. In appreciation for the assistance it provided, Rocky decided to repay the foundation. Dr. Max told the audience that Rocky, on his own initiative, located an Internet developer who contributed his time to establish a web site for the foundation. This site will give background information to those who desire to learn about the foundation.

Dr. Max then said that the foundation wanted to thank Rocky for his help. So, as outlined in the dinner program, Rocky had a life-long desire to visit San Francisco, and Alcatraz in particular, which brought scattered laughter from the audience. Dr. Max said he was seeking a volunteer from the audience to help Rocky fulfill his dream. As a caveat, Dr. Max again reminded everyone that the expectations of the volunteer were detailed in the dinner program.

When Dr. Max looked for a volunteer among this grandly-dressed crowd, there was absolute silence throughout the large ballroom. As if to avoid eye contact with Dr. Max, people at different tables began to nervously chatter with those around them.

It seemed like several long minutes had passed and Dr. Max was still scanning the room in search for a raised hand to save the day. He then stepped off the stage holding the microphone, probably hoping that he could shame someone into responding, but there were no takers.

Dr. Max was becoming nervous. I suspect he never anticipated a silent response and probably didn't know how to handle this dilemma.

I glanced at Rocky and it seemed his face had turned pale, but it was probably my imagination. I really felt sorry for this kid. What a potentially embarrassing situation for Rocky and Dr. Max.

Dr. Max made a tactical error by not having a backup volunteer in the event no one raised their hand. It's like holding an auction for a charitable cause; you have to make sure that a "shill" is in the crowd to start the bidding process.

The gears in my brain were quickly churning. A trip like this for Rocky and probably one of his parents wouldn't cost much and the expense might be tax deductible if it was considered a charitable contribution to the foundation. I could probably use my airline mileage for free tickets since I had tons of unused credits, some of which were about to expire. Most importantly, what better way to make amends with Kathy than to satisfy this young man's wish?

So, much to the relief of Dr. Max and Rocky, I raised my hand.

After Dr. Max spotted me, he rushed to our table and immediately identified me through Kathy's involvement with the foundation. He was elated, but obviously astonished by my response. In fact, he even said that it was such a "pleasant and unexpected surprise" to see me volunteer.

I was asked to stand and Dr. Max then took my hand as he led me to the stage. I turned to look at Kathy before leaving the table – she was absolutely dumbfounded. Her mouth was open and her eyes only registered shock.

I also couldn't help but glance at Kathy's friend across the table; I had a sarcastic grin on my face, as if to say, "Up yours."

When I arrived at the stage with Dr. Max, I was greeted by applause from the audience. They were probably less happy for Rocky and more relieved because I ended a potentially disastrous stunt by Dr. Max.

I must admit I was proud of myself. After all, I made two significant accomplishments in the span of a few minutes. I got recognition for having a charitable nature and more importantly, I was instantaneously switched in Kathy's eyes from a goat to a hero.

After shaking hands with Rocky and Dr. Max, I returned to the table.

I saw that Kathy was smiling as I sat down. I could tell she was equally proud of me. But it was at this point that she leaned over and whispered in my ear something like, "Do you have any idea what you've done?"

Of course I knew; I had finally surprised her in a positive way. So, I nodded in a confident manner about my action. For a few thousand bucks, I had bought the immediate appreciation of Kathy, Dr. Max, Rocky and the audience.

Then I noticed that Kathy began to quietly laugh to herself; if fact, she was forced to cover her mouth to prevent herself from laughing out loud while Dr. Max was giving his concluding remarks. People often react in surprising ways when they are overwhelmed by a good deed.

At the end of the evening, a number of people approached me and thanked me for my charitable heart, including Kathy's friend from our table, who admitted she was surprised by my unselfish gesture.

After everyone at our table left, Kathy was still sitting at the table. I looked at her and she again broke out in uncontrollable laughter, to the point that tears were smearing her makeup.

I really couldn't understand her reaction, but I radiated in the glow of my short-lived fame. This was when Rocky and his father approached me. I exchanged pleasantries with Michael Brooks. After a brief discussion, we agreed to meet later in the week to discuss the "necessary arrangements" for the trip, which I naturally assumed meant my financial obligations.

At this point, quite unexpectedly, Rocky's father gave me an emotional hug and seemed to hold me for a considerable length of time. He even started to cry. This reaction was far more than I expected. I suppose he was not only happy for Rocky, but he was also overjoyed at the opportunity to join him, at little expense.

Unlike his father, Rocky showed absolutely no emotion, which I suppose is understandable. I mean, think about it – first the recognition at the dinner in front of a huge crowd and then my gracious offer; it must have been totally overwhelming for the kid.

As I was hailing a cab, I glanced at Kathy who was standing at the curb. She had this devilish smile on her face – she reminded me of a proud homecoming queen whose boyfriend, the star quarterback, just scored the winning touchdown. Whether I wanted it or not, I had a feeling I was going to get lucky tonight.

While in the cab, she again broke out in hearty laughter; so much so that she was holding her side in apparent agony. I thought she was about to fall on the floor of the cab because she couldn't control herself.

I saw our cabdriver peek through his rear view mirror. I suspect he thought she was totally drunk, thus the non-stop laughter. He simply smiled, probably figuring I had gotten her sloshed so I could take advantage of her once we arrived at our destination.

At one point, there was a short break in the cackling and I think she said something like, "This is hilarious because you are totally oblivious to what you've done." But frankly, I wasn't really sure what she said because some of her slurred words were totally unintelligible.

Then it hit me; she was probably so upset by my tardiness that she drank a few too many during the cocktail hour and continued with wine until I arrived.

She then asked a startling question, which unfortunately was understandable, "How can you possibly a take a week off work with your schedule?"

I stared straight ahead and tried to use my negotiating face by staying cool; I didn't want to show a look of panic. Now I knew or at least hoped she was ripped, to the point that she was irrational.

What the hell was she talking about? I was only going to fund the trip, not take it with Rocky. So, I didn't answer her.

What worried me during the remainder of the drive home was a remote chance that she was actually sober and knew what she was saying.

When we arrived at our townhouse, I quickly grabbed the dinner program which I had placed in the inside pocket of my coat. I told Kathy that I was going to watch the news for a while before going to bed.

I rushed to the family room, closed the door, opened the program and read the fine print of my commitment.

Sure enough, the language was abundantly clear not only had I volunteered to fund the trip for Rocky, but I was also expected to join Rocky for the journey. According to the program, the volunteer would serve as Rocky's "chaperone" for the entire trip.

DAMN!!!

I can't believe I was so stupid. I am the most careful person in the world; one who never makes a commitment without knowing all of the conditions, but now I got myself sucked into something like this. What an idiot! This confirmed that I should never act on pure emotion.

I hadn't even taken a vacation with Kathy for two years, but now, I was expected to take a complete stranger, a moody and ill teenager to boot, on a trip across the country. It served me right because I had tried to be an instant hero and it backfired.

Then it dawned on me that in the excitement of the evening, I had turned off my mobile phone so I wouldn't disrupt the dinner. I wondered about the status of the negotiations. With the luck I was having tonight, the deal probably fell through after I left.

I immediately called Chris, and I was surprised that he was still in the same conference room, even though it was well past 11. He reported that the other side didn't immediately accept my compromises, but after much urging on Chris's part, he convinced them to do so.

What an arrogant little shit – I just bet that's what happened. They probably accepted the compromises without hesitation.

Chris and the other associates were working with the attorneys to finalize the draft agreement to include the changed terms. They hoped to hand deliver the revised agreement to all of the parties in the morning. Chris told me that both negotiating teams agreed to gather at 10 in the morning to review the final changes in the agreement and hopefully conclude the deal at that time.

It was at this point that Chris said he had everything under control and there was no need for me to attend the meeting in the morning. He would handle the remainder of the deal if I want him to do so.

Sure you little creep; so you can take full credit for my transaction – there was absolutely no way that I would miss the meeting. This was the most enjoyable part of big deals from my standpoint; effectively serving as the leader of the band. Finalizing the terms of the agreement with the attorneys, conducting the Board of Directors' meeting to approve the deal and preparing press announcements about the deal.

After the call with Chris, I slowly and quietly went upstairs to the bedroom. I was afraid Kathy would wake up and erupt in laughter through the rest of the night.

Even though my head was spinning, my goal for tomorrow was very clear; I was determined to find a way to escape from this commitment. Given my clever and conniving methods of solving problems, I went to sleep with full confidence that Rocky and Dr. Max were no match for my skills. Those poor guys were lambs compared to me. In the end, they would be thanking me for bowing out.

There was no question that Rocky would take his dream trip; the only open item was who would accompany him. I would still pay for everything associated with the trip, but someone else would have to serve as Rocky's travel companion.

At least I learned something from this evening, which is never agree to volunteer for a charitable cause, other than to pay money.

CHAPTER 4

"MY SOCIAL DEBUT"

BY ROCKY

March 9, 1999 – New York City

Depending on a person's point of view, last night could be considered a wonderful, uplifting experience or a total nightmare. For me, it was a frightening ordeal, and unfortunately, it wasn't a dream. It was all too real.

About a month ago, I told Dr. Max that his medical foundation had aided me so much in the past that I wanted to do something for the foundation, but I didn't have the money to make a big contribution. I told him I would come up with something creative. He smiled, but frankly, I think he was humoring me – I suspect he thought that I would do something like begging door-to-door for contributions or selling brownies in the lobby of my building.

For some reason, I never seem to get any credit for my innovative thinking. This could however be a blessing since no one seems to have high expectations of me – this means that there is very little pressure on me to produce. This is one of the few benefits of being ill.

By the way, before I continue, you should know that sometimes, rather than try to describe another person by their appearance, I say that he or she looks or acts like a well-known personality. It doesn't have to be a movie or singing star – it could be a politician or a world leader, just so it is a person who is easily recognizable by most people.

For example, Dr. Max looks a little bit like Anthony Hopkins, but of course not when he played that horrible cannibal guy in "*Silence of the Lambs*." Dr. Max is more energetic however and reminds me of a person we met in Florida who was trying to sell Dad a condo timeshare. Just like this salesman, Dr. Max doesn't easily accept "no" for an answer from anyone.

Dad looks very much like a heavier version of actor and comedian Steve Martin, including the prematurely gray hair. Unlike Mr. Martin, however, Dad is a soft-spoken, reserved person who rarely shows any emotion; he hasn't even smiled much since Mom's death. Although Dad has a sense of humor, it sometimes takes him a while to find it. As I often tell him, I think he saves his humorous side for guests and family members.

Laura looks and acts like a younger version of Meg Ryan because she is spunky, highly charged and most of the time, very funny, but she can also become highly emotional, at other times. People who first met Laura a few years ago would disagree with this characterization because she was understandably depressed after Mom's death. But now, Laura is a different person and I know she does whatever she can to keep things light and funny for Dad and me.

As for me, Laura and others have said I look a little like actor Michael J. Fox during his "***Back to the Future***" movies, but I act more like Tom Hanks. Not when he played "***Forrest Gump***", but more like his roles in "***Cast Away***" or "***The Green Mile***". I hope they mean that I am a gentle person who is deliberate, cool and even-tempered, with a dry and sometimes offbeat sense of humor.

Anyway, after my discussion with Dr. Max, I went on the Internet to get information about the foundation so I could determine how to best help. Surprisingly, the foundation didn't have its own web site. At first I thought I must have been typing the wrong information since most other similar organizations have a site. When I confirmed this wasn't the case for the foundation, the light bulb went on and I decided to create a web site for the foundation.

Although I consider myself pretty good with computers and have even developed my own web site, I am a long way from being an expert in web design. So, I went through many different kinds of sites and made a list of the best web developers. I then contacted them by e-mail and asked if they would be interested in donating their time and knowledge to create a site for a worthy cause – I gave them a brief description about the foundation's good work throughout the world.

Out of the 42 e-mails asking for help, I received two favorable responses. I selected a developer whose youngest son recently experienced a major medical problem that was diagnosed early and thankfully he was cured without any continuing problems. As a result of this incident, he was eager to help the foundation.

I sent the developer as much information as I could find about the foundation through brochures, newspaper articles and other public material. He developed an extraordinary site geared for potential donors, parents and children. It is a friendly site, with lots of bright colors and easy enough for just about anyone to navigate.

I made an appointment for Dad and I to pay Dr. Max a visit. The purpose of the meeting was a mystery to both of them.

While in Dr. Max's office, I asked to use his computer. I pulled up the foundation's web site, even though it was still in the developmental stage. Dr. Max was truly delighted. I told Dr. Max and Dad the best part – which is that a volunteer from California developed the site at no cost to the foundation.

Dr. Max was so pleased with this unexpected gift that he asked an assistant to join us in his office. He suggested to her that the site's address should be mentioned in all of the foundation's future mailings, including the program for their annual dinner event. He also told her to include my picture and a description of my good work in the dinner program.

Then Dr. Max asked what the foundation could do for me. The polite answer would have been a simple "nothing." But sometimes, I'm so unpredictable that I even amaze myself. I quickly blurted out that I would love to take a trip to San Francisco.

Both Dr. Max and Dad looked surprised; Dad asked, "Why San Francisco?"

There were two reasons, but I only told them one. I said because it looks like such a great place in movies and pictures. I didn't say that it is the first item on my "Regrets List", which I privately told you about in my introduction.

Dr. Max said, "Maybe we can do something to help you get there."

We left it at that and I never expected to hear about this trip again. But two weeks before the annual dinner, Dad came home from work to tell me that Dr. Max had decided to fulfill my wish. At first I no idea what he was talking about and then I remembered the San Francisco conversation.

Dad said that during the foundation's annual dinner, Dr. Max would seek a volunteer to take me to San Francisco, at that person's expense.

I couldn't believe what he just said and I tried to act as if I was elated, but I wasn't. I was actually nervous and very upset. I wasn't really serious about taking a trip to San Francisco. It just happened to be the first thing that came to mind when Dr. Max made his offer. I never expected him to do anything about my request. I just thought he was making small talk.

Knowing Dr. Max, there must be a reason why he was including this trip as part of the dinner program. I suspected there was a hidden benefit for the foundation in arranging this trip. Otherwise, I doubt Dr. Max would have remembered my comment.

This confirmed what Dad has always told me, which is to never say anything spontaneous because it always seems to get me in trouble. I'm truly an idiot for mentioning San Francisco. Why couldn't I have said that I would love to attend a Yankee game? Or maybe I could have asked for a big-screen television. But I knew it was too late to change my request.

In trying to think about an instant excuse for avoiding the trip, I asked Dad, "Would you really allow me to take this trip with a complete stranger?"

I should have known that Dad and Dr. Max had already discussed this subject. Dad assured me that if any of us felt uncomfortable about the volunteer, we could graciously decline by saying there had been a change of heart. Dad hoped I would not be disappointed if this happened, but he and Dr. Max do always have my best interests in mind.

I couldn't say it to Dad, but I would have been delighted if everyone forgot about the whole damn trip. On the other hand, it might actually be better for me if no one volunteered at the dinner because it would create a lot of sympathy from Dad for a long time. He would think that I would be devastated. Which meant that I could probably milk this fiasco for a new computer or television.

Even though I was at first shocked by the idea, I knew that I had a safety net and I could always say that I wasn't comfortable with the volunteer. If there was a volunteer, I hoped it would be someone who was not considered responsible. That would give me the perfect excuse for bailing out.

So, when Dr. Max called me directly to tell me that I would be honored at the dinner for the web site development and that my dream trip would be part of the program, I showed what I thought to be great delight. In fact, I have to say that I put on one of my better performances, but I probably overdid myself when I stopped talking for a few minutes and then said I needed a facial tissue to wipe away my tears. It truth, it was a stupid idea.

The foundation's annual dinner was held last night and instead of looking forward to this event, I dreaded the whole thing. I couldn't wait till it was over, hopefully without any volunteers for my trip.

The first thing that occurred when I arrived was an interview with a newspaper reporter. Dr. Max was going to get as much publicity out of this thing as possible. The reporter asked me many questions and I answered all of them, except for the one about my illness. I told him it is a personal subject and he was nice enough to leave it alone.

Then the reporter mentioned something about attending two San Francisco Giants baseball games during my trip. This was news to me, but I guess Dr. Max thought he was doing me a big favor since he knows I am a baseball fan. But I found out that attending the games had nothing to do with my love for baseball.

The reporter told me that Dr. Max would ask for pledges to the foundation based on the number of runs scored by the Giants and the opposing team during the games I was to attend. He gave me this example: if someone pledges $100 for each run and the total number of runs scored by both teams for the two games equal 20, the foundation would receive a $2,000 contribution from this person alone.

You have to give Dr. Max credit; not only would he get lots of publicity for my trip, but he could also receive big donations through these baseball pledges. He is a smart man who never misses an opportunity to get more money and recognition for the foundation. For that, I very much admire him.

After we finished the main course and dessert was being served, Dr. Max took the stage and talked about all of the good things that have been done by the foundation. His speech was followed by an informative video presentation. He then introduced people in the audience; my guess is that these people must be major contributors to the foundation.

Then it was my turn. I was asked by Dr. Max to join him on stage.

Here I was in my rented tuxedo with all of those lights shining in my face, and I was hoping that no one would notice that I was shaking. I thought for sure I would piss in my pants in front of everyone. You can just imagine a pool of pee forming around me as Dr. Max spoke. He might have electrocuted himself if he stepped in the pee while holding the microphone.

I had no idea what Dr. Max was saying while I was on stage, but I continued to smile while feeling pure fear. He asked me something and I somehow got the courage to answer him, but right now, I don't remember what he asked or what I said. My response must have sounded okay because the audience clapped.

This is when he was glowing in his remarks about my contribution in developing a web site for the foundation. He also talked about San

Francisco and Alcatraz. At this point, he told people to look at the program brochure to see the obligations for a volunteer. I wonder what the program said because people started reading while we were on stage.

Then the big moment arrived and Dr. Max asked for volunteers. It reminded me of an auction, except that the auctions I have seen usually have lots of immediate activity. This wasn't the case in my auction.

When Dr. Max wasn't having luck getting volunteers, I was surprised that I had mixed emotions. On the one hand, I was delighted because it would mean that I wouldn't have to take this silly trip. However, I also felt slightly discouraged because I felt that people were rejecting me rather than the trip itself. I know this must sound crazy, but I was actually a little hurt and embarrassed.

Dr. Max then took the microphone in his hand and walked between the dinner tables. Many people put their heads down as he passed them.

It was like being in class and hoping the teacher wouldn't call on you to read in front of the entire class. For the brief time that I attended school, I never made eye contact with teachers when they were looking for volunteers.

Then out of nowhere I saw a raised hand. My first thought was someone was stretching, but this wasn't the case. A man, who seemed a little older than Dad, raised his hand. Dr. Max spotted him, rushed to the volunteer's table and escorted him to the stage.

Dr. Max was very relieved because this could have been an absolute bomb for him.

I didn't really know how to feel. Instead of looking at this as a "win-win" situation, it was a "lose-lose" deal for me. Before I was introduced this evening, I was very much hoping that there wouldn't be a volunteer. However, once on stage, I was in a minor panic when no one initially raised a hand. I could just imagine the headlines in the morning paper if no one volunteered – "Sick Kid Rejected At Charity Dinner." But I still didn't want to go on the trip.

After the hand was raised, I didn't know whether to smile or cry. I probably looked like a fool because I showed no emotion – I just stood there on stage, staring at the audience. I was so damn close to both victory (for not having to take the trip) and humiliation (because no one wanted me). I wasn't sure which would have been better.

The rest of the evening is a blur. I was introduced to the volunteer, who was identified as Mr. Peter Franklin. The funny thing is that this guy also had the "deer in headlights" look when he arrived on the stage, so I didn't feel alone.

After Dr. Max concluded the event, Dad and I approached Franklin. They exchanged business cards and a few words. Dad then did something that was very uncharacteristic of him – he gave this stranger a bear hug. I thought for a moment he was going to plant a big wet kiss on the guy. Boy, that was embarrassing; it looked like a scene from one of the "***Godfather***" movies when someone thanked the "Don" for a favor. I expected Dad to get on his knees and kiss Franklin's right hand.

While they were hugging, I noticed a woman sitting a few feet from us at Franklin's table; I figured she must be his wife. She made me feel self-conscious because she was quietly laughing to herself.

I thought she was either drunk or there was a private joke between her and Franklin. Then it hit that she may be laughing at me for some reason. I immediately looked to see if my zipper was down, but thankfully it wasn't.

That would have been the topper, to be on stage with my fly wide open and part of my shirt hanging out.

On the way home, Dad said that I was very lucky to have Franklin as the volunteer because he is a well-known and highly respected investment banker. Dad hadn't said this before the event started, but I guess he was beginning to have second thoughts about the trip. But he now feels comfortable; especially after Dr. Max give him glowing information about Franklin.

He also said he thinks this trip will do me a "world of good." He and Laura were becoming increasingly worried that I was becoming a hermit – never leaving the apartment for weeks at a time. He now believes this trip will give me a once in a lifetime opportunity to have a wide variety of experiences.

By the time we arrived at the apartment, I faced the realization that there is a gigantic tear smack in the middle of my safety net.

So I sat down at the computer and typed a list of everything that had turned against me during the evening, including –

1. The publicity for the foundation – it would be embarrassing for everyone involved if I backed out.
2. The whole business about pledges based on runs scored – another unexpected complication.

3. Franklin appears to be the pillar of the community – I can't say that he may be a pervert.
4. Dad is delighted about the trip because he thinks it will be a great experience. I would never want to let him down.

There was no question about it; I'm totally screwed.

I might as well start packing, unless, of course, I get lucky, like maybe my buddy Franklin is forced to cancel if he gets too busy at work. But fat chance this will happen. As a betting man, I would say the odds are ten to one that he won't cancel.

With my luck, Franklin is either a do-gooder who is anxious to take the trip or he is volunteering so he will look like a decent person to his wife and friends. My gut feeling is that Franklin isn't doing this for me – I think he wants to be a hero to someone.

Actually, it doesn't really matter what his motivation might be for volunteering. The point is that either way, I already don't like the guy.

CHAPTER 5

"EVASIVE ACTION"

BY PETER

March 10, 1999 – New York City

I didn't sleep much last night so I took the opportunity to develop my game plan for avoiding the San Francisco commitment.

By five o'clock in the morning, I was confident that I wouldn't be traveling with Rocky. I knew that either my "first attack" or "backup" plan would prove successful.

I woke up before Kathy, took a shower and went to a shop down the street to buy warm bagels, cream cheese and lox. I also bought fresh squeezed orange juice and a bag of fresh coffee beans, which I ground when I returned to the apartment.

I sliced the bagels and presented the accompanying items in a manner I had learned over the years from my firm's caterer. I made coffee and warmed milk, which is the way Kathy likes it.

Kathy came into the breakfast room shortly after eight. She had a curious look on her face; this is understandable since it is rare for us to see each other in the morning, let alone eat breakfast together, particularly during the weekdays.

She didn't say "hello" or "good morning", but rather a terse, "Okay, what's on your mind?"

This was not a particularly good start.

I tried to say something articulate, but I just stammered that I wanted to have breakfast at home since I had plenty of time before my first meeting.

Kathy wasn't buying this explanation, nor would I because it wasn't credible.

To make a long story short, before I was able to say anything about the previous evening, Kathy said, "Look, if you think I'm going to help get you off the hook with Rocky and the trip, you're very much mistaken."

She then took her cup of coffee along with a bagel and left the room without saying another word.

Even though I couldn't see her face as she walked away, the odds are 100 to one that she was smiling as she left. I know she must have been enjoying my torment.

In hindsight, I probably tipped her off with the breakfast approach. This was not a good tactical move because it was out of character for me. She knew I had an ulterior motive from the moment she walked into the breakfast room. Next time I need a favor from her, I will take a different line of attack – she always seems to be more sympathetic when I pretend that I'm feeling sorry for myself.

I actually had a persuasive argument for why she should replace me as the volunteer, but I never had the opportunity to give her my reasoning. First, she could visit a good friend from her college days who now lives in the San Francisco area. Second, I suspected that Rocky would feel more comfortable with Kathy than with me. She would be doing him a favor, not me.

Having failed miserably with the Kathy approach, I quickly regained my confidence and moved to the backup plan.

I picked up the phone and dialed, and much to my surprise, I connected with Jennie on the first attempt. On those few times that I called her in the past, we often exchanged voice mail messages for days.

Like mother, like daughter - instead of saying "hello", she said, "What's the matter?" Her first thought was that someone was ill or had died.

In fairness, I can't blame Jennie for reacting in this manner since I hadn't called since her birthday many months before.

After I assured her that nothing was wrong, I asked fatherly-type questions about school, friends and other stuff, which of course was of little interest to me. She quickly dispensed with these questions with one-syllable answers, like "fine" or "good." Jennie was waiting for the punch line, meaning the purpose of my call.

I told Jennie about our wonderful evening at the foundation dinner and explained that I had volunteered to take a young man with medical problems on his dream trip to San Francisco. But this morning, it occurred to me that the trip would probably be much more enjoyable for her than it would for me. She wouldn't have to worry about missing any of her schoolwork since the trip could easily be scheduled during Spring break.

Even though Kathy couldn't possibly have spoken with her before I made the call, Jennie was well prepared with a quick and succinct response.

First, she informed me that her plans for Spring break had already been finalized. She wasn't going to make any changes for me. Then she said something that I thought was rather vindictive.

Even if she didn't have plans for Spring break, she still wouldn't take the trip because she claims that I once told her, "Once you make a commitment to others, you should always honor that commitment." I told her that I don't remember ever saying such a thing and even if I did, there are always exceptions for extenuating circumstances.

My immediate reaction was that here is a kid who usually can't remember where she last placed her car keys, but she recalls something inane that I supposedly said many years before.

Just like Kathy, my revengeful little daughter must have really enjoyed this moment. The next time they need something from me, I will remind them of how they treated me in my time of desperate need. Believe me, they will pay for this.

Without Kathy and Jennie, I was basically down to the following choices, find another person to replace me or simply excuse myself from the commitment due to extenuating circumstances, namely work. However, this would be my last resort because the ramifications of declining to go on the trip were far too great.

By the time my cab reached the office, I knew that my fate had been essentially sealed - I couldn't seek another volunteer. My dear son Josh has broken diplomatic relationships with me, so he was out. My mother wouldn't be able to endure such a trip with a teenager. I even thought about my assistant, but this isn't feasible since she is a married mother of two young kids.

As I was in the elevator, the solution came to me.

It's actually pretty simple – I'd suggest that either Rocky's father or mother join their son on the trip, at my expense. Rocky would certainly feel more comfortable with one of them than he would with a complete stranger.

The first thing I did when I reached the office was to call Rocky's father to arrange a meeting.

After missing each other playing "phone tag" during the morning, I finally connected with Michael in the afternoon. I told him I had meetings late into the evening, but I could break away early tomorrow. We decided to get together tomorrow night – he suggested that we meet at my house.

I bet Michael suggested my house for the meeting because he is understandably curious about how I live. I would do the same before sending one of my kids across the country with someone I don't know. Maybe if I throw papers and garbage all around the house and come out to meet them in my old pajamas, Michael may decide against the trip. Better yet, I could be dressed in my underwear and watching a porno movie when they arrive. I can't do that because Dr. Max would tell everyone that I'm a deviant. So, I'll have to be on my best behavior.

My mind was relieved and I focused on finalizing the merger, which we expect to publicly announce tomorrow morning.

The good news is that the matter with Rocky is well in hand. He will be joined by one of his parents on his dream trip. Everyone will be happy with the outcome.

Now you can understand why my colleagues often refer to me as the "miracle man." I have an uncanny knack for solving the unsolvable.

CHAPTER 6

"THE MEETING"

BY ROCKY

March 11, 1999 – New York City

When Dad told me he scheduled a meeting for tonight with Franklin, my first reaction was to suggest that they meet in private. However, when I gave it more thought, it occurred to me that I better get to know this man since I might soon be spending a few days with him on the other side of the country.

Actually, I was also secretly hoping he would do something to irritate or frighten Dad or me. Hopefully he'd act weird or get totally blitzed on alcohol. Or maybe, I could do something during the evening to make him have second thoughts about taking an unbalanced teenager on this kind of trip.

When we arrived at his townhouse, I was surprised that it isn't fancy-looking on the outside, but I must admit that it's hard to beat the location – on the upper East side, a couple of blocks from Central Park.

The inside of the townhouse is a different story – it has high ceilings, different colored walls in each room, hardwood flooring and awesome furniture throughout the entire place. Even though every room has great features, my favorite room is Franklin's office, which has a large-screen television, a computer desk, bookshelves covering an entire wall and a view of the Park from a large window. If you put a bed in that room, I could live there forever.

His wife, Kathy (she asked me not to call her "Mrs. Franklin") joined us, which made me feel more comfortable. I wish she would take me on this trip instead of her husband, but I know this isn't possible.

You may be wondering whether Kathy or Franklin remind me of any celebrities. The answer is yes. Kathy is like Meryl Streep, a little in looks, but more in her mannerisms. She is a very nice woman, down to earth, warm and outgoing.

Franklin on the other hand is stiff and businesslike. He showed no warmth during the entire evening. He half-smiled whenever someone said something humorous, but otherwise showed little emotion. Frankly, he seems to be full of himself in many ways and comes off as being incredibly arrogant. To be more blunt about it, he's a classic "know-it-all" jerk.

In a way, he reminded me of Harrison Ford when he played the serious and cold businessman in the movie *"**Sabrina**"* . Mr. Franklin also resembles Mr. Ford in other respects: his size, build, slightly graying hair and overall appearance. I only wish he was like Mr. Ford in the role he played as Indiana Jones or even when he was in the movie *"**The Fugitive**"* .

At one point, I saw that Franklin was trying to get a point across to Dad, but it went completely over Dad's head. Franklin asked whether our family had ever taken a trip to the West Coast. Dad explained that at one time we had planned to do so, but after Mom's death, he never gave it further consideration.

The way Mr. Franklin looked at Kathy, it was obvious they didn't know about Mom's death.

Franklin then said it would be only fitting that Dad and I experience this wonderful trip together.

It was obvious what Franklin was trying to do – when I looked at Kathy, I had the feeling she was also wise to him, which is why I think her mood suddenly changed toward her husband.

No question about it, the way she was glaring at him, my man Franklin was probably in lots of trouble – if I'm right about what Kathy was thinking, Franklin won't get any loving from her for many weeks. He'll be lucky if she thaws out by the summer.

I was starting to feel pretty good because maybe my luck was about to turn. This guy was obviously trying to weasel his way out of the trip. I could conceivably escape the trip or at the very least, Dad would be my traveling buddy. Although I would prefer to stay at home, the next best alternative would be to go on the trip with Dad or Laura.

Dad still didn't seem to understand that Franklin was trying to sneak one by him. But Dad is sometimes too trusting of people and refuses to believe that some have rotten motives.

Even if he could swing it financially, Dad said he still thought it would be a much more fruitful experience for me to see San Francisco through the eyes of a seasoned traveler like Franklin.

He didn't know it, but Dad just killed me with that statement. I had a chance to make a clean break, but it fell apart because Dad couldn't see through this imposter.

So, much to the disappointment of Franklin and myself, it seemed we were about to embark together on this unwanted journey.

Once this was established, it was odd sitting there, the two travelers looking totally dejected and the non-travelers in obviously good spirits.

Since Franklin's stature was elevated even higher in Dad's eyes as a result of the meeting, it seemed I had no viable excuses to veto him as my traveling companion.

After returning home, I just sat in my room and stared out the window for a long time.

Sometimes, when I'm going through a difficult time, I think about Mom and what she would advise me to do given what she now knows about life. When I approach things this way, the problems I may be facing don't seem so insurmountable.

One question that she typically whispers is, "What's the worst thing that can happen?"

In this case, assuming that Franklin is not a pervert or mass murderer, the worst that can happen is only a few miserable days away from the comforts of my home.

Mom nailed it again when she said, "So what?" The trip would be over in the blink of an eye and I would soon be back home with Dad. Besides, even if I had a crappy time, at least I would have something to discuss the next time I had an opportunity to impress a girl, which probably happens for me only once every five years.

I wonder what Franklin is thinking right now? I could actually be wrong about this guy and maybe he was really thinking about Dad and me in offering that we take the trip together and he wasn't trying to avoid the trip. But I don't think so, especially the way Kathy sneered at him. There's no question that something was going on between the two of them that I may never know, but my instincts tell me that this is a man who cannot be trusted.

Let me figure this out in detail. If we leave on a Monday morning, most of that day will be taken up by our flight. I wouldn't have to talk with him during the flight because I could watch movies or read, but I'll keep my headsets on at all times, even if I'm not listening to anything. After we arrive in San Francisco, I would say that I'm too tired to do anything that afternoon and pretend to take a nap in my room. We would eat a quick dinner and return to the hotel within a couple of hours. So the first day won't be bad.

On the second day, we would tour Alcatraz, which is something I want to do with or without Franklin. Since we will be with others during the tour, I won't have to talk to him. After another nap, we would go to a Giants game, where we would eat dinner. We would return to the hotel exhausted. Another day would quickly pass.

I'm sure that on the third day we would tour other attractions in the city, eat lunch and after my nap, go to the second Giants game. We might again eat at the ballpark and return to the hotel late in the evening, so we wouldn't need to spend very much time alone with each other during this day.

The next morning, we would take a return flight home and I would follow the same routine of using the headsets for the entire flight.

The total time away would be four days and three nights. If I followed my plan, Franklin and I would only have a few hours of private time together during the entire trip.

My guess is that from the time we depart on Monday morning until we return on Thursday afternoon, I'll be away for about 80 total hours. The air travel time both ways will be about 10 hours and the nap and evening sleep times would take another 35 or so hours. After at least 25 hours for cab rides, the Alcatraz and city tours and the baseball games, this means that I'll only have about 10 hours total with Franklin, without a diversion.

When I break it down this way, it doesn't seem so bad. I'm sure that with all of his important work at whatever he does for a living, some of those few hours will be devoted to business matters.

With any luck, maybe we won't say more than 100 words to each other during the entire trip. And if things get bad and he becomes a pain in the ass, I could always play the "sick" card. He knows that I'm not healthy so it shouldn't come as any great surprise to the brilliant Mr. Franklin if I don't feel well enough to join him for any particular activity.

After a sleepless night following the big event, I can sleep well tonight knowing that things are not as bad as they first appeared.

Thanks Mom.

CHAPTER 7

"SURRENDER"

BY PETER

March 12, 1999 – New York City

When I arrived at my office, I was sure everyone noticed my foul mood. There were no phony "good mornings" and I didn't exchange any pleasantries with my assistant. I just called her to my office and dictated orders for her and others. She had often seen me in this type of mood and painfully learned that it is best to stay away from me at these times.

Given what I consider to be a rather powerful ability to persuade people, I was disappointed that I failed miserably with Kathy, Jennie and Rocky's father. Last night was a major disappointment because Michael never got my hint about taking his son on this trip.

By the way, I found Michael to be an outstanding person. It was obvious that he has experienced a great amount of pain as a result of his wife's death. Yet, he seems to have his life in perspective, particularly his apparently close relationship with Rocky. From the way he spoke about his daughter, I gather he is in tight with her as well.

Anyway, I feel I'm a good judge of character and Michael is a quality guy who can be trusted with anything. I just wish he trusted me last night and accepted my veiled offer to send him on the trip with Rocky.

Rocky, on the other hand, is difficult to read. He said little to me, but seemed to jell immediately with Kathy. Perhaps there was the intimidation factor. Since I can't even loosen up with my kids, I can understand how Rocky must feel around me. I've tried to kid around with Josh and Jennie, but whenever I do, they look at me in a funny way. You know the look I'm talking about; it's like when dogs tilt their head because they can't understand what a human is saying to them.

What bothered me more than anything about Rocky was the way he seemed to be focusing on me. It was as if he was trying to read my thoughts. Don't get me wrong, it wasn't eerie, but I have no doubt that he saw through my attempt to avoid the trip. There's something concealed inside this kid, but I doubt I'll know him long enough to figure him out.

I have a feeling that Rocky is a disturbed child, but you can't really blame the kid since he lost his mother at a young age and because he is apparently ill. My guess is that he also has low self-esteem, but when you rarely see outsiders, which I gather is the case with Rocky, it's understandable that a person's confidence level is below par.

Thankfully, he's not my problem. I have enough to deal with in my family.

I have made it a habit to check my voice-mail and e-mail messages when I first arrive at the office in the morning. When I pulled up my e-mail, I was surprised to see that Michael had sent this message at 10:39 the prior evening:

Dear Pete:

It was good to meet you and Kathy tonight. Thankfully, you confirmed what I had heard from Dr. Max and I have absolutely no qualms about the trip.

I know what you were attempting to do during our conversation. The answer to the question you were posing is an unequivocal "yes" – I would dearly love to join Rocky on this trip.

Please understand that I very much appreciated your gesture and under normal circumstances, I would have accepted the proposal that you were about to make. However, for Rocky's sake, I graciously decline your kind offer.

When Dr. Max first suggested the trip, I had serious reservations. For one thing, I was worried about Rocky's health. However, since he doesn't have any significant limitations at this point, I concluded that the trip would actually be beneficial.

Let me explain why I pretended that I didn't understand the thrust of your question.

I really believe that Rocky needs a "soul mate" other than his sister or myself. While we are an incredibly close-knit family, Rocky doesn't have any close friends. There is no one that he can confide in outside of his own immediate family.

Believe me, I don't expect you to become Rocky's pal, but perhaps he can gain enough trust and confidence in you that he will be able to open up to others. Since he has been hurt many times by young people who he thought were his friends, Rocky pretty much lives inside his shell, both figuratively and *literally*. He's very much afraid of getting hurt, so he no longer attempts to befriend anyone.

I'm sure you are more than a little curious about Rocky's medical condition. First, you should know that Rocky receives a thorough medical review every three months by a doctor who is an expert on his condition. I don't mean to be secretive about his ailment, but knowing Rocky's sensitivity, I prefer that he tell you directly, if and when he feels comfortable in doing so.

Rest assured that Rocky is not receiving any treatment at the present time nor does he pose any risk to you during this trip. I will, however, give you his doctor's telephone and pager numbers as well as his e-mail address. I will also furnish you with a letter from the doctor describing his condition and a medical authorization form should Rocky need any treatment during the trip.

This brings me to my final point. I don't know what motivated you to volunteer for this cause, but whatever it was, I couldn't be happier that you've done so. Unfortunately, since his mother's death from the same ailment that afflicts Rocky, he is certain he won't have a long life. This is probably true given the current state of medical knowledge about his ailment, which has led Rocky to be preoccupied by this notion of an early death. Consequently, he doesn't plan beyond a few months in the future and he has even gone to the extreme of writing his obituary and planning the music for the funeral service.

I'm hoping that the "fighting spirit" that you have developed in your vocation will rub off on Rocky, even if only to a limited extent. In other words, I don't want him to give up so easily. I believe that caving in to this disease will undoubtedly shorten his life.

As far as the timing of the trip is concerned, after reviewing Rocky's calendar, we suggest the week of April 12th, but of course we understand that your schedule takes priority.

God bless you.
Michael

Now I really feel like a total schmuck.

Here I am using every devious scheme possible to avoid this trip and Michael thinks that I'm a caring person who is thinking about him and his son by offering them the opportunity to take this trip together.

I deal with so many people whose sole purpose in life is to screw others that I often forget there are still decent people out there.

Michael's e-mail essentially reinforced my conclusion that I have a firm commitment to Rocky and his father. There's no backing out now, even if something occurs at the firm that requires my presence.

The first thing I did after reading Michael's message was to apologize to Kathy for my actions the morning after the foundation dinner. It was interesting that she seemed skeptical about my apology, but I really can't blame her. Kathy probably thought I was making another sneaky maneuver to avoid my obligation to Rocky.

After lunch, I called a meeting with my partner Jack Till, Chris and a couple of other junior associates who often work with me. The purpose of the meeting was to review pending projects and to also plan our activities so I could clear my calendar for that week in April.

I asked Jack to join the meeting because we often cover for each other while one of us is on vacation, traveling or engaged in one of our marathon negotiating sessions.

Jack and I joined the firm at the same time and you could say he is my best friend, both inside and outside the firm. I wanted Jack to have a comprehensive look at my outstanding projects. This way, he could easily respond in a fully informed manner should any emergencies arise.

I must admit I have become increasingly concerned about Jack's ability to effectively handle my projects when I'm not available. When Jack and I first met, we were inseparable. His first wife was also very close to Kathy.

After 12 years of marriage and three children, Jack's wife filed for divorce when she found out that Jack was having an affair with his secretary.

Jack then married his secretary and they had a child during their six years of marriage. Well, Jack couldn't help himself and had another affair, which lead to the second divorce.

After a few wild years as a bachelor, Jack surprised us one day by calling from Las Vegas to announce his third marriage. He had met his new bride, who is 18 years younger than him, while they were both seeking professional assistance for their substance abuse problems.

In the meantime, Jack never stopped pissing away money. He truly lives hand to mouth and not only has hefty child support and alimony obligations, but he and his current wife also live very high. They own an expensive townhouse in the city as well as a second home in the Hamptons.

Jack and his wife remained sober for the better part of a year, but then she fell off the wagon and instead of helping her, he joined her. They readily admit they have serious drinking problems, but they seem unwilling or unable to do anything to get help.

Kathy believes they not only drink excessively, but based on her observations at social events, they probably take "recreational drugs." I wouldn't doubt it because Jack often looks "wired" and I've often noticed him popping pill, particularly when we are required to put in lengthy hours.

Earlier in the year, Jack faced problems with the firm's Executive Committee after he failed to meet an important deadline for a particular client's project. That client severed its long-term relationship with the firm as a result of Jack's negligence.

The Committee concluded that Jack should be terminated, not only for this incident, but also for his apparent inability to effectively handle the needs of other clients.

I saved Jack on that occasion, with the understanding that one more transgression would mean immediate severance from the firm.

Jack would undoubtedly be handsomely paid upon termination because of the value of his partnership interest. However, given his personal overhead and lack of savings, I suspect that Jack would quickly squander any windfall he would receive from the firm. At his age and given his reputation, I'm sure Jack realizes that it would be very difficult for him to find a comparable position.

After Jack's reprimand by the Executive Committee, he became like a frightened animal. Instead of working harder and in a more effective manner, the incident had the opposite effect. Jack is now deathly afraid to make critical decisions without first consulting with me or other trusted partners. He also does everything possible to avoid negotiating sessions that involve a large cast of players. His confidence is shot.

I realize that Jack probably can't effectively function within the firm. Perhaps it is wishful thinking on my part, but I'm still hopeful he will regain his confidence if he has a few successes, regardless of their relative size or meaning. For this reason, I want him to know I have complete faith in him and his abilities as a transactional banker and this is why I keep emphasizing that he is my backup during my absences.

In order to calm him down about my absence, I assured Jack that I would remain in constant contact with him during the trip. In addition, I would keep my mobile phone, pager and laptop with me at all times. If an emergency should arise, I could always use the facilities at our firm's San Francisco office.

Having comforted Jack about the trip, I gave my assistant an anticipated schedule so she could make the travel arrangements. I decided to use frequent flier mileage credits for first class upgrades. I can't remember the last time I flew in the back of a plane and I suspect that Rocky has never flown in the front.

In the next few weeks, I will do as much as possible at work to avoid any major lingering projects which could be problematic to Jack and consequently for me.

Through constant contact with Jack and others in the firm during my absence, I expect that his involvement will be minimal, which means I won't have to worry that he'll screw anything up. On the positive side, for Jack, the fact that I trust him during my absence may lead other partners in the firm to do the same. Who knows, maybe he'll eventually redeem himself.

So you see, I'm not as bad as you may have thought and contrary to what others believe, I actually have a heart and I use it at least once every few years. But please don't let anyone know my secret.

CHAPTER 8

"AIRBORNE"

BY ROCKY

April 12, 1999 – New York to San Francisco

At first, it was odd flying with an adult travel companion that I had only briefly met on two occasions. Overall, I may have said all of 10 words to him during those encounters. I will be spending the better part of one week with this guy, yet I know very little about him and he knows practically zilch about me.

Rather than repeat the details about the trip, here is the e-mail I sent to Dad with the particulars:

Dear Dad:

First, I want to say I'm sorry for the way I acted on the way to the airport. I didn't mean to jump all over you every time you made a comment. I was very tired after little sleep and of course, there is the anxiety factor. You should have screamed at me because I deserved it. So, I apologize for being such a pain in the ass.

When you started getting teary at the terminal, I was afraid you would trigger a similar response from me. Believe me, I was just as sad as you, but I didn't want to show it.

The flight was great. You can't believe the legroom in first class. It was as good as watching television while lying on the couch at home. Each seat has its own video screen and I was able to watch two recent movies.

You know that food is not a priority for me, but the lunch was great. We started out with appetizers. I have never eaten caviar and it is actually good when you mix it with hard-boiled eggs, onions and sour cream. But it tastes pretty awful alone – you have to add the other stuff to make it edible.

We had our choice for the main course and I chose the pasta instead of fish or steak. I'm glad I did because my second choice was the steak and I saw Pete's serving – it looked like they barely cooked it.

Dessert was the best part of the meal because the flight attendants came around pushing a cart with coffee and vanilla ice cream, hot fudge and butterscotch toppings, nuts, whipped cream and cherries. As you can guess, I had a hot fudge sundae with everything on it.

As you suggested, I took a nap to maintain my strength and I'll try to do this all week if time permits.

Pete (Mr. Franklin asked me to use his first name) worked most of the time during the flight, except for the last hour when he read a magazine about movies and Broadway shows. Maybe we at least have movies as a common interest. I doubt there is anything else we can talk about because he doesn't seem to be interested in anything other than his work.

No, I'm not being negative already, already; I'm just facing reality.

We were late for our arrival, but I guess we were lucky because the airport had been closed due to foggy conditions most of the day. I'm glad it was clear when we landed because I was able to see San Francisco Bay and some of the bridges.

We were taken by private car to a massive high-rise hotel in a very nice area of the city. You wouldn't believe the view of San Francisco and the Bay from my room.

Dad, you are right, this will be a real adventure.

Love, Rocky

I left out a few details about the flight because it would seem like I'm already whining.

For example, shortly after takeoff, Pete gathered a bunch of paperwork and his laptop as if he was making a private office on the plane. He then put on his headset, but I noticed it wasn't plugged into the arm of the seat. He wasn't listening to anything. So he was either trying to drown out the airplane noise or he didn't want to talk with me during the flight.

To be honest, this was fine with me because I had no interest in speaking with him during the flight. I wouldn't know what to discuss with him since I don't know anything about mergers and stuff like that.

For the first couple of hours during the flight, he read thick stacks of paper that were probably legal documents. Occasionally, he made marginal notes on certain pages, but he mostly read the papers. He then shifted his attention to his laptop and once in a while, he typed something. I don't know exactly what he was doing, but it was clear that he wasn't playing computer games.

The rest of the time during the flight, he had his ear glued to the phone – it was pretty irritating, not just to me, but also to some of the other passengers. They gave him dirty looks because he spoke in a loud voice and threatening tone, but he didn't seem to give a shit about the other passengers.

After lunch was served, he wrote notes on a legal-size yellow pad of paper. While I was enjoying the second movie, he asked me to remove my headset. I could see he was reading his notes as he spoke, or rather, lectured me.

The first thing he said was that I could call him "Pete" instead of Mr. Franklin. Wow, big deal – this would be the thrill of the trip!

Second, based on what Dad said about me, he knows that I'm an "obedient" young man. It sounded like he was talking to a housetrained dog. Then he said he "fully expects" me to act this way during the trip. He can't afford any embarrassment. Then came the warning that if I don't behave myself, we would return "forthwith" on the first flight back to New York.

I have two comments to make about this warning. First, I wouldn't mind returning today if possible. Second, what the hell does "forthwith" mean? I suspect it means immediately, if so, why didn't he just use this word instead of trying to impress me with his vocabulary.

That's when he said that I should not hesitate to be open with him. If I'm ever tired or prefer to do something else, I should make this known. He said that he's not a mind reader. I could have told him that because I'm not even sure he can read his own mind. In fact, he probably doesn't have a clue as to what people mean even when they tell him directly. He doesn't strike me as the kind of person who patiently listens to others. Boy, I'd hate to be one of his kids; I couldn't imagine a father like this who thinks he knows everything. It would be unbearable.

Then, he said something that really surprised me. Since we don't know each other, he thought it would be "interesting" for us to share little known facts about ourselves. This way, we can learn about each other during our short time together. I suspect that this was Franklin's sneaky way of trying to find out about my medical condition without asking me directly.

I said fine, but I honestly thought it was a lame idea. Why should I share anything with a guy that I'll probably never see again after this trip? Especially with such a conceited ass like him. I mean, if I really thought he was interested, I wouldn't mind telling him about myself. But instead of pissing him off, I said it was a great idea. He'll probably forget anyway so I won't have to worry about "share and tell" time.

I think this was basically the end of the discussion, but I really wasn't sure. So, in order to cut off this lecture, I quickly changed the subject by asking Pete whether he counted the number of drinks the passenger across the aisle had during the flight. I bet he had at least six drinks, all vodka on the rocks.

I then suggested a bet to Pete. I doubted that this guy could have any more drinks because he was barely able to make to the bathroom. Since we only had about one more hour before our scheduled landing, I thought this was a pretty safe bet. In fact, I was hoping the guy would pass out when he came back from the bathroom.

Pete took the opposite view by betting that he would have at least two more drinks before we landed.

Well, I lost the bet. This guy actually had three more drinks. At one point, the attendant had to go back to the coach area for the last two small bottles of vodka since she had run out in first class. Then this man passed out and he was still snoring as people were exiting the plane.

When we landed, I had a feeling that Pete was surprised by the size and weight of my suitcase. He must know how to pack because he only brought a small carry-on and a light garment bag, plus his attaché case.

We were picked up by a black Lincoln and driven to a hotel in the Embarcadaro area of San Francisco. Pete was on his cell phone during the entire drive from the airport to the city.

What I didn't mention in my note to Dad was my concern about sharing a room with Pete. It is bad enough to travel together, but there's no way that I was going to share a room him. I never mentioned it to Dad because I didn't want him to think I was complaining. But thank God, we had separate rooms and believe me when I say the view from my room is as awesome as I told Dad in the e-mail. I took a couple of pictures from my window to show Dad, Laura and my new friend, Kathy.

After Pete showed me to my room along with the bellboy, he told me he needed a couple of hours to make phone calls. Since his room is across the hall, he said he would knock on my door when it was time for dinner. By winning the bet on the plane about the vodka drinker, he was given the right to select the type of food we would eat for dinner.

After unpacking, I sat in the chair next to the window and enjoyed the view of San Francisco. It's hard to believe that I actually made it to California.

As I sat there, I thought about Mom and what she said to me before I left for this trip. This is when I decided that I should enjoy this trip as much as possible. After all, the hard part is over, meaning the long days of anticipating the departure. But I really can't complain because the flight was fun, especially sitting in first class, watching my personal video screen and eating a hot fudge sundae.

So far, everything is going as I had hoped. Pete and I said very little to each other during the flight and I have confirmed that he will be focused on business. This means that we will have very little interaction. After we see the sites, visit Alcatraz and take in a couple of Giants games, we will be returning home on Friday.

The only disappointment was when Pete said that instead of returning on Thursday, we would go home on Friday. I'm sure he told Dad, but this wasn't my understanding. However, I'm not going to complain. I'm sure we'll do something fun on Thursday. One additional day isn't a big deal. After all, like Mom always said, I have to look at the positive side and this trip could be the opportunity of my short lifetime.

By the way, I know Pete won the bet and could choose whatever restaurant he desired, but I wish he had the decency to ask whether I like seafood.

Of all the things he could have selected in this city of great restaurants, he picked a seafood place. I don't like most seafood but thankfully, I loved the clam chowder, bread and shrimp cocktail. So even a potentially disastrous dinner turned out to be okay.

It was actually a pretty good day. Well, maybe that's going too far – let's just say it wasn't as bad as I expected.

The best part is that Pete completely forgot about sharing secrets with each other after dinner.

I'm so tired that I won't even change my clothes. I just want to get to sleep in preparation for my big day tomorrow at Alcatraz.

CHAPTER 9

"SPEECHLESS"

BY PETER

April 12 – New York To San Francisco

Be careful what you wish for!

Before the flight, my wish was that my little package, Rocky, wouldn't be hyper or constantly interrupt me while I was working. Actually, I wish he had said more. Except for the wager he proposed about a drunken passenger, Rocky hardly made a sound during the entire flight.

If his silence continues throughout this trip, it is going to be a very long few days. But I guess I can't win because I was either going to have a non-stop talker or a mute. It's probably better to have the latter than the former.

The flight was uneventful. I caught up on a number of projects and read all of my e-mail. I even had a chance to read my favorite entertainment magazine.

During the flight, I think I scared Rocky when I laid out the ground rules for the trip. I hope I didn't come across as too abrupt, but I thought we should set the record straight at the very beginning. The most important rule is my expectation that he behave himself at all times. I made it clear that I won't put up with any crap from him.

Actually, instead of being intimidated, Rocky just stared at me and if my hunch is right, I think he believes I'm an absolute jerk, or maybe something even worse. I get the same kind of blank look from Josh when I give him advice.

I'm so used to traveling that I pack very lightly and rarely check in my baggage. Rocky, however, checked in his suitcase and believe me, it's a monster. I could barely take it off the conveyor belt at baggage claim.

I don't have any idea what the kid packed in his suitcase, but it's incredibly heavy. I mean, he had a separate backpack with his laptop and books, so the suitcase must be full of clothes and personal items. Maybe he brought along his complete library of San Francisco and Alcatraz movies.

My guess is that Rocky has enough clothes in that suitcase to last a month. In a way, I can't blame him because he probably has no idea what to expect and he wants to be prepared for any occasion.

I'll stop bitching because it could be much worse. I would be really pissed off if he wore baggy jeans that hung five inches below his waist and oversized shirts that could fit a 300-pound offensive lineman. At least he won't embarrass me if we go to decent restaurants.

Really, I have become a very negative guy and nothing ever seems to please me. Kathy's right because I'm never satisfied and the problem is that it's getting noticeably worse. Imagine what I will be like when I'm in my sixties. I'm on track to become a very mean old man, the kind that kids in the neighborhood avoid at any cost. I don't think I was always this way, but I honestly can't remember ever being any different.

I have no right to take out my frustrations on Rocky because he must be scared to death traveling with an unfriendly stranger who is older than his father. I really need to lighten up for his sake.

Actually, the day went better than expected. As I said, it was as if Rocky wasn't even on the flight with me. I was able to get most of my work done on the plane and by the time we arrived at the hotel, I had already returned two telephone calls from the car. After we checked in, I took care of a conference call from my room. With my laptop and phone, I had a portable office. So, there is no need to worry about work.

When I unpacked, I looked at a sealed envelope that was given to me at the airport by Michael Brooks. The label is marked, ***Andrew Michael (" Rocky") Brooks – Medical Information***.

Apparently, it contains a medical authorization form, a copy of a medical insurance card and a letter from a doctor giving the status of Rocky's condition. Michael asked me not to open the envelope unless there is an emergency. Michael thinks that Rocky might eventually explain his condition to me after we develop a relationship.

Given the short amount of time we will spend together and the expected lack of conversation between us, I doubt we will ever establish a close relationship. Quite honestly, I'm mildly curious about Rocky's condition, but on the other hand, it really isn't a big deal if I ever know.

The chances that Rocky and I will see each other again after the next few days is slim to none and I would bet on none, except maybe at a foundation function.

Since I won the bet with Rocky about the vodka-drinking passenger, I was given the honor of selecting the restaurant for our dinner and since we are in San Francisco, I chose an outstanding seafood place. When I saw Rocky's face while he was reading the menu, it occurred to me I should have asked if he likes seafood.

Rocky was polite enough not to say anything unkind about the restaurant or the food he was served, but judging from his look, he probably would have preferred to starve rather than eat the seafood.

As hard as it may be, I'll have to consider Rocky's favorites when it comes to food, and not my preferences. Even if it means that we'll eat fast food every night during this trip.

This is probably the first of many mistakes on my part, but it could have been far worse. I was actually thinking about taking Rocky to my favorite sushi bar where they specialize in squid. With sushi as his only choice, he might have asked to return home on the "red eye" flight. Come to think of it, this may an effective tactic if he starts to piss me off. I'll just pick food that I know he will hate – I wonder whether he likes Indian cuisine?

At dinner and on the way back to the hotel, Rocky was still reserved. I tried to spark his interest by bringing up various subjects, but all I got was one-word responses. The only time he showed any spirit was when we talked about tomorrow's tour of Alcatraz. I still can't figure out his fascination with Alcatraz – maybe Rocky is a closet criminal at heart.

When we returned to my room, I saw the message light blinking. It was a telephone message in my room from Jack telling me that a draft merger agreement was being sent to me by fax to the hotel. He said he needs my comments before 10 in the morning, Eastern Time. Since the agreement will probably be over 50 pages, this means that I'll need to wake up in the wee hours of the morning to begin my review. It's going to be another night of little sleep.

As I drank Scotch from the mini-bar, I realized that I objected far too much to this trip. Rocky seems like a decent kid and I suspect he will be low maintenance. After all, the next few days will pass quickly and we will soon be returning to New York. Most importantly, I will remain in constant communication with my office and I have little to worry about with my projects in Jack's hands.

While this may not be my ideal trip, I can already tell that it isn't going to be horrendous or time-consuming. I have to apologize to Kathy for acting like a selfish brat because a few days away from the office won't be the end of the world.

Sometimes, I look in the mirror and find it hard to believe that I've become such a self-centered ass. Who knows what Rocky's condition is but one thing is for sure, it will end his life prematurely.

I might as well make the best of this adventure, if for no other reason than for Rocky's sake. This is the kid's dream trip and I'm not going to ruin it for him. I also must think about Michael – he placed his faith in me and I won't let him down.

If Josh were in the same situation, I would certainly want someone to make the effort to fulfill his dreams. It isn't too much to ask for me to take this trip with Rocky, but unfortunately, I stopped thinking about others a long time ago, including my own family.

But in all honesty, there are other reasons for making this a successful adventure. First, it's important for Kathy to see me as a good soul, even though she will no doubt be suspicious of my motivation.

The other reason is admittedly vile. One of the calls I made when we first arrived at the hotel was to Al Roberts, who is a New York-based media relations person. He has represented the firm and many of our clients for years. It occurred to me during the flight that I should make "lemonade out of lemons", or however that expression goes. After giving Al background information about the trip with Rocky, he immediately reached the same conclusion. Both the firm and I would get a tremendous amount of media mileage from this good deed.

Al will prepare a press package during my absence and once we return, he will schedule media interviews for Dr. Max, Rocky and me. My firm's senior partner will send copies of favorable print articles to our major clients.

I know what you may be thinking, but at least the foundation will receive tons of free publicity from this coverage. In addition, Rocky will get his 15 minutes of fame and if he is so inclined, he will draw sympathy for his medical condition. This information might result in increased funding for research and donations to support groups for those afflicted by the disease.

I have to be careful how I orchestrate this media effort. If Kathy finds out that I contacted Al, she will be livid. So, I'll pretend that someone in the firm called Al without my knowledge.

As I stared out the window from my hotel room, I must confess that in hindsight, I wasn't proud of my call to Al. However, it's too late to reverse this action because Al already sent me a fax with copies to members of the Executive Committee laying out his game plan for maximizing media exposure.

Over the past few years, I've become distraught about my distasteful business maneuvering. The scary thing is that these actions just happen, as if they're automatic and without any resulting pangs of guilt on my part. But when I later reflect on what I've done, I'm often repulsed.

The critical question is whether I regret my offensive deeds so much that I am willing to trade my business successes for the possibility of failure. Unfortunately, it's all become a game and winning is the only goal. Nothing less will suffice.

I probably have to accept the fact that I'm at the point of no return. I believe that my phenomenal success in recent years is a direct result of my increasingly heartless and conniving tactics. But it still tears me apart.

Ned asked Rocky and I to be honest and disclose everything to you. So, in keeping with this request, you should know that I already made an unsuccessful attempt at violating the rules we first agreed on with Ned. Because I couldn't tell what Rocky was thinking today, I called Ned to find out, but true to his word, Ned wouldn't give me any hints. He suggested that I ask Rocky directly.

This is a perfect illustration of who I am. Always trying to secure an unfair advantage.

CHAPTER 10

"ESCAPE TO ALCATRAZ"

BY PETER

April 13, 1999 - San Francisco

For whatever reason, Rocky was a completely different person this morning. There was a look of excitement on his face and he was far more expressive, both verbally and with his body movements.

I have to constantly remind myself that this is a reserved teenager who most likely has little self-confidence and I shouldn't push him. What Rocky doesn't know is that I'm probably as nervous as he is.

At least I now know what I could always fall back on if there is a lull in our conversation; Alcatraz is the key to a meaningful dialogue with Rocky. If I were Michael, I'd be very worried if Rocky takes a similar interest in serial killers. Hopefully, he won't want to visit members of the Manson family while we're in California.

I guess it doesn't matter because it's not my problem if Rocky has a dark side. At least he's showing spunk today and that's all I can ask for.

I don't care how callous a person may get; I have to admit that it's still refreshing to see something new through the eyes of a young person. It reminds me of the time Kathy and I took Jennie and Josh for their one and only trip to Disney World. The excitement on their faces said it all.

Unfortunately, Kathy saw far more of that than I did with our kids. On one occasion while the kids were both less than 10 years old, Kathy rented a house on the coast of Maine for part of August. I worked longer hours than usual to make sure that all of my critical projects were completed before I left for Maine.

The day before we were to leave, I received an urgent call from the chairman of one of our major clients. He had been approached by a competitor to discuss a possible merger and asked me to join him for a meeting on the West Coast the following day. I suppose I could have told him about my vacation plans, but I didn't. This project and my client were more important than a vacation.

Before talking with Kathy, I arranged to take a "red-eye" flight to California. I explained the situation later to Kathy while I was packing.

To her credit, she went to Maine without me.

After that missed vacation, I promised myself it wouldn't happen again. Thankfully, I didn't make the same promise to Kathy, because some years later, a similar office-related emergency prevented me from joining the family in South Carolina.

As a consequence of my work schedule, I often missed experiencing new places through the eyes of my children. I now realize those days are lost forever.

This morning, between a few calls to and from my office, Rocky gave me an abbreviated history lesson on Alcatraz.

I wasn't aware that Alcatraz had been a military prison from the mid-1800's until it was converted to a federal prison in 1934. According to Rocky, the prison was the government's response to the post-Prohibition, post-Depression era. The concept was to create a prison where difficult-to-manage prisoners could be placed in one facility.

One of the first occupants of the prison was the infamous Al Capone. I guess when Capone was first housed in an Atlanta federal penitentiary, he remained in constant contact with his family and colleagues who stayed at a nearby hotel. Capone was able to continue to manage his "operations" in Chicago through these contacts. He was also able to bribe prison officers while in Atlanta in order to obtain special privileges, such as a personal radio and expensive furnishings in a carpeted cell.

Based on Rocky's research, this all ended when "Big Al" joined the first official shipment of prisoners to Alcatraz in 1934. There he was assigned menial jobs and apparently treated like any other prisoner.

Throughout breakfast, the cab ride to the terminal and the boat trip to Alcatraz, Rocky described some of the other notable prisoners who had resided in Alcatraz, including "Machine Gun" Kelly, Doc Barker and Robert Stroud, the so-called "Birdman of Alcatraz".

Since it turns out that Rocky and I both enjoy movies, we talked about Burt Lancaster's role in the movie "***Birdman of Alcatraz***".

According to Rocky, Stroud was a very violent man. In the early 1900's, Stroud murdered a bartender in Alaska because the victim had failed to pay a prostitute for whom Stroud was pimping. While in the first penitentiary, Stroud assaulted a hospital orderly and also stabbed a fellow inmate.

Following these acts, Stroud was transferred to Leavenworth Penitentiary in Kansas. After being refused a visit by his brother, he "lost it" and stabbed a prison guard to death in front of over 1,000 inmates while in the mess hall. This offense resulted in the death sentence, which was commuted to life without parole by President Wilson at the request of Stroud's mother.

Due to his violent and unpredictable nature, Stroud was then placed in a segregation unit away from other inmates and most prison officers.

It was during this time that Stroud found an injured bird in the recreation yard and this is when he developed an interest in birds. Over the duration of his 30 years at Leavenworth, Stroud authored two books on the subject after having raised about 300 birds within his cells.

While the study of birds made Stroud more humane, his continuing violation of prison rules led to a surprise, middle of the night relocation to Alcatraz in 1942. He spent most of his 17-year residence on the "Rock" in the prison hospital and he was rarely heard from by the outside world. Stroud died in another prison in 1963 without ever seeing the Burt Lancaster movie.

The most fascinating part of my short course in Alcatraz history was Rocky's description of some of the escape attempts. If Rocky's information is accurate, there were a total of 14 attempts involving 34 prisoners while Alcatraz served as a federal prison. Twenty-three prisoners were caught, six were shot and killed, and five were reported missing and believed to have drowned.

In the movie "*Escape from Alcatraz*", Clint Eastwood played the role of Frank Lee Morris, who supposedly masterminded the most famous escape attempt. Morris became a seasoned criminal after serving in penal institutions virtually all of his adult life. He ended up in Alcatraz after attempted escapes from other institutions.

Morris had two accomplices in this escape, brothers John and Clarence Anglin, who were serving lengthy sentences for bank robbery. The Anglin brothers and Morris had previously met at the Federal Penitentiary in Atlanta. The Anglins also wound up in Alcatraz after various escape attempts.

Morris and the Anglin brothers, together with another neighboring cellmate, developed an elaborate escape plan involving lifelike dummies and the use of over 50 raincoats to make rafts and life preservers.

After months of preparation, Morris and the Anglin brothers made their move. The fourth member of the group was left behind because he wasn't able to loosen the grill from his cell that led to their escape route. The three men climbed to the rooftop and then down some piping to the ground. That was the last time the three men were ever seen.

Although no bodies were ever found, it is unlikely that the men survived. According to the prisoner who was planning to join the other three, the group planned to steal a car and burglarize a clothing store. However, there were no reports of such crimes in Marin County for the two weeks following the escape attempt.

I don't know if Rocky was telling me fact or fiction, but he had read that on the same evening of the escape, a despondent man jumped from the Golden Gate Bridge – several people saw this man jump. Even though the Coast Guard responded quickly, his body was never found. So, the fact that the bodies of the three prisoners were never found doesn't necessarily mean they were successful in reaching land.

This briefing of Alcatraz history actually peaked my interest in the tour; but unfortunately, I had to detach myself from the group in order to respond to an urgent pager message from my office.

Although I can't be certain, I had the feeling that Rocky was either disappointed or upset when I left the group. Actually, he probably didn't give a damn whether I stayed or left.

The Alcatraz tour was not nearly as important as seeing young Mr. Rocky so animated. This is one impressive young man, particularly the way he expresses himself when he chooses to speak. Even though he apparently lives a cloistered life, he certainly has a knack for communication.

On the return boat ride from Alcatraz, an older gentleman approached me while Rocky was standing along the side of the boat taking pictures of the "Rock." He thought Rocky was my son and I expected him to complain about something that Rocky had done while I was away from the group.

Not so, however, he said that Rocky politely interrupted the tour guide on several occasions, mostly to ask questions, but at least twice to expound on the guard's description of a particular event or prisoner. I guess this guy and some of the others in the tour enjoyed Rocky's antics, but apparently the tour guide didn't appreciate Rocky and he seemed a little miffed. Now I really regret missing the tour.

While returning to the hotel, I took a call on my cell phone. Rocky sat silent after I completed the call and then asked whether all of the calls I receive or make are absolutely critical. His tone was sharp when he then asked, "Would the world come to a complete stop if you don't immediately return a call?"

I tried to explain to him that in my business, events move very quickly and a few moments' delay could mean success or failure for a transaction that could be worth billions of dollars.

Having said this, however, I knew this was bullshit and the way Rocky looked at me, I suspect he felt the same about my answer. By and large, emergencies are self-made and typically, a short delay in responding won't make one bit of difference.

This is when Rocky issued a challenge. He said that I'm so addicted to my cell phone that I couldn't avoid using it for three straight hours. Rocky first suggested a three-hour period starting at one o'clock this afternoon, but I told him I needed more time to give my office advance notice not to call me. We compromised and settled on 9:00 a.m. through "high noon" the following morning.

I feel comfortable with this bet because I don't expect any pressing issues tomorrow morning.

Having decided on the bet, we next had to agree on the winner's prize. I suggested that the winner could select the type of food for Thursday night's dinner, since we would be eating at the baseball park tonight and tomorrow evening.

Since Rocky was so confident that he would win, he wanted a far more significant prize. Rocky said that since we haven't planned any activities for Thursday, the winner could select our activity for that day, "within reason, of course."

This time, I wasn't going to blindly commit to something, so I asked if he had any particular activity or place in mind. Rocky said that when (not if) he wins, we would rent a car on Thursday morning and drive to the Monterey Peninsula area for the day. He said something about Pebble Beach being on his "list", just like San Francisco. I didn't dare ask about his "list", but I will in due time.

Although it would make for a long day, I thought this sounded fair. If planned right, I could probably visit my sister, Amy, for lunch since she lives in Santa Cruz.

However, we won't even have to consider Monterey because there is absolutely no way I will lose this bet. To insure victory, I gave my office specific instructions – no one is to call me during those three hours unless it means life or death.

If someone does call, I won't answer. I'll check my voice mail messages after "high noon" and then return the important calls.

I told Rocky that if I win the bet, we would take a leisurely drive to Napa to visit some of my favorite wineries.

The bet was settled and we shook hands.

After making a number of calls that afternoon and early evening, we went to the ball game.

I must admit that I didn't focus on the game because by and large, I find professional baseball games to be incredibly long and awfully dull. I even brought newspapers and magazines along in case I got bored. After two hot dogs, three beers and lots of peanuts, I actually had a reasonably decent time. But instead of watching the game, I enjoyed watching the crowd. Rocky was upset after I missed a critical play; I couldn't tell him that two attractive young women distracted my attention.

The weather was bad that evening and the howling winds at Candlestick are not an exaggeration. I was ill prepared for the cold conditions. When I saw the forecast early in the day, I thought a sports jacket would be sufficient. But it was so cold that I ended up buying a Giants jacket for Rocky and a sweatshirt for myself and this still wasn't enough. I froze my ass off.

I should buy gloves, ski hats and maybe thermal underwear for tomorrow night's game.

When we returned to the hotel, I remembered one of the ground rules I had established the previous day during our flight, namely to share something about each other on a daily basis so we could get to know each other better.

Instead of going directly to our rooms, we went to the coffee shop. Rocky ordered a vanilla shake and I had a root beer float, probably the first one I have had since Josh was Rocky's age.

Rocky asked me to go first with my revelation.

I'm not sure what I was thinking when I proposed this sharing concept. I guess Rocky was so quiet in our prior meetings and during the flight that I thought it would be an icebreaker. But judging from his changed personality today, this suggestion was probably unnecessary. I don't think

Rocky would have cared, but I didn't want to back out; otherwise, I might lose what little credibility I have with him.

I decided to be cautious in what I said and expected him to do the same since we were only going to spend two more days together. I doubted he would reveal any deep secrets and I certainly wasn't about to do so.

I played it safe by telling him about my love for movies and theatre. Had I the balls to tell my father, I probably would have majored in theatre arts in college. It was still my desire to go back to acting in some form or another, not professionally but with a community theatre group, once my work schedule permits.

So the worst thing Rocky could tell people is that Pete was scared of his father and is a "closet" entertainment lover.

Rocky told me his little secret and believe me, it was not much more enlightening than mine. But, I'm not comfortable sharing Rocky's disclosure since it may have been told to me in confidence. Maybe Rocky will tell you his little secrets. I hope he does because Rocky needs to open up to others since I doubt he will with me.

I can't figure this kid out and I doubt I will ever get the chance in the short time we will have together. He is a complex young man and I have a feeling that inside his seemingly cool exterior, there is a large, caring heart. But then again, I have little experience with teenagers and for all I know, Rocky could easily be a totally insensitive kid who hides his anger because of his medical condition.

If I were asked to make a wager about Rocky's personality, I would bet a month's pay that he is a quality person, from head to toe. However, I've been wrong in the past when judging people and he could easily be fooling me.

CHAPTER 11

"BREAKING THROUGH THE ROCK"

BY ROCKY

April 13, 1999 – San Francisco

Dear Dad:

This was another interesting day. First, the tour of Alcatraz was everything I had expected and more. The only disappointment was its size; it seemed much smaller than I expected.

Although it was a mild day temperature-wise, I still can't see how anyone who isn't a great swimmer could get across the bay. Those three guys who tried to escape from Alcatraz couldn't possibly have survived. The water is way too cold and the currents far too strong. After seeing Alcatraz, I now understand why the prison authorities felt it was "escape proof."

Pete and I are getting along fine and I really felt more comfortable with him today. He seemed to take more of an interest in me, especially when we talked about Alcatraz and the movies that are based on the prison. But there's one thing that really started to get me pissed off today. I know I shouldn't say this, but Pete has a problem with his cell phone. He's like a teenage girl who's addicted to her phone. We should get Pete together with Laura so they could have a record-breaking phone marathon.

I thought he would enjoy the Alcatraz tour, especially after I gave him a history lesson about the prison, but he left the tour to take a "call." I don't think every call is critical, but I guess I'm probably underestimating Pete's role in the corporate world.

Maybe this whole investment banker thing is a front and Pete is really a mafia chief - every time he makes an important call, he's ordering another hit or working on a drug buy.

It's doubtful he would ever admit this, but I have a feeling Pete answers every call because it makes him feel like an influential guy and that everyone is anxiously waiting for Mr. Big to make some momentous decision. For all I know, the people in his office could be asking him what they should serve a client for dinner.

The more I'm around Pete, the more I'm convinced that he's full of himself. It must be some kind of insecurity thing because someone who has high self-esteem wouldn't try to make himself seem so important.

Don't get me wrong, he's an okay guy, but I'd hate to be his son and it would be even worse to work for him because he's damn rude on the phone to people in his office. That must be part of his insecurity, because no one has the right to push people around the way he does. I don't care if you're the President of the United States, people should be treated with respect.

While we were taking the boat to Alcatraz, I was tempted to grab the phone from his hand and throw it into the bay. It's really irritating trying to talk to someone when his phone constantly interrupts you.

I know you wouldn't want me to make bets with Pete, but I have a feeling he's a gambler at heart. Besides, we're not betting with money. We bet that he wouldn't be able to stay off his cell phone for three straight hours. This is a sure win for me because he doesn't have the willpower to resist. He's a classic cell-phone junkie.

After I win, we will take a trip to Pebble Beach on Thursday. If by some miracle he wins, we will be heading to the wine country in Napa, which honestly sounds boring.

By the way, I'm sure you told me, but I thought we would be returning to New York on Thursday. Pete mentioned that Thursday is an open day and we will return on Friday. This isn't a major issue, but I was mistaken about our return date. I'm telling you this in case you also think we are coming back on Thursday.

The Giants game this evening was great, except it was very chilly.

As I told you before I left, this is the last year the Giants will play at 3Com Park. You were right when you said they had changed the name from Candlestick Park.

An employee of the hotel who helped us get a private car for the game suggested that we wear warmer clothes because of the cold and windy conditions at the ballpark. Pete ignored him, which turned out to be a stupid move.

The driver said that your favorite player, Willie Mays, could have been the all-time home run king if he had not played at Candlestick. He believes the wind often knocked down high fly balls that would have been home runs for Mays in most other parks. He's probably right because the wind was terrible tonight.

Next year, the Giants will move to a new park that is being built closer to the city, near a place called the China Basin Channel. Our driver took us by the new park and told us that some home runs to right field would fly right into the channel. Maybe you and I can plan to take a vacation on the West Coast next year to see a game at this park. Yes, this is not an imposter writing to you – it's your son Rocky talking about planning something for next year. I bet I never cease to amaze you.

The game was not very exciting because there was little to cheer about after the sixth inning. The Astros got ahead by a score of 4 to 2 in that inning and eventually won the game 7 to three. There were only two home runs and both were hit in the ninth inning; one by Barry Bonds. The Astro pitcher, Mike Hampton skunked the Giants for seven innings, allowing only two hits.

The only time there was an exciting play, I turned and saw Pete looking in a different direction. He missed the action on the field, but it turned out that his eyes were glued to two young women who were sitting below us. He's so conceited that he probably thinks women find him attractive. Other than possibly his mother, I doubt that any woman would think he is handsome, probably not even Kathy. She must have married him for his money, but it sure wasn't for his charm or good looks.

By the way, the total attendance was 9,425. I couldn't believe it since the park seats at least 60,000 people. This is probably why it didn't seem very exciting, but at least there were very few people in the food and bathroom lines.

Speaking of the game, I forgot to tell you that I received an e-mail from Dr. Max telling me that the foundation had received pledges totaling $1,225 for each run scored in the two games. Since 10 runs were scored tonight, the foundation will receive contributions of $12,250 for this game alone.

One final thing before I fall asleep.

During the flight yesterday, Pete suggested that in order for us to get to know each other, we would each share something that is not commonly known about ourselves.

I really didn't like the idea, but I'm sure you would have wanted me to go along with him. I understand that Pete is trying to get to know me better and I can't really fault him for making this effort, but he could have been more creative. For a guy who is supposed to be so very bright and successful, I must say that he hasn't impressed me one bit with his brainpower. I honestly think that many people like Pete who have high up positions in the business world are overrated. However, I'd bet my computer that Pete doesn't think so – he probably believes all of the crapshit that people tell him about his greatness. What absolute crap because he doesn't even come close to you in intellect.

Just so you're not surprised in case he brings it up, I told Pete that other than you, I don't have any real friends. I realize that a couple of guys come over once in while, but they're not friends in the true sense. Most of the time, I think they're more interested in my computer games than they are in me.

Please don't be sad about this, but because of my health, it's very hard to have true friends. I wish it could be different, but I've accepted this as my reality.

Thankfully, I couldn't have a better friend than you.

I can't repeat what Pete shared with me because anything I tell him will remain confidential. Even though it wasn't said, I expect he would want me to do the same with information he gives me.

I may be kidding myself, but I really think I made a little progress with Pete today. Since we visited Alcatraz, it seems only fitting to say that I "broke through the rock" and got a small peek into Pete's inner workings. Plus, Pete was more open and he actually tried to make funny comments, but I didn't understand his dry sense of humor.

On the negative side, Pete isn't patient like you and he seems to think he's hot stuff, especially when he deals with people whom he considers to be beneath him. Unfortunately, he thinks this about most people and I'm sure that your son is member of this group.

It may all be hogwash (notice I didn't say "bull____", which is what I first typed), but tonight Pete said that he had an enjoyable day and is pleased to be on this trip with me.

I'm exhausted and will sign off, but don't be concerned about me because it's a good kind of tired.

Love you Dad.
Rocky

CHAPTER 12

"LOSING BUT WINNING"

BY PETER

April 14, 1999 – San Francisco

Although I was initially pissed off at Jack, I really couldn't blame him. The poor guy is scared of his shadow, or more likely, of the imposing shadow of the firm's Executive Committee. He realizes that he is under a magnifying glass.

Rocky's three-hour phone abstinence bet started this morning while he and I were having breakfast at the hotel. I left my phone on to monitor the telephone numbers of the callers so I could return the calls later. This turned out to be a serious mistake.

While we were riding in one of San Francisco's famous trolley cars on our way to Fisherman's Wharf, my phone vibrated, signaling a call. I checked the screen on my phone and saw that the call was from Jack's office.

I figured he would leave me a voice mail message that I could retrieve immediately after I won the bet. But within a span of 20 minutes after the first call, there were three others from Jack's office. By this time, we had reached the wharf.

At first, I restrained myself, but by the fourth call, I felt that something must be terribly wrong. I had no choice but to return Jack's call.

Rocky had a hard time containing his elation. I later told him that no one likes a winner who gloats.

Jack's secretary answered and immediately after I asked for Jack, she apologized for making the calls. She had received instructions from my assistant, but said that Jack insisted she place the calls. It was obvious she was worried about her job security.

I assured her that she did the right thing by following Jack's orders.

When Jack picked up the phone, his first words were, "Are we having fun yet?" Jack always had a way of disarming people, but lately, even his charm wasn't working its usual magic.

I was far from pleasant with him and so said, "Jack, if this isn't critical, I'm going to cut your balls off."

This probably wasn't the right thing to say in front of Rocky because he may have doubts about what I really do for a living.

According to Jack, the calls were indeed important because they were made solely for my benefit.

Jack explained that he had received an e-mail message earlier this morning from the president of the international division of a Los Angeles-based client. Even though Jack and I had represented this company in various transactions in the past, it was primarily Jack's client.

In short, the president told Jack that he had scheduled an introductory meeting with a group of executives from a Japanese conglomerate. Our client and the Japanese company are considering a significant joint venture to manufacture diagnostic medical equipment.

Jack was told that if our client doesn't enter into such a venture, no doubt the Japanese company would then try to form a similar venture with our client's most significant competitor.

The meeting will be held on Monday morning at our firm's office in Los Angeles.

I knew what Jack intended before he finished his explanation, but I give him credit because he made it seem like he was doing me a favor rather than the other way around.

Jack said that since he was up to his ears with a variety of critical projects, it wouldn't be possible for him to make the trip. So, we had two choices, either send an associate or I would have to take the assignment. He thought it would be better for the client relationship if I attended the meeting.

Here was Jack's rationale for his repeated calls: instead of flying back to New York on Friday and then returning to the West Coast on Sunday, Jack suggested I stay in California over the weekend.

By making the calls, he said he was thinking of me – he'd hate to see me travel coast to coast if it could be avoided.

I doubt that Jack has a ton of other projects that prevented him from making the trip. But it's clear from the sound of his voice that he is so uptight, I felt that given his current state of mind, this trip would probably do him far more harm than good.

I thanked Jack for his consideration and apologized for barking at him when he first answered my call.

There was no question that I would handle the Los Angeles meeting. It would be a mistake for the firm to send an associate to an important meeting involving this important client.

This meant that Rocky and his father would have a decision to make: Rocky could either join me on a flight to Los Angeles and then return to New York on Tuesday or, if he preferred, Rocky could return to New York "solo" as scheduled on Friday morning.

If they weren't feeling comfortable with these options, I could return with Rocky on Friday and easily fly back to Los Angeles on Sunday evening. I had taken many similar trips in the past, so it wouldn't be a problem to do this again if Rocky or Michael preferred this approach.

During lunch at the wharf (not seafood, but an Italian restaurant at Rocky's request), we discussed the alternatives.

Rocky had another idea.

Because I lost the telephone bet and we were already going to Pebble Beach on Thursday, Rocky suggested that instead of returning to San Francisco, we could continue by car from the Monterey Peninsula to Los Angeles. This way, we could drive along Highway 1 through Big Sur, Morro Bay, Santa Barbara and other coastal communities on our way to Los Angeles.

I have to give him credit, for a kid who has never been to California, he is very familiar with the state's geography. I wouldn't be surprised if he knows the history of every stop along the way.

I had no problem with Rocky's proposal. After all, if I stay on the West Coast without Rocky, I would have Friday, Saturday and Sunday to kill before the Monday meeting in Los Angeles. In addition, the drive would give me an opportunity to see the California coast for the first time, visit Amy in Santa Cruz and possibly see my retired partner in Santa Barbara.

Rocky called his father and explained the situation to him. From what I could tell, Michael must have asked Rocky for his preference and Rocky said he would like to drive down the coast with me.

Rocky then handed me the phone. Michael asked for my thoughts and I told him I also preferred Rocky's plan. After I convinced Michael that Rocky would not be a burden, he agreed that this detour would be another valuable experience for Rocky. However, I sensed a slight hesitation from Michael, probably because he may be concerned about Rocky's health or maybe he just missed him since they have a close relationship.

DIVIDED ROADS

After we finished lunch, we walked around the wharf for a while. This is when an unfortunate incident occurred. I must confess that after losing the telephone bet, I was ticked off. I didn't mind the idea of going to the Monterey area on Thursday, but I just hate losing, regardless of what may be stake. Maybe this is what set me off.

A homeless old man approached us and politely asked for pocket change. At first, I just shook my head. That should have been the end of the encounter, but not for me. I lectured the guy, telling him to clean up and get a job. He was right to look at me as if I was crazy. To compound matters, Rocky took a buck from his wallet and gave it to him.

After a few moments of silence, Rocky said, "If you won't give street people money, that's your option, but you don't have to demean them with a lecture. Boy, you've got a major problem in dealing with people."

Rocky is right.

That incident darkened an otherwise decent morning, despite the loss of the telephone bet. I can't explain why I treated the old man in such a crappy manner; I wish I could find him to apologize.

From the wharf, we went to a sporting goods store to buy gloves and ski hats in anticipation of another chilly night at the Giants game.

The remainder of the afternoon was spent at our San Francisco office, where I reviewed faxes and e-mails and Rocky used the Internet to research places we would see on our drive to Los Angeles. I had given Rocky the choice of returning to the hotel or staying with me at the office and to my surprise, he chose the office.

That evening, we attended the Giants game, which was far more exciting than the prior night. Unfortunately, the excitement wasn't on the baseball field. It was in the stands.

During the sixth inning, a foul ball was hit on the first base side behind the dugout. The ball landed a few rows in front of us, hit an empty seat and fell to the ground. A kid was about to grab the ball, but suddenly a man who was sitting in the last seat across the aisle pushed his way through the crowd and got to the ball before the kid.

This man then raised the ball in the air, as if claiming victory. As you can imagine, this bully received a chorus of boos from the sparse crowd.

He didn't seem to care and went back to his beer-drinking buddies, still holding the ball in the air to taunt the crowd.

At the end of that inning, I went to the concession stand for coffee and hot chocolate. While in line, I thought that by analogy, I'm no better than the guy who stole the ball from the kid. In my business, I'm the bully who doesn't care what it takes to get the prize.

As I returned to my seat, I saw Rocky talking with a stadium usher and an armed security guard. At first I thought they were concerned that Rocky was sitting alone, but it turned out that Mr. Rocky was in trouble.

The usher explained to me that "my son" was caught throwing peanuts at a man a few aisles below us – his target being the beast that had stolen the foul ball from the kid in the prior inning.

I said there must be a mistake, but the usher detailed Rocky's crimes. The usher saw him throw one peanut, then a couple more. Well, this started a virtual riot because others saw Rocky throwing the peanuts and joined him in pelting this guy with food and other items. Then people from the upper level threw stuff at the bully and an older woman sitting behind him poured beer over his head.

When I looked at the ball stealer, he had mustard and catsup on his shirt and what appeared to be food scraps in his drenched hair. He was yelling obscenities at Rocky, me and the other fans around us.

The guy could have killed me with one punch if provoked – this is not an exaggeration, his arms were thicker than my legs. I would have flown further than a Barry Bonds home run had he connected with my chin. But when I saw it was relatively safe, I screamed at the guy, calling him a whale and a bully – I suggested that next time, he should pick on someone his own size, not an innocent little kid.

My outburst made matters worse and the offending fan's eyes popped out and it seemed like he began to foam at the mouth because he was absolutely livid. He began to charge towards me, but was thankfully grabbed by the security guard, who needed assistance from two uniformed police officers.

After the ball-stealer pushed one of the officers to the ground, he was tackled and handcuffed. As he was ushered away, he threatened to do something to me that I don't think is physically possible – he said he was going to push my head all the way up my ass.

Anyway, Rocky was viewed as the instigator of this mini-rebellion. At first, there was talk about taking us into custody, but they only wrote our names down and then led us up the stairs. As we were being "escorted" out, I heard a chorus of boos, but I think they were directed at the usher and security man rather than to the fans' hero, Rocky.

All of a sudden, Rocky took off his cap and waved it in the air. This brought cheers from the fans sitting near us and in the level above. Rocky got his first few minutes of fame at 3Com Park and I was booted out of an event for the first time in my life, but it was kind of fun being a kid again.

Even though I was actually pleased that we left the game early, I couldn't appear to condone Rocky's action. While we were in the car returning to the hotel, I didn't say anything for the first few minutes, which Rocky apparently interpreted as my disappointment in his behavior.

Before I could say anything, he apologized, but said the "big ass" deserved to get showered with food since he stole the foul ball from a little kid. We then had a brief discussion about the "behaving" rule, but the truth be known, I thought Rocky was courageous to pull such a stunt against this bully. It was actually pretty funny to see this guy covered with crap, but he scared the hell out of me when he started to charge up the stairs in my direction.

When we arrived at the hotel, we followed the same ritual as we had the prior evening by visiting the coffee shop for a late night snack and sharing our personal secrets.

I felt I owed it to Rocky to tell him about this trip and my misunderstanding of what volunteering entailed. I thought he would be disappointed, but he enjoyed the story, particularly after I told him I was now pleased to be with him on this adventure.

Then he told me something funny. When we were speaking after the dinner, he noticed that Kathy was laughing and he first thought that his fly was open. When he found it wasn't, he still thought Kathy was having fun at his expense. Now he understood her reaction.

He is an odd kid; he said he now likes Kathy even more because of her sense of humor and the fact that she enjoyed seeing me in a state of panic as I tried to think of a way to avoid the trip.

It felt good to get this off my chest. My real intention was to explain my mood when he and Michael visited our house. I confessed I was trying to escape my duties.

My mother always told me "things happen for a good reason." I was becoming convinced that taking the trip with Rocky, losing the telephone bet and accepting the Los Angeles assignment are events that were all meant to be. By the end of the trip, I hope that Rocky will have benefited from it. At least he will have realized his goal of visiting San Francisco. This alone is worth the trip.

I very much doubt this trip will do anything positive for me other than the recognition I will undoubtedly receive for serving as a volunteer. This trip will be a useful subject to bring to the attention of our clients to show that our firm not only does great banking work, but we also honor our civic duties. Beyond that, there is little for me to gain and frankly, I'm just looking forward to returning to my routine in New York.

After we changed our travel plans, we called Ned to tell him that we wouldn't be returning to New York this week. Instead of being disappointed, he was delighted because it gives him even more material for his book. So, everyone seems pleased.

CHAPTER 13

"SERIOUS ADDICTION"

BY ROCKY

April 14, 1999 – San Francisco

When I returned to my room after a full day of activities, I pulled out my laptop to send an e-mail to Dad to give him a complete update.

After logging on, I noticed Dad beat me by sending the following e-mail earlier in the evening:

Dear Rocky:

I hope you're doing well and keeping up your strength with all of the activities.

It occurred to me that I might have made a mistake when you and Pete called to talk about driving to Los Angeles. I apologize in advance if I placed you in an awkward situation.

Although you pretended otherwise, I know you were not thrilled about taking the trip to the West Coast with Pete. In a way, I feel that I may have influenced you far too much. Believe me, if I did, I was only concerned for your well-being. Nevertheless, I may have indirectly pushed too hard, and if so, I apologize.

I wish you had been honest with me. If this trip was so uncomfortable for you, all you had to do was tell me. You know I would never have forced you to go.

Today, when you and Pete called, I initially thought that it was your idea to tag along with Pete to Los Angeles. However, given your silent hesitation about taking the trip to San Francisco in the first place, it dawned on me that you might just be acting polite by agreeing to join him on a drive to Los Angeles.

I should have spoken with you privately about continuing with the trip. With Pete sitting next to you, perhaps you didn't feel comfortable expressing your point of view. In other words, I trust you weren't agreeing to continue to Los Angeles just because you think this is what I would prefer. My preference is for you to do whatever you want to do.

Rocky, you rarely hold back your thoughts from me or anyone else, so please be honest. If you prefer to return to New York directly from San Francisco, this would be fine with me. In fact, I have mixed emotions. On the one hand, I would like you to gain as many favorable experiences as possible but on the other hand, I miss you terribly and wish you were with me.

It is now your choice to make. If you prefer to return this week, I will be waiting for you at Kennedy. However, if you would like to join Pete and go on to Los Angeles, I will be anxious to hear about your continuing adventures through e-mail messages and telephone calls.

Love you,
Dad

Well, knowing Dad and how he worries about me, I wouldn't be surprised if he wakes up early tomorrow to check the computer for a reply from me. Even though I was very tired, I owed him a response.

Here is what I said:

Dear Dad:

Thanks for your concern about my continuing on to Los Angeles with Pete.

If you asked me before we left New York about the possibility of extending the trip to go to Los Angeles with Pete, I would have said absolutely not, because the trip is already long enough.

Now, having gone this far and after becoming more comfortable with Pete, I would very much like to join him for the drive to L.A. After all, it's only a few more days and I have a lot more energy than I had anticipated I would. I will probably sleep for days when I return, but right now, I feel that I want to keep going.

If this is acceptable to you, I will continue on with Pete. However, if you are having second thoughts by the time you receive this e-mail and prefer that I return to New York, I'll come back on Friday.

You asked me to be honest with you and I expect you to do the same with me.

As far as our activities today, there really isn't much to report.

We got a chance to see Fisherman's Wharf in the morning and stayed there for lunch.

I told you about my bet with Pete concerning the use of his cell phone; well he lost. What I didn't understand is why he left the phone on during the three-hour bet period. He should have turned it off. Maybe he's so addicted to the phone that he can't help himself.

He doesn't like to lose, so he said that under the circumstances, the outcome wasn't meaningful since we are going to drive down the coast in any event.

One thing's for certain, Pete sure is a sore loser. He pouted for hours after he lost the bet. He even took out his frustrations on a poor old homeless guy who asked us for money. Pete was very rude to this man. His reaction was totally out of line. I think he became even more pissed off when I gave the homeless man a dollar.

You won't believe this, but I felt comfortable at Pete's San Francisco office this afternoon. I was treated like an important person and was given the office of a partner who is away on business. The furniture in the office is great, just like you'd see in a movie, and the view is even better than the one from my hotel room. It looks directly out towards the Golden Gate Bridge and Alcatraz.

After our time at the office, we then went to the second Giants game, but this time, we were better prepared to deal with the cold weather.

We ended up leaving the game in the middle of the sixth inning because it got so cold. The score was four to two in favor of the Astros when we left. The Astros ended up winning the game six to three. There were more home runs in this game, including a towering shot to the right field stands by Barry Bonds. The attendance was still very low, something like 11,000. In a way, I can't blame the Giant's fans because the wind and cold weather make it miserable for fans, especially at night games.

I don't think our early departure from the game will forfeit the pledges made to the foundation. Dr. Max said the pledges are based on the number of "runs scored at the games I attend." Pete and I interpret this condition in the same way; money will be donated based on the total number of runs at games that "I attend."

As a result of these pledges, the foundation stands to make nearly $25,000. Dr. Max was clever to think about this kind of pledge. He had nothing to lose and everything to gain for the foundation.

When we returned to the hotel, Pete and I spoke again about our "secrets".

This time, he shared something with me about this trip. I can't reveal much, but like me, he also wasn't thrilled about coming on the trip. Now, just like me, he is beginning to relax and enjoy himself.

Dad, thank you for nudging me to take this adventure. It's already been a great experience, even though my travel partner is like a two-headed dog. Unfortunately, the ill-tempered rottweiler is usually on duty and the gentle golden retriever rarely shows himself. In the long run, I hope for his sake that the retriever wins the battle between the two, but this is unlikely because of the rottweiler's strength.

Love,
Rocky

I suppose that I really should have told Dad about the incident at the ballpark. I know Pete said he would keep it to himself, but by all rights and based on our open relationship, Dad should know. But when you think about it, there was no harm done and it gave us a good reason to leave that windy park and boring game.

I have no regrets about my action at the game tonight. I only wish I had done it when that jerk first stole the ball from the kid. I probably would have received even more support from the fans while the incident was fresh in their minds. Frankly, this is all "rationalizing", as Dad often says to me when I try to explain something that went wrong.

I was also scared to tell Dad about the ballpark fiasco because I know he would have been concerned about my making Pete's life miserable. But in truth, I have a feeling that Pete enjoyed himself a little, at least until the guy came after Pete. That's when Pete looked scared to death. He even stepped behind me so I would shield him from attack.

There is no question that Pete is going through some kind of an internal conflict. At times, I can tell that he wants to do the right thing, but then all of a sudden, the ugly half reappears and takes over. This is what must have happened when he lectured the homeless man. I mean really, does Pete think that the homeless guy would say, "You're right, I'm going to clean myself up and get a job." Knowing Pete, he may be deluded enough to think that he can actually influence a homeless person to turn his life around.

I think Pete is hopeless, but time will tell. I'm not about to give up on him just yet. He's definitely a real challenge, but I like it when the odds are stacked against me. That's why I chose the name Rocky.

CHAPTER 14

"CRUZ-ING"

BY PETER

April 15, 1999 – San Francisco to Monterey Bay

By the time we met for breakfast, Rocky had already been awake for several hours. He had showered, completely packed and was excited about the activities for the day ahead.

I first told him about a change in plans and hoped he wouldn't be too disappointed. Instead of passing through Santa Cruz on the way to Monterey and Pebble Beach, we are now going to Monterey first and then doubling back north to Santa Cruz to visit my sister, Amy. Since she urged us to stay with her for the night, I didn't want to disappoint her. So, I canceled our hotel reservations in Monterey.

As I told him about these change, I was concerned that Rocky might feel awkward about staying at Amy's house. To his credit, Rocky seems flexible and he didn't show any sign of discomfort with the revised plan. But honestly, I still can't figure him out because at times he becomes vocal, like about my telephone use and how I treated the homeless person, and at other times, he either holds back his feelings, or he could be just totally indifferent about certain matters.

After we left the hotel, we rented a car for the drive to Los Angeles.

Normally, I would have selected a large, "boring" gray or white sedan, but while at the counter, Rocky spotted a car in the lot that was more suitable to his taste. After he determined that it was available for rent, he asked whether we could rent that car. Since he won the telephone bet, it was only fitting that he not only select our "free day" destination, but also our mode of transportation.

So Rocky and I drove away in a bright red Mustang convertible, but despite Rocky's request, I refused to put top down in the cold, overcast weather.

Since I had driven in the Monterey area only once before, Rocky served as my navigator with roadmap in hand. As he was reading the map, he often called out the names of areas that are familiar to him, usually through movies or major news events.

When we passed the San Francisco Airport, Rocky noticed on the map that we were approaching Stanford University.

I asked whether he had any interest in visiting various campuses during our trip. His response was surprising, not just in what he said, but also in the way he said it. Since he didn't think he would be attending college, there was no need to waste our time touring campuses. I probed a bit more, but it was obvious this is a sensitive subject. Michael had told me that Rocky's tutors believe he can qualify for a top tier university if he desires, but he's emphatic that college isn't in his future.

When I suggested that he keep his options open, Rocky said something like, "I doubt I'll live long enough to attend college." Michael had prepared me for Rocky's preoccupation with his mortality. However, I had not seen any obvious signs from him until this conversation.

The interesting thing is that he was not morose when he made the comment about college. On the contrary, he was rather nonchalant and continued to read the map as if nothing odd had been said.

I guess I could have challenged him when he made this statement, but since I know nothing about his condition, it would have been presumptuous for me to say anything at this time. So, I politely dropped the subject. However, when I saw the Stanford sign, I turned off the freeway. I lied to Rocky about the purpose of my detour by saying that my son is considering various schools and I had promised him that I would visit a variety of campuses whenever I travel to California.

Rocky shrugged his shoulders, but I think he knew exactly what I was doing.

Seeing Stanford brought back memories of my senior year in high school. I had been accepted to Stanford, but I never saw the campus because Princeton had become basically a given.

I wonder if a campus visit at that time would have changed my life. You just never know how the smallest things impact decisions that have long-term implications. Suppose I took a tour in my senior year and my guide was a pretty Stanford junior – that alone could have given me enough balls to confront my father.

As we drove around the Stanford campus, Rocky pretended to be totally disinterested, but to my surprise, he asked me to park the car. He said that he wanted to use the restroom, but as we walked around, I could tell that he was enjoying the campus. At one point, he deviated from the walking path and went directly towards a girl who was reading while sitting on the lawn. He told her that he had applied to the school and asked her a series of questions ranging from academics, athletics, and campus life, to the dorms.

I wonder whether he would have asked these questions if there was a guy lying on the grass – probably doubtful. Now I see another side of Rocky, the "ladies' man."

After visiting Stanford, we continued south towards Monterey, arriving in Carmel around lunchtime. After a meal in Carmel, we took the famous 17-mile drive through the Monterey Peninsula.

In order to better appreciate the scenery, I put the top down on the Mustang, although it was still rather cold. We both pulled out additional clothing from our suitcases in order to properly "layer" ourselves for the chill.

We stopped at several spots along the way to view the natural beauty and local sea life. I suspect that Rocky would have preferred more time to watch the otters and sea lions, but I'm always anxious to move on. Kathy claims that I'm a restless guy who's so determined to get to my destination that I often miss the beauty of the journey. She applied this statement to more than just driving trips – it was my life in a nutshell and unfortunately, Kathy is always right.

The beautiful scenery mesmerized Rocky. It's truly breathtaking with the contrast of the ocean against lush trees and golf courses. At one point, Rocky asked me to stop at a local real estate office - he ran from the car and returned with a handful of brochures describing local homes that are on the market.

A real estate woman followed him out to the car. I guess that in the short time he was in the office, Rocky told her I'm his father and that I'm in the process of selling my software company for $600 million. Don't ask me how he arrived at this number because I have no idea, but I'm sure there's a logical explanation.

I noticed that Rocky was watching my face while she talked – I think he expected me to either blow his cover or become irritated about his creative fabrication. But I just went along with his story by telling her that my son shouldn't have said anything since the media always seems to know my private business. I took her card and told her I would be calling after I concluded the sale of my company.

I added one more thing for a little spice – that we already have three homes and I'm interested in something in the area with at least 5,000 square feet with an unobstructed view of the ocean.

As we drove off, I suspect she was mentally calculating her commission on the sale of a multi-million dollar property.

I asked Rocky why he felt it necessary to lie to this nice woman. As you might have guessed, he had a reasonably good answer. After he asked her for one of the many free brochures on the table in her office, she rudely told him that they are only available for clients of the agency. This is when he spontaneously came up with the software mogul idea.

You have to give this kid credit; he's pretty damn quick on his feet.

I like his style – with his ability to convincingly mislead people, Rocky would make a great trial lawyer.

Our next stop was the famous Pebble Beach Golf Links. What a truly unbelievable looking golf course, and it is actually more spectacular than it appears on television.

While we were in the golf shop to pick up a souvenir scorecard for Rocky, I bought Pebble Beach logo golf shirts for both of us and a golf hat for Rocky. I also bought a windbreaker for myself since I thought it might be useful as we continue to drive to Los Angeles with the top down.

After the 17-mile drive, I took Rocky to the Monterey Bay Aquarium. Again, Rocky knew about the aquarium and educated me about its history based on what he had learned yesterday while using the computer at our firm's San Francisco office.

I must say this was one hell of a generous gift to the community by the famous Packard family since the original cost of the facility was $55 million.

It was interesting to learn that the aquarium was designed in the style of the original cannery building that once occupied the site. Usually, I take little interest in such exhibits, but the abundance of plant and sea life was truly impressive, particularly the "Mysteries of the Deep" tanks.

After the aquarium, we finally headed to Amy's house, which is located about 40 miles north of Monterey. While on the drive, I thought I should give Rocky a little background about Amy so he could be better prepared to deal with her many eccentricities. So I gave Rocky a "briefing" on Amy – oddly enough, he responded by saying he liked Amy even before meeting her. This kid seems to gravitate to offbeat people.

I had no idea what to expect for our accommodations at Amy's since it had been at least 15 years since I last saw her in Santa Cruz. At that time, she was living with three other hippie-type women in an old, dilapidated house in the center of town.

After getting directions from a gas station attendant, I found the house and much to my surprise, it was a restored Victorian home that had been converted into a bed and breakfast inn. At first, I thought I had the wrong address. I knew this was the right street, but perhaps I had incorrectly jotted down the number of her house.

I was tempted to call Kathy to ask for the address from our book at home, but I decided to approach the house and ask for Amy. If she didn't live there, perhaps the residents would know of her and direct me to the right location.

Well, it turned out to be the right house because Amy answered the door wearing an apron. I gathered we had interrupted Amy while she was cooking for guests at the inn.

To make a long story short, Amy has owned the inn for over three years, but she was reluctant to say anything to the family, particularly Mom. She said that given her unconventional background, no one would believe she could make anything of herself, particularly in a business, so she was waiting for the right occasion to tell us.

Not only did Amy own the inn, but she also used the little inheritance she received from Dad's estate to buy the house next door, which she converted to a boarding house for senior citizens. Amy got the inspiration for the senior home after volunteering at a local convalescent facility; the conditions depressed her so much that she was determined to do something positive to help the elderly.

True to her idealistic nature, Amy has always given a helping hand to those who have little voice or support in our society.

Amy was kind enough to make room for Rocky and me in two of the six guest rooms in the inn. The other four rooms were occupied with guests.

After Amy showed us to our rooms, she led us down to the kitchen where she was baking muffins and bread for tomorrow's breakfast.

I couldn't believe this was "aimless Amy", as I often called her. Amy was always a bit of a rebel. She had transferred from a small liberal arts college in Massachusetts to UC Berkeley during the height of the movement against the Vietnam War, but she didn't bother to inform Mom or Dad before she made the decision to transfer. As you can imagine, her transfer was not well received, particularly by Dad, who was a staunch Nixon supporter.

For some reason, Amy was always able to get away with murder, maybe because she was the only one of the three of us who had the courage to test our father.

Amy was kicked out of boarding school after she and some of her classmates spray-painted their school colors on the rival school's bus. For some unknown reason, our parents didn't discipline her after this incident. If I had committed the same offense, they would have gone nuts. But Amy was always considered the baby of the family and the rigid rules for Maggie and me never applied to her.

During her Berkeley days, Amy was arrested on three occasions for involvement in demonstrations; once, she and a few others broke into the administration building during the evening hours. She told us later that they had planned to occupy the building until all U.S. troops pulled out of Southeast Asia.

Like many of her classmates, Amy never graduated from Berkeley. In fact I have serious doubts whether she was even enrolled after her first year.

The family lost touch with Amy for months at a time during the early 1970's. We knew she lived in communes in New Mexico and Oregon, but we rarely heard from her, unless she was in need of money.

Always unpredictable, Amy unexpectedly showed up at our parent's house in 1978. Since no one was home, Amy used the house key that was always hidden under a potted plant on the front porch. It's amazing that she remembered about the key or anything else for that matter since she had "experimented" with so many different kinds of hallucinatory drugs.

You can imagine Mom's reaction when she arrived home to see what she thought was a "hippie" intruder sleeping on the couch in the family room. She was about to slug Amy over the head with my old baseball bat when fortunately she recognized the bracelet she had given Amy on her 20th birthday.

Amy apparently had enough of traveling and communes and she wanted to return to college. When I first saw Amy, I didn't recognize her because she had lost a great deal of weight and looked years older than her age. Amy was a mess – she left home as an energetic nineteen-year-old and returned home as a woman who had experienced a lifetime in a short period of time.

After Amy took a few months to get herself together, she ended up at NYU and earned a degree in sociology. After graduation, she accepted a two-year assignment with the Peace Corps in Africa.

Since Amy was never comfortable in New York, or any big city for that matter, upon her return from the Peace Corps, she settled in liberal-minded Santa Cruz where she opened a bookstore with her former Berkeley classmate. This was what she was doing when I last visited her in Santa Cruz.

Given her uninhibited nature, Amy spoke to Rocky as if she had known him for years. The poor kid was asked a barrage of questions within minutes after first meeting her, but he held his own and never became intimidated. It'll be interesting to see if Rocky can dodge the questions she will pose during our stay by her penetrating style of interrogation. She must have learned this technique from the cops because of all her arrests.

Amy told us that her regular helper was ill so she needed our assistance in the kitchen. She gave us aprons and taught us the fine art of baking muffins and breakfast breads.

We were then given a full tour of the common areas and some of the guest rooms at the inn. It was a sight to behold: The paint and wallpaper in each room matched the bedroom appointments and each room was furnished with restored antiques. It is hard to believe that my little sister has made such a success of her life.

At dinner, we joined Amy for dinner with the senior citizen group at the adjoining house. Again, this house is fully restored, but the furniture is not nearly as ornate as at the inn. It's a simple place, but the walls throughout the house are painted in bright, lively colors. I'm sure the residents prefer this house over a cold and sterile convalescent facility.

This is when Rocky and I met Frank. He may have told us his last name, but I honestly don't recall because I was so focused on the huge cigar that was sticking out of his mouth. You might describe Frank as the "house father" because he is responsible for the chores, cooking and social activities at the senior home. He also serves as the driver for the group, taking them on errands and for medical treatment. Amy told us that Frank gets free room and board as well as a few hundred dollars a month for his assistance.

From what we gathered from Frank and the others, the seniors are all assigned the responsibility of cleaning their rooms and adjoining bathrooms. On a rotating monthly basis, two people are also responsible for maintaining the living room; another two take care of the kitchen and the remaining three tend to the garden area.

Amy had basically taken her commune experiences and applied them to this senior home, but you can't knock it since all of the "inmates" seem happy.

I used the word "inmates" with Amy because it wouldn't be natural if she didn't get pissed off and throw something at me every once in a while – I had to do something to agitate her.

While it was expected that every senior would be physically able to do their own chores, one of the guests had suffered a mild stroke a few months ago and could no longer handle his responsibilities. Rather than ask him to leave, the group voted to keep him in the home and each person was allocated some of his duties.

Amy has turned these innocent seniors into a bunch of flaming Socialists.

As you would expect, the seniors sometimes bicker over little things, like which television program they will watch, but Frank told us that generally speaking, they have become as close as family. According to Amy, they are even closer because some of the guests rarely receive visits from family members.

I must admit that Frank has a flair for cooking. We were served pot roast, mixed fresh vegetables, mashed potatoes and biscuits. Even though Rocky and I were full, we couldn't refuse Frank's special apple pie.

After dinner, Frank joined the parade back to Amy's inn. I don't know if it was the brandy, the laid back Santa Cruz atmosphere or inhaling the second-hand smoke from Amy's "special stash", but I felt like we were in a group therapy session. Little did I realize how "heavy" this session would become.

During a lull in the conversation, Rocky mentioned that he and I were sharing private information in order to better know each other. For once, I wish Rocky had kept his mouth shut.

As I expected, Amy loved the idea and she asked to join us tonight because she "doesn't know much about her cute older brother" and suspects he knows even less about his "darling little sister."

I was hoping that Frank would leave, but he just sat and didn't say a word. When I suggested that his joining us would not be a sensible idea, I was soundly defeated by a vote of three to one.

Then came the unexpected.

To my surprise, Rocky asked to go first. In keeping with my commitment, I won't reveal what he said, but I now know about his "list".

After hearing this information from Rocky, I decided to accept Michael's challenge to help his son face life with a more positive frame of mind. This kid has truly given up and will probably never fight his ailment, whatever it may be.

While Rocky was speaking, Amy and Frank became more than interested bystanders. They listened intently to everything Rocky was saying. My only disappointment was that Rocky continued to speak in a general manner about his "ailment", but given the audience, this was not the appropriate time for him to give specifics.

As Amy lit up another joint, I was hoping Rocky wouldn't notice, but it's hard to ignore the smell.

When Rocky finished, Amy took center stage. I was actually glad she did because her ramblings would give me enough time to consider what I would say to the three misfits about myself.

Amy first said that her revelation is not a secret and I could share it with Mom and Kathy if I desired. Then came her bombshell.

When Amy was at Berkeley, she became pregnant by her then boyfriend, a guy named David. Despite David's pressure for her to abort the pregnancy, Amy decided to continue. Sadly, as a result of her lifestyle, she suffered a miscarriage. As for David, he fled to Canada in order to avoid the draft. She never heard from him again.

Maybe it was because of her third shot of brandy and the two joints she had just finished, but she broke into tears, saying this was her biggest regret in life - not having a child.

There were other long-term boyfriends and one short-lived marriage, which is also something she never told us about, but she never got pregnant again.

Now that she is nearly fifty, Amy said that she misses a child even more today than in the past. She doesn't want to end up like the people in the senior home next door – alone and without visitors when she reaches a ripe old age.

I tried to break the mood by saying that when we reached that age, she, Kathy and I could start our own little commune in New Hampshire. We could even grow marijuana for medicinal purposes.

After a couple of moments of silence, Frank said, "You think that's a regret, listen to this one." Frank seemed determined to "top" Rocky and Amy with his disclosure of past demons.

He was on a roll and went on for quite a long time, sharing his story in vivid detail, as if it happened yesterday. He started by telling us that he and his wife had two girls, Christine and Carol, who were two years apart. Frank was a construction worker in the Los Angeles area and admitted that he was an alcoholic in his younger years.

After a weekend binge, he became verbally and physically abusive with his wife. She called the police and after he returned from jail, all of his belongings were laying out on the front porch.

His drinking became even worse for a while, but he then stopped, or so he thought.

On a May weekend in 1968, while they were separated, Frank's wife reluctantly granted his request to watch the girls while she visited her ill mother in San Diego. Frank picked up his daughters on a Friday night and the more he saw of them, the sadder he became. He realized he was a rotten husband and father.

The next day, he took the girls to Venice Beach, even though the weather was still relatively cool. While sitting on the beach watching his daughters frolicking in the sand, he was approached by a former drinking buddy who was armed with a six-pack of beer.

To make a long story short, Frank first refused his friend's offer for a beer, but as the sun became warmer, he finally relented. The first bottle led to another and he finished the third before his friend left for work.

With the combination of three beers, the bright sun and not having eaten since the previous night's dinner, Frank became drowsy and fell asleep on the sand.

He has no idea how much time passed, but he suddenly awoke when he heard his older daughter frantically screaming. By the time he regained his senses, he realized that his younger daughter had been swept out to sea. Apparently, the whitewash from a large wave hit her while she was focused on a sand crab.

Since it was May, there were no lifeguards on duty. Frank asked for help from the few people who were walking in the area, but none of them had seen his daughter. He jumped in the water in a futile effort to find his daughter, but there was no sign of her.

By the time emergency help arrived, it was far too late. To make matters worse, his daughter's body was never located.

As a result of this incident, Frank was charged with child endangerment and he entered a guilty plea without retaining an attorney. Since this was his first offense, Frank received a relatively light sentence. The judge apparently concluded that Frank had already suffered enough and would have to live with his own torture for the rest of his life.

After his release, Frank became a drifter. He figures that he traveled through 21 states over the next 24 years until he returned to California six years ago.

While he was first on the road, he sometimes took menial jobs in the construction industry. After traveling the country for several years, mostly hitchhiking, he landed in Santa Fe, New Mexico, where he worked as a dishwasher in a family restaurant. When the cook's assistant failed to show up on a busy Friday night, Frank received a "battlefield promotion" to the position of a cook's assistant.

After a year with this restaurant, he again had the urge to move and his next stop was Colorado Springs, where he became a cook in another café. This is when he learned the art of cooking. He said he loved to experiment with new dishes and would usually offer at least two special lunches each day.

While in Colorado, he became sober and finally weary of traveling; he decided to settle down. After a horrible Colorado winter, he returned to California where the weather offered a more suitable climate for his retirement. Following a short stay in San Francisco, Frank longed for a quieter life in a smaller community, which led him to Santa Cruz.

After a few odd jobs, he took a position helping Amy at the inn and then began "supervising" the senior's home.

Frank has not seen his older daughter since that tragic day at the beach. His wife divorced him, remarried and passed away a few years ago as a result of cancer. She never spoke with him after the incident.

Frank's surviving daughter has remained in touch with him through letters and pictures. Frank pulled out his wallet and proudly showed us a picture of a woman flanked by two boys, who appeared to be in their teen years.

In every letter, his daughter, who is a single mother, invites Frank to visit her and the boys. Frank said it would be too painful for him to do so.

What was particularly surprising was the fact that Frank had not told anyone about his history since he left prison. Why us and now is a mystery, but he said it was good to finally "release", particularly to Amy, who had become like another daughter.

After a long pause, I sensed that the three of them were looking at me.

Since everyone had been so open, I couldn't say anything trivial in nature.

I told them that I have not talked to Josh for nearly two years – from the time he dropped out of college.

Kathy keeps in touch with him on a weekly basis. So, I know he lives in Park City, Utah where he earns his living as a ski instructor during the season and as a fishing guide in the off-season.

The reason I stopped our communication was because of what I considered to be an utterly stupid move. As I told my audience of three, "How's he going to prosper in life without a degree?"

Sensing this information wasn't nearly enough, I continued by also revealing that I no longer speak with my other sister, Maggie.

While Rocky, Frank and Amy may not be understanding about cutting off communications with Josh, I thought they would be more sympathetic about my reasons for discontinuing my relationship with Maggie.

At a Christmas family reunion a few years earlier, Maggie was constantly badgering Mom, who for some reason could do nothing right in Maggie's eyes. Maggie had acted the same way with Mom from the time she entered college by always bitching at her, even about the most insignificant matters.

At one time, Maggie shared with me that she felt that our father's constant absence was due to Mother, but I knew that Maggie was far from correct. Our father's life was his work, not his family, and Mother had nothing to do with his priorities. Regardless, I couldn't convince Maggie that she was mistaken.

During that reunion, I let her initial caustic remarks directed at Mom go unanswered because this had become Maggie's normal operating procedure. However, later that evening, while we were opening Christmas presents, Maggie unleashed a horribly hurtful remark at Mom. This resulted in Mom's tearful departure from the room.

After a string of profanities, which I now regret, Maggie didn't say a single word to me, but her husband, a philosophy professor named John, simply got up and directed her and their son Brian to pack up their belongings.

John never liked anyone in the family and the feeling was mutual. I don't think he was protecting his wife, but rather using my outburst as an opportunity to leave our house and extricate himself from our family. John always treated Maggie and Brian like dirt. As a result, Maggie lost what little confidence she may have had after she married him. Brian became an angry young man because he also couldn't stand John's insensitive treatment of his mother.

Instead of helping Maggie, I made matters even worse for her with John.

I tried to convince them to stay, if only for Mom's sake, but it was no use – they left the house and took refuge at a hotel.

I have not spoken with Maggie since that day.

There was a seemingly long, uncomfortable silence in the room after I finished my story. I had no idea what the others were thinking, but I suspect they where probably critical of me for being so very stubborn. Unfortunately, I can't disagree.

Thankfully, Amy broke the tension by announcing that we should all get to sleep since we need to wake up early to prepare breakfast for the guests. From this comment, I gathered she expects Rocky and I to help her in the morning.

Amy then gave Rocky a hearty hug – she has always been the most affectionate child in our family. A true "love child" from the day she was born.

After saying good night, we all went quietly in our different directions.

As I sat in my room, I reflected on Rocky.

He is an enigma – at first I thought he was a reserved kid who shows no emotion. But I couldn't be more wrong. The way he talked and listened, particularly to the attention-starved seniors showed me a tender side.

The same is true when he demonstrated his obvious sympathy to Amy and Frank after they told their stories.

I have underestimated the depth of this kid – I just wonder what's really going on inside his head.

I doubt anyone really knows, perhaps not even Rocky.

CHAPTER 15

"UNVEILING ANOTHER LAYER"

BY ROCKY

April 15, 1999 – San Francisco and Monterey Bay

Dear Dad:

It is late Thursday evening and I'm sending you this e-mail from my room in Amy's place inn in Santa Cruz. You will remember that Pete mentioned that his sister, Amy, lives in Santa Cruz. What he didn't know until today is that Amy operates a successful bed and breakfast inn. In fact, she has two businesses – she also owns a small home for senior citizens next door to the inn.

I'll try to keep this short because I'm very tired and I don't want to tie up Amy's telephone line, although I doubt she will be making or receiving any calls at this late hour.

My room at Amy's inn is outstanding, full of restored furniture. My place is called the "blue room" for obvious reasons. Everything in the room - the walls, bedding, towels and picture and mirror frames are blue. Even the telephone is blue.

It was a great day today, starting with our selection of a Mustang convertible for the trip to Los Angeles.

Pete took me for a quick drive around Stanford University. He made up a lame excuse about touring the campus on behalf of his son, but I know he thinks he can pump me up to consider attending college in the future. There is no need to debate with him, so I'll just go along with his fantasy. Anyway, he probably doesn't realize that based on what he revealed tonight, I caught him in a big lie about touring campuses for his son.

I have a feeling that Pete is so delusional that he thinks he can convince me to think about attending college. Little does he know that pushing junior guys around at work as he often does on the telephone doesn't make him Mr. Persuasive.

The Monterey Bay area is far more beautiful than I expected. Even though it was overcast and a bit windy, we had the top down for the entire drive through the Pebble Beach area.

When you consider retirement, you should seriously think about this area, despite the weather. Actually, I think the overcast weather makes it even more appealing.

We ate lunch in a small community called Carmel and then took the 17-mile drive that you once mentioned to me. Pete then took me to the Monterey Aquarium, which is also on the "must see" agenda when you and I return to California.

Although I had a sense that Pete first doubted his decision about contacting Amy, there was no question that he was glad he came. Amy is a real kick – an upfront person who doesn't hold back what she wants to do or say. Even Pete seems to let her take charge during our conversations.

Even though I would guess that Amy is in her mid- to late-forties, she acts like she is in her 30's. She looks and acts like Bette Midler – she's energetic, outgoing and always smiling and cracking jokes.

We had a great night with her and an older man who works for her - his name is Frank. He is a sad little man because of his difficult life, but he maintains a great sense of humor. He also says whatever's on his mind.

*Frank looks like George Burns of 20 years ago when he did the "**Oh, God**" movies, but he acts like Walter Matthau, particularly in his role in "**The Odd Couple**." Maybe he reminds me of Mr. Burns because even though Frank told us that he stopped smoking a long time ago, he constantly chews on a large, unlit cigar. It's like a pacifier for him.*

By the way, I told you about Pete's idea to share little known information about each other on a daily basis. Today, I told Pete about my "Regret List", which I should have shared with you before.

There is really nothing mysterious about the list. Some time ago, I prepared a list of 15 items – places I would like to see or things I want to do before I see Mom again. Notice how delicately I communicated the concept of death.

The reason I selected 15 is because too many people have a top 10 list and 20 items are excessive.

Dad, believe me when I say that none of this is morbid to me ... it's just reality.

When I'm on my deathbed, I will review the 15 items. They will be the things I will regret not having seen or done during my life.

By the way, there will always be 15 items because whenever I accomplish a particular thing, it is removed from the list and a new item takes its place.

Today, I told Pete about five of the items: (1) to visit San Francisco, (2) to play golf at Pebble Beach, (3) to have my writing published in a well-known magazine or newspaper or used for a movie script, (4) to see Tahiti and the neighboring islands and (5) to finally see you retired, relaxed, happy and not constantly worrying about me.

I'll tell you the other items on this list when I write you this week. You should think about preparing your own list and please Dad, think of yourself for once. There must be things you want to do and places you would like to see during your lifetime. Don't say no, you can't possibly be that boring.

I'm not sure what the agenda is for tomorrow, but I assume we will continue south along the coast. Pete will decide the course and I'll navigate.

This journey has become enjoyable and I don't mean just the sightseeing – this whole experience has been an eye-opener.

Love you,
Rocky

P.S. – I forgot to mention that Pete took only two calls today on his cell phone. To my surprise, he turned it off while we were at the aquarium. Maybe he's making a little progress.

Before I completed the e-mail, I thought about sharing with Dad the things that Amy, Frank and Pete discussed tonight after dinner. But then it occurred to me that this would probably alarm him; he may think that I'm in the company of extremely bizarre people.

How could I tell Dad that Pete doesn't speak to his son or sister, that Frank's child died because he was drunk, or about Amy's past?

I also will never tell him Amy lit up a couple of joints while we were talking and that she gave me a small glass of brandy after dinner. If he knew any of these things, he would want me to return home on the first available flight.

I'm not making light of what each of the three shared this evening. They were all in pain as they told their stories, but I really felt sorry for Amy and Frank in particular.

I didn't want to say it in front of the others, but Amy should consider adopting a child. I know it isn't easy to adopt a healthy baby, especially for a single woman her age, but I remember reading that there aren't enough homes for older children. Maybe she can qualify for a child who is hard to place.

When I return to New York, I'll research adoption opportunities for Amy in the San Francisco area and send her copies of what I find. The worst thing that can happen is that she'll toss the stuff away.

As for Frank, he needs the courage to see his daughter – he can't let this go much longer because of his age. Maybe I can find a way to help him.

I doubt anyone can help Pete because he is a stubborn man – I can't see him giving an inch with his son or sister. He'll have to work out these relationships on his own.

I had mixed feelings with the seniors next door. On the one hand, it seems they have little contact with friends or family members. On the other hand, they have a quality home, good food and the support of the others in the home. I can tell you one thing – if I was a senior citizen, I would much rather live in a place like Amy's home than a retirement facility where the guests are treated like a herd of cattle.

I remember seeing a convalescent facility when we visited Grandmother – they are more depressing than a hospital. Most of the people waste away in their beds until they are escorted to the next life. I know those who are religious tell us that there is a reason why some older people linger for long periods of time in poor health, but since I'm not very religious, I have my doubts.

Speaking of this – what possible reason was there for my mother to be taken away from us at such a young age? As a betting person, I would say that some people have health problems that are not associated with poor diet, lack of exercise, environmental factors or heredity. In some instances, like my mother's case and mine, it was just poor luck. There are no hidden messages or spiritual meanings in such a death, but as some people say, sometimes bad stuff just happens and there isn't anything that can be done to prevent it. It doesn't matter whether a person is good or bad, someone somewhere determined that it was checkout time.

Dad and Laura get upset when I talk this way because they're convinced that a higher being had good reason to prematurely take Mom away from us. I know that religious people feel the same, but I wonder whether these people would feel this way if they had my disease.

Now, if my dying will help others, then I would agree that the sacrifice is worthwhile. However, I suspect that I'll quietly pass away, a few people will attend my funeral service and they will then return to their normal lives. So, what's the purpose of my death?

Actually, because of my philosophy on this subject, it's hard to become bitter. To me, it's like betting on a baseball game – sometimes the odds are very much in favor of the team you select, but they just have a bad day and lose. So, Mom and I are two people who were picked at random, but instead of winning the lottery, we drew the only short straws.

I have never talked to Pete on this topic, but I'm willing to bet that he shares my view on this subject. He is a cynical person and probably agrees that sometimes, bad things just happen and it doesn't matter how good or healthy a person may be. Now you can adjust the odds by doing proper things like watching what you eat, exercising and not smoking or drinking. But in the end, some people will get cancer regardless of how carefully they may have lived.

Enough of that – I hope you don't get the impression that I have no faith. On the contrary, I very much believe in God. But I must admit that I'm not really sure there is a "grand plan" for our lives – however, I'm still open-minded on this subject.

I got diverted while I was talking about the senior citizens. I shouldn't go any further because I will then get on my soapbox about giving terminally ill people an opportunity to determine when it is appropriate for them to end their lives in a peaceful manner. Mom, for example, shouldn't have suffered as she did at the end – there is absolutely no rational reason for a goodhearted and kind person like her to have lingered in great pain and discomfort in her last weeks.

This is what concerns me the most – the agony I'll feel before I finally close my eyes. Seeing the tunnel and light that people speak about when they have after-death experiences is no problem – it's the part leading up to the big event that is bothersome. I wish that doctors could give me the option to enjoy my last bowl of ice cream, take a magic pill and quietly drift away. This would not only be ideal for me, but it would also minimize the suffering for Dad and Laura as well.

As Dad and Laura know, if you get me going on a subject that I feel strongly about, it's hard to stop me. Since I've rambled so much, you can tell that these issues are important to me. I have to say that it feels good to communicate them to you because I can't say anything like this to Dad or Laura. Whenever I do, it makes them sad to think about Mom and the realization that I may soon join her.

CHAPTER 16

"LOST BALLS"

BY ROCKY

April 16 – Monterey Bay

Dear Dad:

I have more time tonight to write since I found a second phone telephone line at Amy's inn, so I can give you more details about our activities.

I didn't realize I had overslept this morning until I heard a knock on my door. Pete came into the room in an excited state and spoke very quickly. He was already dressed and ready to go. This is the first time I have seen this kind of enthusiasm from Pete.

He woke up early and spontaneously decided to make another change in our schedule. Instead of continuing towards Los Angeles today, he wants to play golf. He already called the pro shop at Pebble Beach and will join a two-some for an 11:18 tee-time. I looked at the clock near my bed and saw it was about 8:20.

Pete gave me the choice of either riding with him in the golf cart at Pebble Beach or staying with Amy for the day. I was glad to hear that he wanted me to join him, but the decision was entirely mine.

As you can imagine, this was a "no-brainer". I quickly jumped out of bed, showered, got dressed and ate a couple of the blueberry muffins we baked yesterday.

Pete drove quickly to Pebble Beach so he could practice on the driving range before teeing off. While on the drive, I told Pete that I have played the Pebble Beach course hundreds of times on my computer and I know every fairway, sand trap and green on the course. I also mentioned that I practice putting balls in my bedroom for hours at a time. I offered my help in managing this difficult course and helping him read the greens. But he politely declined – actually, now that I think about it, he was condescending and said that playing a computer game isn't anything like playing a real course. So, I didn't help him even though I saw him make mistake after mistake.

Dad, speaking of putting in my room, this reminds me, maybe I could move into Laura's bedroom since it is larger than mine. After all, she is away for practically nine months out of the year and this way, I can increase my putting range to 14 feet.

Anyway, when we arrived at Pebble Beach, Pete rented a set of clubs and bought a pair of golf shoes. He had planned to purchase six balls, but the guy behind the counter suggested that he buy at least a dozen. Pete whispered to me that he wouldn't need that many balls, but he humored the guy and bought a dozen.

While he was at the driving range, Pete let me use the rented putter on the practice green. At first, I was hitting the ball too hard because the green is much "faster" than my carpet, but after a while, I got the feel of it. When Pete returned from the range, he asked the pro shop for another putter, in case I had an opportunity to putt on the course.

We met our playing partners on the first tee, a married couple from Toronto celebrating their 30th wedding anniversary at Pebble Beach.

Before teeing off, our partners made a wager between themselves, which we understood is their habit. Pete turned to me and asked, "Alright, Mr. Gambler, let's make a bet." You should know that I first said that you don't like me to bet, but Pete said that it wouldn't be for money, so it's okay. Interesting argument.

Pete suggested the terms of the bet - he said that, based on his golf abilities, shooting below 100 was a "sure thing". After seeing his practice swing, I had serious doubts, especially since this is such a tough course. In the short time I've known Pete, I can see that he tends to exaggerate, especially about his abilities. It must be some kind of insecurity thing. Well, the claims about his golf abilities were another stretch.

You would have been proud of me because I knew this wouldn't be a fair bet. Although I didn't say this, I could see there was no way he would break 100, unless he stopped playing after the 15th hole. I gave him a break by betting that he couldn't shoot below 105. He accepted the challenge and I could tell from his smug look that he was certain he would win this bet.

Now we had to determine the prize. He suggested that we could delay our departure for another day from Los Angeles, which would give us a free day on Tuesday. Whoever won the bet got the right to determine what we'll do that day.

We shook hands and I was immediately thinking about what we would do on Tuesday

On the first hole, a 339-yard par four, Pete hit a 3-wood about 190 yards, straight down the fairway. He was pleased with the accuracy of his drive, but not with the distance – this was when he made the first excuse, this time about the unfamiliar clubs.

Every time he had a shitty shot, he complained about the clubs or something else, such as: his sore feet because of the new shoes; the balls were not the kind he ordinarily uses; the absence of a caddy to read the greens; and the unfavorable weather conditions. I'm surprised that Pete didn't blame our playing partners for playing too slow or me for distracting him from playing his typically brilliant game. Some people just can't accept responsibility for their mistakes and Pete is the king of that group.

He gave the most creative excuse after he hit two balls into the ocean – the reason for those two horrible shots was his "slippery" new glove. Give me a break! The reason that those balls went into the ocean is because he has a crappy golf swing.

So, back to the first hole – Pete topped the second shot and then hit the third one in a sand trap to the right of the green. This is when it got funny. He hit the ball out of the sand trap, it flew over the green and landed on the fly in a trap on the other side of the green. The ball never touched any part of the green.

After he finally holed his ball on the first hole, I was ready to record his score of nine. But Pete argued that I should only record seven strokes because of an "index equalization rule" or something like that. Based on his handicap, Pete said that the maximum score he should take on any hole is three over par.

I had no choice other than to accept what Pete was saying, although I had my doubts. So, I reluctantly scored only seven strokes instead of nine on the hole.

By the way, I later found out that what Pete had said about this rule was not true. I don't think he was intentionally cheating I'll give him the benefit of the doubt by saying that he probably doesn't know the rule very well.

While Pete was preparing to tee off on the second hole, a 439-yard par 5, I did the math based on Pete's maximum stroke rule. I figured that if he hit the scored maximum on each hole, his score would be 126. So, I was still comfortable with my bet.

By the time we reached the 5th hole, Pete had already lost four balls and he was 12 over par. But the scoring was charitable because he never took any penalty strokes for the lost balls. He called these bad shots "mulligans", which must be another one of Pete's convenient rules.

Pete shot a legitimate two over-par on the 156-yard 5th hole. He actually hit a decent tee shot, just off the green, but flubbed his chip shot and three-putted the green. Actually, let me correct my statement – it wasn't legitimate because he had four putts, but he said the last miss didn't count because he rushed his short tap-in putt so we wouldn't delay the group behind us. Naturally, this time, it was the putter's fault, not his.

The next four holes all run along the ocean. Pete hit a couple of more balls on to the rocks or the beach. By the 9th hole, he had already lost six balls. So, the pro was right in suggesting a dozen balls for 18 holes.

I had a hard time containing myself on the 9th hole. Pete hit a reasonably good drive and his second shot, a fairway wood, traveled 180 yards. He was on the green in three shots, about 15 feet away from the hole. Pete actually had a chance for a real, honest to goodness par. But he choked and hit the putt so hard that the ball rolled completely off the green. At that point, he was probably 60 to 70 feet from the hole. He three-putted from there, for a score of seven on the hole.

You can safely say that Pete was more than a little pissed after that hole. He took the putter shaft over his knee and would have broken it, but then remembered that it was a rental club.

What was even more frustrating for Pete was the fact that our partners, who are a little older than he is, kept hitting the ball straight down the middle, although not far. They didn't lose any balls and putted well, even though this was also their first time at Pebble.

Pete ended up with an "adjusted" score of 57 on the front nine. I'm sure that our partners beat him, but I never saw their scores.

I think Pete saw me quietly snickering after he four-putted on the 9th hole. This is when he became even more irritated and said, "Okay hotshot, let's see if you can putt better than me on the back nine."

Another challenge accepted and this time, the winner would choose our activity for Monday night in Los Angeles. I selected a Dodgers baseball game and Pete chose an evening at the Music Center.

We were even in our putting contest after the first four holes on the back nine with 10 putts each.

Pete finally got lucky on the 184-yard 12th hole. He actually hit a terrible tee shot; a five-wood that never got higher than five feet off the ground. But, he got a friendly roll and the ball ended up within 12 feet of the pin. It was what our Canadian partner called a "seeing eye ball."

Pete then holed his putt for a birdie. It was pure dumb luck, but he was now one ahead in the putting wager.

On the 14th hole, we had a near-tragic incident. Our partners stopped their cart at a safe location to watch Pete hit his second shot. But we all found out that there are no safe places when Pete is hitting. He hit a shot that I didn't think was physically possible – instead of going straight, it took a hard right and actually went backwards. It made a loud noise when it hit our partner's cart. If it had been a couple of inches higher, it would have hit the Canadian man. From then on, the Canadians were always directly behind Pete or sheltered by a tree. It was scary.

On one hole, I believe it was the 15th, Pete hit his ball in a deep, greenside sand trap. Our partners were chipping on the other side of the green, so they could barely see Pete in this deep sand trap – all they could see was the top of his head and the movement of his club as he swung.

Pete hit his first shot "fat" and the ball stayed in the trap. He hit two more and the same thing happened. He was so frustrated that he picked up the ball and threw it onto the green. The ball landed within 10 feet of the pin.

We laughed, but our partners thought that he actually made a great show out of the deep sand trap. Instead of admitting that he threw the ball, he responded by saying it was a "lucky shot." What a cheater!

The 18th hole is a real killer: a 538-yard par 5, which runs entirely along the water. By the afternoon, the wind had picked up making it even more difficult to play the course. He tried to hit the ball hard by taking a mighty swing – but unfortunately for him, he only hit the very top of the ball. As a result, he didn't even reach the ladies' tee. He also topped the second shot, sending it all of 30 yards. The woman playing with us was over one hundred yards ahead of him on her first shot and he was still hitting his third. Talk about embarrassment.

Pete never asked for his score while he was playing; but I knew that he had lost the first bet after the 17th hole since his total was already 101,

DIVIDED ROADS

even with his "maximum stoke rule" and without recording any penalty strokes.

Needless to say, his score on the 18th was again the maximum, giving him a total of 109. He had exhausted his supply of a dozen balls by the 15th hole and was forced to borrow five more balls from our partners for the remaining three holes.

It was funny to see Pete today because during our trip, he has rarely said a curse word, but he more than made up for it at Pebble. He unleashed a string of profanities, including "son of a bitch" and other things which I shouldn't repeat. He apologized twice to our playing partners for his language. At one point, when he hit two straight shots to the "fish", he yelled out a horrible curse. Our female partner couldn't help herself and laughed uncontrollably as her husband drove their cart away.

Dad, don't get me wrong. Pete is really a good guy, but he obviously hates to lose.

By the way, I won the putting contest. It pissed me off, however, because I heard Pete tell our playing partners that he intentionally lost the contest. What pure crap! He can't admit that he is just a lousy putter.

I exchanged addresses and telephone numbers with the couple from Toronto. Pete barely said goodbye to them because I think he was humiliated by his performance. For him to be beaten by an older lady must have been a tremendous blow to his ego. But I doubt that anyone will ever learn about this loss from Pete. I wouldn't be surprised if he bribes me to buy my silence.

Before we drove back to Santa Cruz, Pete checked his voice mail messages and returned a call to Jack, his partner.

It was funny because Pete told Jack he had a great day at Pebble and actually played "reasonably well" despite the rental clubs. He then described his "professional quality shot" on the 12th hole, which earned him a birdie on the hole. He said that his tee shot flew high and landed within a couple of feet from the pin.

After the call, I said he must have had a "mystery" shot because the one he described to Jack was totally different from the crappy one that rolled more than half the length of the fairway. He smiled for the first time since the first hole and said, "Every golfer embellishes a little." If this was a small embellishment, I'd like to hear what he considers to be a gigantic lie.

It was an unpleasant return drive to Santa Cruz. Pete didn't say a word because he was still stewing about his embarrassing golf game. I said something like, "Hey listen, it's just a game. You can't expect at good showing your first time out at Pebble." But he coldly responded, "I don't want to discuss it." This man has a dark side and you sure don't ever want to screw with him. So, I kept quiet for the remainder of the trip.

Before we got back to Amy's place, Pete insisted on driving by the University of California in Santa Cruz. Because of his black mood, I figured that this was no time to argue with him.

Before dinner, Frank asked me to join him at the beach to watch the sunset. I know I don't know Frank, but he doesn't strike me as the type of person who takes much interest in a sunset. As we walked to the beach, he surprised me even more by telling me that as he watches the sun setting, he often communicates with his daughter, who drowned when she was less than 10 years old. Even though I'm not an expert, this sunset was absolutely gorgeous. The sun looked huge and after it set, the sky had a bright orange afterglow. Neither of us said a word for a while; we quietly enjoyed nature's grand finale for the day. Then Frank said, "Goodnight Carol."

You won't believe where we ate - at a homeless shelter!

Amy and Frank volunteer their time at a local shelter one evening a week, usually Friday nights. Amy gave us a choice of helping at the shelter or eating out at a restaurant and then joining her later at the inn.

Pete left the decision to me and I selected for the shelter.

Even though I'm glad I made this decision, believe me, Pete and I worked hard. Pete was assigned the task of cutting vegetables and I ladled out food to the guests.

It was an eye-opening experience. I thought it would be mostly older people, but there were many guys who were your age or younger. There were also more women than I had expected; mostly older, but one woman brought three young kids with her.

It was a sad sight. I kept glancing at Pete, who would occasionally look at the people, but most of the time, he focused on his chore. For some reason, he avoided eye contact with the people at the shelter.

Frank stood next to me the whole night and we talked a lot about his background and his daughter, who he has not seen for many years.

When we got back to Amy's inn, I was asked to share five more items from my "Regret List" with Pete, Amy and Frank.

Here are the next five: (1) to attend the Kentucky Derby; (2) to visit Paris; (3) to drive a sports car around a race track; (4) to see Polar Bears in their natural environment; and (5) to fall in love with a beautiful girl (I got a lot of crap from the three others for this one).

Now it's confession time. While Pete and Amy were in the kitchen, I was alone with Frank in Amy's family room. I don't why I said it, but in a weak moment, I suggested to Frank that he join us tomorrow for our trip to Los Angeles so that he can finally visit his daughter. He smiled and said, "maybe."

I doubt very much that he will accept, but I know I shouldn't have said anything to Frank without first talking with Pete. In a way, I hope he doesn't accept because I think Pete will be pretty unhappy. And after what I saw this afternoon of his ugly personality, I don't want to do anything to piss him off.

It's getting late and I need to be up early tomorrow so we can start down the coast.

Tell Laura hello for me. I hope she can join us when we come to California.

Love you,
Rocky

Again, I omitted something from my note to Dad. The disclosures from Frank and Amy this evening would have really sent him into a panic.

They are great people with big hearts, but they have had their share of problems in the past.

Pete, on the other hand, was a bit more reserved in his revelation this evening. I suspect he probably felt he went too far last night when he spoke about Josh and Maggie. I also think that the golf game fiasco still has him bummed. He just hasn't been the same since we left Pebble Beach. Or maybe, this is the "real Pete" and the other guy who has been traveling with me is an imposter.

Everyone has his or her fair share of issues in life and I'm by no means alone.

CHAPTER 17

"PLAYING FROM THE ROUGH"

BY PETER

April 16, 1999 – Monterey Bay

Dear Kathy:
 Greetings from tranquil Santa Cruz.
 I tried to reach you twice today, but you are probably busy helping your mom decorate her new place.
 I'm glad she finally moved; the other apartment was larger than necessary and it brings back too many memories of your dad. Please assure her that I will pay for her new furnishings.
 Thanks for arranging to have my suit and other clothes delivered to the hotel in Los Angeles.
 Based on what we saw yesterday and today, you and I definitely have to visit this area for an entire week. It is truly beautiful and I know you'll enjoy the sights, as well as the shopping.
 You have always said that I'm never spontaneous. Well, you would have been proud of me today because instead of driving to Los Angeles, I decided to play golf at Pebble Beach.
 Even though I didn't play as well as I could have and totally embarrassed myself in front of Rocky and our playing companions (a Canadian couple), it was a thrill to play this course. Even for non-golfers, it is a sight to behold.
 I know you're not interested, but I had one great hole; I actually shot a birdie after hitting a professional type shot and sinking the putt. I missed a hole-in-one by only a few inches. Best shot of my life.
 Had I played with my clubs instead of rental clubs, I would have done much better. As it turned out, I shot slightly over 100, which isn't bad since my attention was often directed to Rocky rather than on my golf game.
 When you speak with my mom, tell her that she would be very proud of Amy. It may have taken her nearly 50 years, but Amy has finally

settled down. I'll give you the details when I return, but Amy is actually running two successful businesses.

Now that Amy is a tax-paying, small businessperson, you would think that she has tempered her liberal views, but not so. She has moved even further left, which I didn't think possible. I swear that one of her two businesses is based on Socialist ideology.

For the first time in decades, Amy is finally at peace and seems happy with her life. She actually looks younger than the last time I saw and her general style is very becoming; she dresses much better than the past when she used to wear her homemade creations.

While at Amy's, we met her employee, a colorful older man named Frank. He is quite pleasant, but apparently life hasn't always been kind to him. Amy rescued him, just like she has so many other people in her life.

I wonder what happened to the three Franklin children – two started out stable, then got screwed up; the third was screwed up but now is stable. I suppose that a psychologist would disagree by saying that Maggie and I were really the troubled, insecure ones and Amy the stable child, even during her turbulent hippie years. We know one thing for sure, the big heart and compassion went to Amy.

You will never believe what Rocky and I did this evening. We helped serve dinner at a homeless shelter and I must confess that it was an overwhelming experience. I never realized that all it takes is a series of adverse events and there you are, destitute and on the streets. So many of them are mentally ill as well and should be receiving help, but as Amy said, many institutions were forced to close because of government cutbacks. For once, she and I agreed on something because many of these people desperately need help.

No doubt you will be surprised about something else. When we were flying from New York, I suggested to Rocky that each day we share something about ourselves daily to help us learn more about each other. I was hoping that he would open up more, especially about his health problem, since he was so very quiet during our first two encounters. I suppose I was also playing child therapist by hoping that if he hears "private" things from me, he might be less intimidated by me. Don't laugh, but he might also see that I'm actually human.

During the past few days, I have not only learned more about Rocky through this exercise, but also more about myself.

When I told Rocky about my relationship, or lack thereof, with Josh, I felt pretty foolish. In truth, my attitude developed because I was not only worried about Josh's future, but I suppose I was also embarrassed to tell people that my son is a ski instructor, rather than on a professional track at a prestigious university. Yes, I readily admit you have been right; this has been a big mistake on my part. My massive ego has again clouded rational thinking.

Anyway, during the course of our sharing period last night, we had two additional participants, Amy and Frank. I will tell you when I return about their stories, but they would both make great movie scripts.

The revelations from them tonight were thankfully far tamer. In Amy's case, she was arrested last year after she chained herself to a tree in order to save an endangered owl whose survival is threatened by logging activities.

Frank always has to top the others with his stories, which I assume are true. Like Amy, he also has a criminal past.

While drifting through Texas many years ago, he became desperate for food. After getting drunk with two other guys, the three broke into a convenience store and stole food and $540 from the cash drawer, which they split equally.

After Frank settled down in New Mexico as a cook, he found the telephone number for the convenience store and spoke with the owner, who claimed that it was his store when the burglary occurred.

Frank told us he then sent the owner $200 in cash to make amends for his criminal act.

I wish I could share Rocky's thoughts with you, but I promised that whatever he reveals will remain confidential.

Kathy, one more thing I need to tell you. I'm very sorry about trying to extricate myself from this trip with Rocky. Whether knowingly or not, I made a commitment when I raised my hand at the dinner. It was foolish and cowardly of me to try to have you, Jennie or someone else take this trip.

I know you will have a hard time believing me, but I'm actually glad I came with Rocky. I think you may be absolutely correct in your initial reaction; Rocky is a great kid with a huge heart. However, there are times when he shows a vindictive nature that possibly suggests a hidden anger. On the other hand, I have the impression that he only shows this trait when he feels that someone has been wronged. I will explain what I mean when I see you – remind me to tell you about our ejection from the second Giants game.

There are so many other things that warrant my apologies to you, but I'll save those until we are together, even though we may need an entire day to cover everything.

I know what you're probably thinking after reading this e-mail - either Amy has shared one of her funny little homemade "cigarettes" with me or I'm totally drunk. I admit I had a little brandy tonight, but I'm by no means drunk nor have I smoked anything. For a change, I'm speaking to you from my heart. You may have vague memories of a time before I became an insensitive ass that I actually spoke from the heart.

I will call you in the next few days.

Love,
Pete

I think I know how Kathy will react after she reads this e-mail – she'll think that I've temporarily flipped out, but that the "real" Pete will reappear once I return to New York.

The big question is, who is the "real" Pete? Over time, I've developed a persona as a cold-blooded, but incredibly successful, dealmaker.

When I think back to my personality through the early part of my career and compare it to who I am today, there is no question that I'm a different person. For one thing, I know that I was far less self-absorbed by my importance in college and even for the first few years of my working career.

I seem to remember that I once had a deep concern for the feeling of others, but this is no longer true. Now, I'm simply a hired gun who has one thing in mind, namely to deliver the best results for my client, irrespective of what this may mean to others, including my family and members of my firm. But when I'm truthful with myself, which doesn't occur often, I realize that I'm more concerned with my personal success rather than the client's interest. Yes, most often the two parallel each other, but not always.

The change wasn't sudden – it evolved gradually over time. I noticed that when I played the role of an enforcer, people paid more attention to what I had to say. It was a natural high and the feeling of power was intoxicating.

The interesting thing is that this transformation probably wasn't necessary. Perhaps I wouldn't have moved up the ladder quite as quickly in my firm, but had I maintained my true personality, I probably would have ultimately succeeded in this or another profession. But the operative word is "probably" – once I got rolling and received accolades for my "no prisoners" approach, I didn't want to take the risk by reverting back to the "other Pete."

I guess you could say that at the beginning it was like an acting assignment. But I got so good at playing the role that I was essentially "type cast" – I became the character I was imitating and afraid to accept any other role. Now, I doubt I would even know how to play life any other way since I have been this other character for such a very long time.

The real tragedy is that this role not only became my "game face" for the business world, it totally consumed the rest of my life. Let's take today, for example. I admit that I was humiliated by my showing on the golf course and I don't mean my atrocious play, which is attributable to a number of factors, including the lack of practice and the difficulty of Pebble Beach. The most significant component is the simple fact that I'm just not a very good golfer, but I would never admit this. I just make all kinds of creative excuses for my poor performance.

My real embarrassment today relates to how I acted both on the course and afterwards. I was constantly cursing, threatening to break clubs and I even took credit for a shot out of a sand trap, even though I actually threw the ball instead of hitting it from the trap. As if this wasn't bad enough, I told our playing partners that I pretended to lose a putting contest to Rocky. Why couldn't I have been truthful and said what really happened – he simply beat me. I even cheated by not counting all of my strokes. And then on the drive back to Santa Cruz, I pouted like a kid who struck out four times in a Little League game.

After all, it's just a stupid golf game, not life. Why do I feel the need to win at everything? Even with my relationship, or lack thereof, with Josh, I expect him to apologize to me and not the other way around. But apologize for what? I'm the one who stopped speaking to him because I am embarrassed to tell people that my son is a college dropout.

In a way, my transformation to this evil side was probably easier for Josh and Jennie and more difficult for Kathy. The kids have never really seen the "gentle Pete". Only Kathy knows that he once existed.

I'm scared because I don't like who I've become and worse yet, I doubt I can bring back the Pete that Kathy once knew.

CHAPTER 18

"TRES AMIGOS"

BY ROCKY

April 17, 1999 – Santa Cruz to Morro Bay

Dear Dad:

I'm typing this e-mail from my motel room in a small coastal community called Morro Bay.

Before I tell you about what we saw and did today during our drive from Santa Cruz, there is something that you need to know.

In my last e-mail, I told you about a man named Frank who works for Amy. I mentioned that I probably shouldn't have invited Frank to join us on the drive to Los Angeles because I had not discussed it with Pete before making the invitation. But I never expected Frank to accept, so I didn't think it was a big deal.

Well, you can probably guess where this is heading.

When I got up this morning, I was surprised to see Frank having his breakfast at Amy's inn, instead of the senior home, where he usually eats his meals. I also noticed two bags near him, one brown shopping bag and a white plastic garbage bag. It looked like the bags were full of clothes and other personal things. At first, I thought it was Frank's laundry.

Amy was serving the other guests at the inn, so she didn't say anything to me, but I noticed her smile as she glanced at Frank.

To make a long story short, Frank decided to accept my offer and he asked Amy for a week off so he can visit his daughter in Los Angeles.

There was no turning back because Frank had already talked with his daughter and told her he would be arriving this coming Sunday.

My first thought was, "Oh shit, wait till Pete finds out." After seeing him so pissed off yesterday after the golf game, I thought he would flip out when he found out about Frank.

I tried to pretend that I was pleased by Frank's decision, and I probably would have been under normal circumstances, but I doubted that Pete would be very happy about another passenger, especially Frank.

Now Pete would be baby-sitting two people, neither of whom has anything in common with him.

Within a few minutes, Pete joined us in the breakfast room.

During this trip, I have found that Pete is typically not a morning person. Actually, now that I think about it, Pete isn't an afternoon or evening person either. He is generally in the same serious mood all the time, unless he really gets pissed off, like he did at the golf course, then he explodes.

However, this morning was different - he seemed pretty happy and even said good morning to Amy, Frank and me. This was followed by an even more incredible statement when he asked, "Isn't it a great day outside?"

I thought to myself that it may be great outside, but it won't be very good inside in a couple of minutes.

Pete sat down and immediately went to the business section in the newspaper. I really didn't know what to say so I just kept staring at Pete while he was reading. I was looking for the right opening, but it didn't come.

Frank naturally assumed that Pete knew about the invitation, so he didn't think there was anything unusual. He just continued to eat his muffin without a care in the world.

Amy obviously knew what was happening and it was clear that she didn't want to get involved. She stayed in the kitchen when she wasn't serving the guests and judging from her furtive glances in our direction, I think she was enjoying this moment. She probably was curious about how her big brother would react to this situation. She wasn't the only one interested in Pete's reaction.

Without looking away from his paper, Pete asked Frank why he wasn't eating at the seniors' home next door. Frank either didn't understand the question or didn't hear Pete and kept eating.

After a moment of hesitation, I said to Pete, "Guess what, Frank decided to join us on the trip to Los Angeles."

If I wasn't scared, I would have enjoyed Pete's reaction because it was classic. He slowly put the paper down and stared at Frank and then at me, but he didn't say a word. He then looked at Amy, who quickly ducked into the kitchen.

His response was, "I'm sorry, what did you say?"

I repeated my statement and you will note the way I artfully dodged the issue by saying, "Frank decided..."

I certainly didn't lie because it was Frank who made the decision to join us and visit his daughter.

Pete said something like, "Well, this is quite a surprise, but Frank, you know we have a pretty small car and I don't think it'll be comfortable for such a long trip."

This is when I spoke up and volunteered to sit in the back seat.

After a few seconds of silence, there was little that Pete could say at this point, other than a reluctant "okay." He then just shook his head and went back to the newspaper.

I really didn't know what he was thinking, but he seemed to accept the situation much better than I had expected.

So, you can imagine the next picture with the three amigos in the Mustang, Frank in the front chewing his cigar and me in the back with Frank's two bags next to me.

Pete didn't say much during the drive, but I really think he was enjoying himself with the Mustang, navigating the twists and turns of Highway One.

Dad, there's no question that sometime this year or next, you, Jennie and I have to take this same trip. Pete has been very patient in stopping at various scenic spots for me to take pictures, but even when I blow up these digital images on the computer, they won't do justice to the natural beauty. Everywhere you look, the scenery is awesome.

I was worried at first that Frank would monopolize the conversation during the drive, which would have driven Pete crazy, but he was pretty quiet. In fact, we often drove for miles without saying anything. We were either enjoying the sights or deep in our own thoughts.

We stopped several times along the way. The first stop was only about an hour after we left Amy's house when Pete decided to put the top down on the Mustang "in order to enjoy the environment." But I knew exactly why he put the top down and it didn't have anything to do with the sights - it was because of Frank. I know I shouldn't be so crude, but it seemed like within five minutes after we left Amy's, Frank started letting off loud and smelly gassers. He didn't even try to disguise them; they just exploded one after another in a synchronized manner like a series of fireworks. No wonder one of the women in the senior home called him "the Gas King." I thought it was because Frank said he once worked in a gas station while drifting. If Pete didn't put the top down, I was going to ask him to stop for a gas mask.

When Pete saw that Frank was getting cold, he reluctantly offered to put the top up on the Mustang. But Frank said no, so Pete gave him the Giants' sweatshirt and told him to keep the shirt after he found out that Frank is a big Giants fan.

I know that Pete has plenty of money, but he's been very generous on this trip and I doubt if I can ever repay him.

It must have been a pretty odd site to see a middle-aged man, followed by a teenager and a George Burns look-alike chewing his cigar and wearing a Giants' sweatshirt. I suppose we could easily pass for three generations - a grandfather, son and grandson.

I don't know whether Pete had intended to do this all along or it was another unexpected detour, but when he saw the sign for Hearst Castle, he quickly turned in that direction without saying a word to either of us.

When we arrived at the Hearst Castle parking lot, Pete asked Frank and I whether we wanted to take a tour. Another non-decision – this was really a big bonus. I really doubt that Pete wanted to see the Castle and I think he was doing this for me. Maybe he's not as self-centered as I thought.

By the way, I offered to pay for my tour of the Castle, but Pete wouldn't accept.

Since we were all first-time visitors, it was recommended that we take Tour One, which gives a pretty broad overview of the Castle and surrounding grounds.

We saw five rooms of the main house (Casa Grande), including the "Assembly Room" , which is the largest of four sitting rooms. However, my favorite room in the main house is the "Morning Room" , which is a smaller sitting room filled with antiques and tapestries.

I really didn't get much out of the gardens. Don't get me wrong, they are awfully nice, but it's hard to get very excited about marble sculptures and plants, even though some of the flowers were starting to bloom.

You wouldn't believe the guesthouse we toured. It is called "Casa Del Sol" , which is an appropriate name since it faces the sunny coastline. The house contains 18 rooms and we were able to visit four bedrooms and four bathrooms.

The Neptune and Roman pools were also part of our tour and each one is incredible. The Roman pool is indoors and the roof of the structure is covered by very fancy glass; I think the tour guide said it is Venetian glass.

Frankly, much of the Castle, other buildings and pool areas are so ornate that I think Pete probably used the right word when he described them as being "gaudy". If this means "too showy", then Pete is right.

Hearst Castle would have to be another one of our stops – except next time, you and Laura can take Tour One and I'll take a different tour.

By the way, this time, it was Pete who gave a history lesson - not about the Castle itself, but on William Randolph Hearst and the Hearst family. Pete had written a paper about Mr. Hearst while in college. As Pete said, Hearst was truly a "multi-faceted" individual.

From what Pete said, Hearst was born to wealth and apparently inherited the land on which the Castle sits. His father made his fortune in the mining business; William made his money primarily in the journalism field, specifically through the ownership of a wide range of newspapers.

As it turns out, Hearst shares common interests with Pete and me. For one thing, he excelled in journalism, which as you know is what I would love to do in life if I'm given the chance. He was also interested in drama in college, much like Pete. In addition, he was involved in the movie business and produced over 100 films.

By the way, we were told during the tour that the Castle represented the fulfillment of Hearst's dream to build a dwelling similar to what he had seen in Europe as a youngster. It took a total of 28 years for him to complete the Castle.

After the tour, we continued south on Highway One. We drove through a little town called Cambria and then stopped for the day in Morro Bay.

During the drive between Hearst Castle and Morro Bay, Pete talked virtually nonstop about one of his favorite movies, **"Citizen Kane"**. I remember you rented this movie for me a couple of years ago, but honestly, it didn't make very much sense to me at the time. Now that I know more about Mr. Hearst, the movie will probably have more meaning.

I still don't understand why Orson Welles kept mumbling the word "Rosebud" in the movie. Do you? I'll remember to ask Pete.

Pete should become a movie and stage critic because he gives a good, thorough description of what he has seen and certainly has strong opinions about his likes and dislikes. Maybe I should recommend this as a second career if he ever retires from his banking business.

I really didn't know what to expect when Pete said we would stay for the night in Morro Bay, but just like the other towns that we have seen along the coast, it is what Laura would describe as a "cute little town."

I know you become sad when I say these things, but I wish Mom had been able to see the California coast. She would have enjoyed it far more than me, particularly the little shops in each town. I know it's painful to talk about Mom, but I guess it doesn't hurt to always keep her in our memories, wherever we go.

Anyway, just like in San Francisco, there is an "Embarcadero" area at Morro Bay, but it is only a couple of blocks total in size. I guess this town was once a prosperous commercial fishing industry, but it's now a tourist area.

You have probably seen pictures of the town's famous landmark, a "rock" that is nearly 600 feet high and over 50 acres at the base. The person who owns the restaurant where we ate tonight said that the rock was the last in a chain of extinct volcanoes.

I guess the rock was even bigger at one time, but some of its side faces were removed in order to provide material for a breakwater and to also build a jetty to connect the rock to the mainland. Thankfully, Morro Rock is now a protected historical landmark.

Since we didn't have reservations, it was difficult to get three rooms during this busy tourist weekend. So, we settled on one large "suite", consisting of one bedroom and a sofa bed in the living room area.

Pete and I made two bets, both decided by coin flips. The first was to decide the sleeping arrangements. I lost the bet and will share the bedroom tonight with Frank. Actually, I would have preferred the sofa bed. I just hope that Frank doesn't snore all night like he did in the car when he took a short nap.

The other bet related to who would have first access to the phone line to do e-mails. I lost this one as well.

At dinner, we took the time to share more of our "innermost secrets", as Frank calls them.

I went first by telling the five remaining items from my "Regret List". They are: (1) to skydive at least once; (2) to take a cruise through the Panama Canal; (3) to watch the whales migrate in Mexico; (4) to be an uncle for Laura's children (even though she says she will never get married); and (5) to have another best friend, in addition to you.

Since I have achieved the San Francisco objective, I'm considering replacing it with one of two things, either a hot air balloon ride across a few states or scuba diving where there is a variety of sea life. I still need to research both before I make my decision.

I can't really say that the Pebble Beach item was satisfied because I didn't actually play the course. So it'll remain on the list.

After Pete spoke (I will keep his thoughts confidential), it was Frank's turn.

I really think that Frank is enjoying this exercise, either because he wants to finally get some things off his chest or he might just be getting a kick out of being in the limelight. One thing is for sure, whether his stories are fact or fiction, Frank has clearly won the prize as the best storyteller.

I don't think he would mind if I share this with you, but I'll give you the condensed version – otherwise, your already tired son will be typing for hours.

It seems that after Frank settled down in Santa Cruz, he contacted a friend in Southern California whose name is Myrna. She had been close with Frank and his wife before they divorced. According to Frank, Myrna couldn't keep a husband; she was divorced from two and also twice widowed.

Frank renewed contact with Myrna in order to get updates about his daughter and her two children. Myrna, however, thought that Frank had a romantic interest in her, which is why she constantly called and wrote him.

Anyway, Frank claims that at one point in time, Myrna visited him in Santa Cruz and she was truly hooked on Frank. (This is easily understood because with his perpetual three-day growth, a cigar hanging out of his mouth and his ever-present soiled white tee-shirt, Frank is one irresistible hunk of a man.)

Well, Myrna suggested that Frank return to live with her in her fully paid-for home in the Los Angeles area. Myrna told Frank that with one of her late husband's monthly pension checks and her other sources of income, they could live very comfortably. She didn't mention marriage, but Frank assumed this was part of the bargain.

After considering the idea for a while, Frank decided against Myrna's proposal and he remained with Amy in Santa Cruz.

Here is the punch line. About a year after the rejection, Frank heard from his daughter that Myrna won $18 million in the California lottery.

According to Frank, however, the relationship probably wouldn't have worked anyway because Myrna never stopped talking. Frank believes that he would have either committed suicide or left Myrna long before her lottery jackpot.

Frank's daughter told him that after winning the lottery, Myrna bought a house in an area called La Jolla and married a tennis teacher who is at least 20 years younger than she is.

Even though Frank has had a totally rotten life, he never gets downhearted – he is constantly laughing at himself and about life. He is the exact opposite of Pete because Frank finds something to joke about wherever we go and always has a pleasant greeting for people.

The only negative thing that occurred today happened after dinner. Pete went up to the room to do his e-mails and Frank and I stayed in the lobby of the motel so we could watch television without disturbing him.

As we were talking to a very pleasant woman behind the counter at the motel, a man pulled up into the parking lot in a big, old beat-up car which Frank said needs a new muffler. The car was loud and obnoxious and its owner was even worse. In fact, he was totally gross.

The woman's personality changed when she saw the car. It turns out that he is the night manager of the motel and I guess he gets pretty nasty with the women employees.

We got a glimpse of his personality when he yelled at the counter woman shortly after he first arrived. I really don't know what he said, but it wasn't pleasant. The next moment, he came up behind her, whispered something in her ear and was holding each of her breasts with his big hands.

She pushed him away and called him a "crude bastard". Frank saw what he was doing and yelled, "Knock it off, asshole."

The night manager's face got really red and he shouted back, "Mind your own business, old man." He then went into the inner office and we could hear him laughing to himself.

As this woman was leaving the motel after finishing her shift, Frank asked her why she puts up with the night manager. She shook her head and said that as a divorced mother of two, she has to stick around because it's a good paying job and she is less than a mile from her apartment.

As she got to the door, she turned around and added, "Whom would I complain to - that little shit is the owner's son." She called the guy "Dirty Little Harry."

Judging from his size and sloppy look, this is probably an appropriate name.

Before Frank and I left the lobby area, we saw "Harry" in action again when he chewed out a Hispanic maid because she apparently hadn't cleaned the office to his satisfaction. She had tears in her eyes as she quickly left the lobby area.

I don't understand why people have to be so mean to others. These women seemed very nice and there is no reason for this jerk to treat them in such a rotten manner. Harry is probably so insecure about himself that he takes out his frustrations on those who can't defend themselves.

Well, enough of "Dirty Little Harry" – he won't ruin a perfectly nice day. People like that often get paid back for their bad behavior.

Frank and Pete are sleeping, so I'll now turn in. We have a long day ahead planned for tomorrow.

Love,
Rocky

I felt that for the first time, I didn't hold anything back from Dad.

After all, I couldn't say anything about my "commando raid" since it hasn't been accomplished yet.

One of these days, I'll probably get in lots of trouble for my retaliatory actions, but in all honesty, what's the worst thing that can happen to me if I get caught?

I doubt that anything could be worse than my own prison.

CHAPTER 19

"STRANGE BEHAVIOR"

BY PETER

April 17, 1999 – Santa Cruz to Morro Bay

When I logged onto my laptop this evening, I was surprised to see a message from Kathy, particularly since I had spoken with her by phone when we stopped for lunch.

This is what she wrote:

Dear Pete:

I was planning to write you today after I read your e-mail this morning, but I later changed my mind.

However, that was before your call this afternoon, which changed my mind again.

I'm probably not making sense, but if you think you're already confused, wait till you read the rest of this note. Your head will no doubt be spinning by the time you finish. But why should you be spared, because that's exactly the way I feel.

I have such mixed emotions about you and this trip that it's very difficult to communicate my feelings in a logical written message, but here it goes.

Probably the best way to show you why I'm in such a confused state is to recap everything that has happened since you first found out about your mistake at the foundation dinner (don't even think about trying to deny your error, because you screwed up, Mr. Smart Guy):

1. *You didn't want to go on the trip and you tried to convince Jennie and me to bail you out. What was particularly insulting was your cheap attempt to get sympathy through bagels and cream cheese. You're slipping because I would have at least expected you to bribe me with expensive jewelry.*

2. After the first day of the trip, you told me that things were okay because Rocky took little time from you, so your work wouldn't suffer. You didn't even care about Rocky and true to form, you only focused on yourself and your damn work.
3. Then you told me about your idea to share secrets with Rocky, yet you never talk with your kids or me. Now, you're revealing secrets about yourself to a teenager that you only recently met.
4. You said something about getting kicked out of a Giants game – what am I supposed to think about that?
5. The next thing I hear is that you suddenly decided to visit Amy and you stayed with her for two nights, but this idea repulsed you when I suggested it some time ago.
6. You visited the Monterey Aquarium, but you could never spare the time to take your kids to a place like an aquarium or zoo.
7. Then you're sharing your secrets not only with Rocky, but also with Amy and an elderly man named Frank.
8. You suddenly decided to play golf at Pebble Beach – I can't remember the last time you made a spontaneous decision to do something fun for you or the family.
9. You helped prepare food in a homeless shelter – you won't even allow me to donate money to a local shelter because you think most of the beneficiaries are not worthy. To use your exact words, "they're lazy bums."
10. You thoroughly enjoyed the ride around the Monterey area, which again is a vacation that I suggested, but you said it would be utterly boring.
11. You're transporting a complete stranger to see his long-lost daughter in Los Angeles.
12. You decided on a whim to tour Hearst Castle – I thought you would have preferred a root canal rather such a tour.
13. You're driving in a Mustang convertible with the top down – those few times that you and I have traveled, you always insist on a Lincoln or another large car so you can look important. And usually, you wouldn't allow the kids or me to even open up the sunroof.
14. You finally admitted that you may have been too harsh with Josh, but instead of telling Josh or me, you reveal this information to three other people, two of whom are virtually unknown to you.

15. You're showing Rocky college campuses, but you didn't have the time to take your own son or daughter for a single campus tour, even though they asked you repeatedly to join them.

Now, please don't misunderstand me. I couldn't be more delighted that you're making special efforts to please Rocky. He's a fine young man and deserves to enjoy himself in every way possible.

I'm also not begrudging Frank. I called Amy after we spoke on the phone to make sure you haven't flipped out and she told me about Frank – it seems he's suffered terribly and I'm proud of you for taking him to his daughter.

Also, I'm absolutely delighted that you are finally enjoying yourself. It seems that you have not had a moment of pleasure in so many years that I can't remember when you last smiled or laughed. I also have no memory of when you last did something in a spontaneous fashion.

As you always tell the kids and me, get to the point – well, here it is:

I HONESTLY THINK I'M JEALOUS OF ROCKY, AND EVEN FRANK, TO SOME EXTENT.

You've shared more of your inner feelings with them, and Amy, than with me in a very long time; in fact, it's been so long that I can't even remember what we discussed.

Rocky has seen you in a way that neither your children nor I have had a chance to experience – at least not for the past couple of decades.

I'm torn with happiness and sadness at the same time.

Do you think that you may be going through some kind of mid-life crisis?

I don't want you suddenly going off the deep end as a result of your constant stress level. I'm actually starting to fear that you will hurt yourself when you get back to the horrible treadmill at the office.

I can't believe that it took Rocky, Amy, Frank, Alcatraz, Pebble Beach, a red Mustang convertible or maybe a homeless shelter to get your attention, but in the end it doesn't matter. I don't care what the catalyst may have been or that it succeeded after I failed – the important thing is that it may help you to inch a little closer to the man I once knew and someone the kids have never met.

I'm sure you won't remember, but in January, I tried to "schedule" dinners with you on two occasions, but you were forced to cancel because of work-related crises. I doubt that any of the major superpowers experience as many emergencies as your firm. In any event, I asked to reschedule because I had something important to discuss, but you never suggested another date for dinner or even asked what was so important.

I hate to talk about this in an e-mail, but I know that when you return to the office, you will be immediately engulfed in urgent activities. By the way, despite your complaints, I think you relish in all of the attention you receive whenever you return to the office after being away for a while. Everybody wants a small piece of Pete. Your ego would be terribly crushed if you suddenly were not in such demand.

What I tried to tell you in January was that after Josh and Jennie went off to school, I began to have serious doubts about our marriage. Don't get defensive because it wasn't anything you did; on the contrary, it's what you don't do any longer. In order to objectively analyze the situation, I met religiously with a therapist for three months. You wouldn't have known because I paid for this from the separate "slush fund" you generously established for me with your last bonus.

Instead of going into detail about my thoughts, feelings and emotions during this soul-searching process, here is the "bottom line" of the outcome. I chose to stay with you for three basic reasons. First, and most importantly, I still love you, despite how you have progressively changed. Second, I still have hope for you and us. And third, I realized that although our relationship has soured, it still isn't so bad. I appreciate that this is not a rousing endorsement, but it's reality. Notice I didn't say I am staying for the sake of the kids because I don't think they would be surprised if we split.

Thankfully for both of us and for the kids, I knew early on in our marriage that I would have to make my own happiness. If I were the type of wife that depended on her husband for her joy, we would be in big trouble.

You know that I'm a pragmatic person and believe me, I would never expect a dramatic change in your behavior, but I would gladly settle for a small and yet permanent detour. Ideally, you've arrived at an intersection with divided roads and you're thinking about taking a different route from your recent past.

Sadly, what will probably happen is that we will again lose you to the corporate black hole. But for your sake as well as ours, I dearly hope this won't be the case.

Whatever happens, you know I love you and I always will.

Love,
Kathy

It was a dagger in the heart; a punch in the stomach. This note hurt because it is so very accurate.

It would have been better if Kathy were so upset that she became irrational. Instead, she was logical, which is something I can't fight.

If she wanted me to feel guilty, then she has succeeded far beyond her wildest dreams.

It wasn't easy preparing this response.

Dear Kathy:

Do you remember the time when two of my partners were so drunk at the firm's Christmas party that they got into a fistfight after they found out they were both having affairs with the same secretary?

I walked away from that party with a broken nose after I intervened between the two prizefighters.

Well, your e-mail did the same thing, except this time, the punch was far more painful.

First, I'm not suffering from any kind of crisis, nor have I flipped out.

Second, much to your surprise, I really can't disagree with anything you said in the note.

Actually, after reading your list of things that have happened since the foundation dinner, I have to admit that my behavior appears more than a little bizarre. In fact, it's downright scary to think that I've done all of these things.

Prepare food in a homeless shelter for people who should be working? Not me.

Sharing secrets with people I hardly know? Never.

Enjoying my visit with Amy? Not a chance.

Renting a red Mustang convertible and driving with the top down through the Monterey Bay area with a kid and an old man? Not in my lifetime.

I'm even finding it hard to believe that I've done these things. But the point is, I have done them and even more interesting is that, by and large, I've enjoyed myself. Maybe that's stretching it - at least I haven't hated the experiences.

I hope you believe me when I say that your note proved timely.

During dinner, we each shared some other thoughts. Someday, I'll tell you Frank's because he is by far the most entertaining person in our therapy group.

Anyway, this is what I told my two traveling companions – I feel horribly guilty because you should be driving down the coast of California with me.

More to the point, I also said that instead of sharing my feelings with others, I should be talking with you – letting you know these and other things that are inside me.

You should know that I haven't been bottling things up, but for some reason, when I'm with Rocky, I just open up – with thoughts that aren't even conscious to me. Don't ask me to explain, because I simply don't understand why his presence brings these things out. And it not just me because I doubt that Amy and Frank would have shared their past experiences if Rocky wasn't present.

You touched on something in your note that I can't answer, which is, how will I act when I return to the New York grind?

I wish I knew. I'm not going to make any promises because when I have in the past, I've let you down far too many times. However, I can honestly say that there will be some favorable changes, but to what extent remains to be seen.

Well, I've exceeded my half-hour limit with the telephone line. It's now Rocky's turn to send an e-mail to Michael.

Kathy, I love you more than you will ever know. I'm just sorry that I haven't lived up to expectations, either yours or mine. You certainly deserve better treatment than I have given you.

All that I can ask is for you to keep pushing and not give up on me. I'm not yet convinced that your dear husband is a lost cause – very close perhaps, but I still have hope for redemption.

Pete

I stretched the truth with Kathy because quite honestly, I'm not sure I can be saved.

Given my history, if I were Kathy, after reading my response, I would say, "What a bunch of crap", because that's probably what it is. You see, I don't even know if I'm truly sincere. My response could be phony because it's the most expedient way to get Kathy's sympathy. On the other hand, maybe these words truly reflect how I feel.

I just don't know any longer who's speaking and whether the things said are genuine.

CHAPTER 20

"THE REUNION"

BY ROCKY

April 18, 1999 – Morro Bay to Los Angeles

Dear Dad:

It was a long day, especially for Pete because he was behind the wheel for many hours. But it was a special day in many ways.

You won't believe where I am right now – I am typing away on my laptop from our hotel in **BEVERLY HILLS!!!**

We are staying in Pete's favorite hotel since his offices are located nearby, at a place called Century City.

Now to the details of today's events.

When Pete and I woke up this morning, we couldn't find Frank. He disappeared during the night and two bags of clothes were also missing.

Pete said he wasn't surprised that Frank fled because it would have been difficult for him to face his daughter after so many years.

I went to the lobby to look for Frank while Pete was getting ready and the night manager, my friend "Little Dirty Harry", told me that the "old fart" walked away from the motel early in the morning.

After I showered and packed, we drove up and down the streets of Morro Bay looking for Frank, but without success.

We asked about Frank at a couple of gas stations, but no one had seen him.

After nearly one hour of searching, Pete suggested that we eat breakfast and then look a little longer before heading south.

We went back to the coffee shop near our motel and we spotted Frank alone in a corner booth, drinking coffee.

Pete was right, Frank got cold feet about seeing his daughter. So, he got up around four o'clock and quietly left the room. He never thought he would see either of us again, unless Pete visits Amy in Santa Cruz.

He walked a few blocks to the main road and hitched a ride with a truck driver traveling north on Highway One.

By the time they reached Cambria, which is about 15 miles north of Morro Bay, Frank asked the truck driver to let him off. He crossed the street and was lucky enough to persuade another trucker to give him a ride back to Morro Bay.

I asked him why he changed his mind.

He said that the first trucker had a picture of his two grandchildren mounted on his dash. This is why Frank returned – he said if he didn't continue with this trip, he could never live with himself. He had already missed far too much. He can't make up for lost time, but he can start fresh.

By the time he returned to the motel, we had already checked out. He wasn't sure whether he would find us, but even if he didn't, he was determined to continue on his own, even if he had to walk to Los Angeles.

Frank then confessed that he had fallen off the wagon during the early morning hours. I'm sure Pete and I had the same thought, but it turned out that Frank wasn't talking about alcohol. He had three cigarettes with the first truck driver.

Before we took off, Pete asked the cook at the café for driving directions for another campus tour, this time to Cal Poly State University at San Luis Obispo. Pete just won't quit with the campus tours. I understand his intentions are good, but enough already!!

He is starting to piss me off. I think Pete missed his calling - he should have been a college recruiter.

After driving through the Cal Poly campus and the "downtown" area of San Luis Obispo, Pete made another one of his unexpected moves; he quickly veered off the main road into a shopping mall parking lot.

The maneuver was so quick that both the driver and passenger of the car behind us flipped us off (gave us the finger) as they flew by us. Judging from the way Pete made this sharp turn to the mall without giving a turn signal, I think it was a split second decision.

It was actually funny to see two fingers in the air in the passing car– one on each side, as if they were saluting us.

Pete parked the car and without saying anything, led us to a large department store in the mall. Frank shrugged his shoulders, but we just followed the "Pete Piper".

To make a long story short, we walked away with a bunch of new clothes for Frank: a sports jacket, three pairs of pants (no jeans), four shirts and shoes. Pete also bought golf-type shirts and jeans for himself, and walking shorts and swimming trunks for me to use in Los Angeles.

After we finished shopping in the department store, we walked through the mall. Again, Pete didn't say a word, but he had a determined look. We stopped at a place that said "unisex" haircuts. Pete gave the hairdresser two $20 bills and he asked her to take care of his "father".

While Frank was getting his hair cut, Pete and I bought a couple of other items, including a suitcase for Frank's clothes. I got an adapter to play my portable CD player through the car stereo.

After his haircut, Frank used the mall bathroom to change into his new clothes. Dad, he looked totally different – transformed from a grungy "old fart" to a handsome senior.

As we continued our drive, I asked Pete whether I could listen to my CDs on the car stereo using the adaptor with my portable player. He hesitated, but said for only 30 minutes every couple of hours.

He didn't say it, but he probably thought that I listen to hip-hop or rap music. But after I played the Beatles, Rolling Stones, Doors and Fleetwood Mac, he eliminated the time limit.

I was surprised to hear Pete sing solos with the CDs. He wasn't bad, but when Frank joined him for a duet, it was awful. Frank doesn't know the words and he either gets them completely wrong, or he just hums.

We stopped for a few minutes at another campus – this time, the University of California at Santa Barbara.

For once, I didn't mind the campus detour. If I ever consider attending college, UCSB would have to be one of the schools I will keep in mind. The location is great and the kids were all riding around on bikes, wearing shorts and tee shirts. You should see the girls!

Dad, don't get the wrong idea. Pete's former partner in Santa Barbara told me that the school has a good academic reputation – so the school is appealing even without friendly girls wearing skimpy tops. It seems like a great school at an ideal coastal location.

Remember I said I could see you retiring in the Monterey Bay area? Well, now I have another location for you to consider: Santa Barbara. It is warmer than Monterey and just as pretty, but the price of housing is ridiculous. I suppose you can always become a butler or caretaker at a wealthy person's estate. I wouldn't mind living in the servant's quarters.

We ate lunch with Pete's former partner, who retired in Santa Barbara six years ago. He has absolutely no regrets about moving here from the East Coast.

Even though Pete told me that his partner is Frank's age, he looks at least 10 years younger with his youthful manner and tan. I should have asked him if he knows of anyone who needs a butler or chauffer.

By the time we left Santa Barbara, I was already tired, but the day was still far from over.

We encountered heavy traffic south of Santa Barbara and this continued all the way to Los Angeles. We were moving at a good pace, but I've never seen so many cars in my life. These Southern California people must live in their cars.

When people refer to the large metropolitan Los Angeles area, I never had any concept of how massive it really is. I thought we would drop Frank at his daughter's and then travel a short distance to our hotel, but it took us nearly three hours to reach his daughter's house from Santa Barbara. The traffic was horrible – plus Frank didn't help by getting us lost a few times before we found the right street. He refused to let me look at the map because I think he was just stalling for time.

It was incredibly sad to see Frank's reactions as we got closer to his daughter's house. He trembled and his voice was shaky. He was so nervous that I thought he was about to jump out of the car and walk back to Santa Cruz.

When we finally found his daughter's house, Pete parked in front and waited for Frank to get out of the car. But he didn't. None of said anything; Frank stayed in the car and stared at the house.

I thought Pete would finally say something, but he didn't know how to handle the situation.

Thankfully, the front door opened and a woman came out with two young guys following her.

Pete opened the driver's side door, but Frank stayed in the car. Pete and I stood outside the car and we were all looking at Frank, who sat completely frozen, looking down.

I'm not sure Frank would have moved if his daughter hadn't opened the car door.

Then we saw a flood of emotion as Frank got out of the car.

His daughter cried as she hugged him and the two boys then joined their mother.

At first, Frank didn't know how to react. His arms remained at his side while his daughter and the older grandchild hugged him. After the youngest grandchild joined his mother and brother in embracing his grandfather, Frank began crying like a baby.

We never entered the house because Pete thought we would be interfering with a family reunion.

As we drove to Beverly Hills, Pete said little. But that evening, while we were eating pizza at a place around the corner from the hotel, he said that the reunion was his most emotional experience in many years. This comment surprised me – I thought he was quiet because he was thinking about tomorrow's meeting. I never expected him to be so affected by Frank's reunion.

A few moments passed and then he said something else, which I think is okay to tell you – his exact words were, "I can't believe I've wasted all this time."

He didn't say another word until he asked for the check. He just kept looking out the window and sipping his beer. It was hard not to feel sorry for Pete.

By the time we returned to the hotel, we were both so tired and drained that we didn't even think about sharing any secrets. But in reality, he said it all during dinner.

With every day that passes, I get more insight into Pete. Sometimes, it isn't a very pretty picture. We tend to paint someone in a certain way by how they live and act, but first impressions, however, are often wrong.

In Pete's case, I had him pictured completely wrong – I thought he is a guy who has everything going for him – but I now think that he is an empty soul. Compared with Pete, I am very blessed.

I doubt that I can help him in the short time we will have together. I guess the best thing I can do for him is to listen when he decides to express himself, like he did tonight.

He is old and wise enough to figure things out by himself. He doesn't need the help of an inexperienced teenager.

I bet I know what you're thinking right now – I should stay out of Pete's business. You're right as usual and I'll do just that.

I am so exhausted that I am about to fall asleep before I sign off.
Goodnight, Dad.

Love,
Rocky

I wonder if Pete will say anything to Dad about what he saw this morning at the parking lot of the motel. I doubt it because he probably doesn't suspect anything.

Even if he does, there isn't any direct evidence to connect me to Dirty Little Harry's car. The fact that Pete's shaving cream was missing doesn't prove anything. I could never be convicted of a crime based on such weak circumstantial evidence.

After I finished my e-mail to Dad, I stayed in bed and thought about Pete's reaction to this afternoon's reunion between Frank and his family. It is hard to explain, but I'm becoming convinced that Pete is not really a tough and calloused individual. A person who is so insensitive would never have been affected by what we saw this afternoon. Instead, such an individual would have been concerned about arriving late at the hotel.

The sad thing for Pete is that since he has this image, it is very difficult for him to openly show any compassion. Maybe Pete feels that if his inner side is revealed, people will not view him as being so fearsome.

What a horrible situation for anyone to be in – you have to basically hide your feelings in order to protect your reputation. If this is true in Pete's case, I guess you could say that he is a "closet humanitarian".

It could be much worse –Pete could be a phony person who pretends to be a kind and gentle person, but who is really an insensitive jerk. I prefer a person who disguises a soft interior with a rough exterior than the other way around.

CHAPTER 21

"DEEP IN SORROW"

BY PETER

April 18, 1999 – Morro Bay to Los Angeles

What the hell is wrong with me?

When I got to the room after dinner, I really wasn't sure what I wanted to do. I watched television for a while, but found nothing of interest.

I then opened the package of background information from Jack for tomorrow's meeting. I tried to review the first page a number of times, but I couldn't focus on anything I was reading.

I really wasn't sure why I was feeling so low, but I guess it was a combination of many things, including sheer exhaustion. It was a very long day with lots of driving, not so much in distance, but more in time, particularly in heavy traffic once we arrived in the Los Angeles area.

I'm sure my mood wasn't helped by my downing two beers at dinner and a Scotch from the mini bar when I returned to the room.

But it was more than all of those things; for some reason, seeing Frank reunited with his family really hit me hard.

It was fortunate that it was too late to call Kathy, because I would have slurred my words or worse yet, I may have started weeping. That would have clinched it; she'd probably think I'm suicidal if I suddenly broke down while describing Frank's reunion with his family.

I concluded it would be better to send her a note. If I don't like what I have written, I can erase it before it is sent. Maybe by writing things down, I will have a better idea why I feel the way I do.

Dear Kathy:

I am writing this letter to you late at night from Beverly Hills.

After your e-mail of yesterday, I'm not really sure how wise it is for me to send you this note, but I need to put my thoughts down in writing so I can better understand what is happening to me.

First of all, please don't worry about me. I'm just feeling a little melancholy, maybe because I'm tired after driving over eight hours.

I know it is unusual for me to share my emotions with you, but as I told Frank and Rocky, better with you than with people I hardly know.

I suppose that because of my tough guy image, I think that showing an emotional side exhibits weakness. Unfortunately, this is the way I grew up, so I don't know any better. Now that I think about it, I honestly don't ever remember seeing Father in an openly sorrowful state, other than when his mother passed away.

Before I start with the "heavy" stuff, let me continue the saga of the three road misfits.

When Rocky and I woke up this morning, we couldn't find Frank. We later determined that he slipped out of our room while we were sleeping.

It turns out that Frank had understandable misgivings about seeing his daughter and as a result, he almost chickened out. But, by a strange turn of events, he returned after a 30-mile round trip in two trucks. Frank changed his mind about retreating and when he returned from this short detour, he was even more determined to see his daughter and his two grandchildren.

By the way, I forgot to mention that when I was about to shave this morning, I couldn't find my shaving cream; I was certain I had brought it with me from Amy's place. I looked for the cream in the cabinet below the bathroom sink, but it wasn't there. What I found, however, was the outside wrapping for three toilet paper rolls. This was indeed strange, but since I was more focused on Frank, I didn't give it another thought.

As we were leaving the parking lot of the motel, I noticed a car parked outside the manager's office that was totally covered with toilet paper and shaving cream. The evening dew had made the paper stick to the car and something had been written on the windows. On the front windshield, someone wrote "jerk" and the word "pig" was on the back window.

After Frank saw the car, he laughed so hard that he couldn't stop. It reminded me of your outburst in the cab after the foundation dinner – except in his case, Frank began to cough uncontrollably until Rocky saved him with a bottle of water.

Rocky didn't say anything, which gave him away. He should have at least showed some interest in the car. I suspect it was another vendetta by Rocky – this young man doesn't show it, but he has a mean streak. I better not cross him because he wouldn't hesitate to put a contract out on my head.

Anyway, neither of my passengers took credit for this terrorist act. I suppose you can say that the motto in our red Mustang is, "Don't ask, don't tell."

We made a short stop in a town called San Luis Obispo to do the impossible: to convert Frank from his typical grubby self to a kindly looking senior statesman. New clothes and a haircut helped, but he refused a shave and wouldn't part with his ratty looking cigar.

Before lunch with George Silva in Santa Barbara, I took Rocky for another campus tour. For once, I think he enjoyed himself, but more for the scenery than the campus. He loves to look at the ladies.

Kathy, you wouldn't recognize George because he looks years younger than he did the day of his retirement party. When George excused himself to go to the men's room, I made a comment to Frank and Rocky about how youthful he looks compared to the last time I had seen him. I made the mistake of saying I thought George must have had cosmetic surgery.

After George returned to the table, Rocky embarrassed me – he told George that I was wondering whether he had a facelift. Thankfully, George was flattered but said that his youthful look is the result of more sleep, lots of golf, daily exercise and reading tons of books that he put aside while working.

He said he hasn't felt this good in decades.

I don't care what George claims; he definitely had a face job and probably liposuction to reduce his beer gut. The way he was talking, I wouldn't be surprised if he has an entire mouth of phony teeth.

After Santa Barbara, we drove for a seemingly endless period of time. It didn't help that we were lost a few times, thanks to Frank's directions. I started to think he was intentionally giving me misinformation because he didn't want to face his daughter.

This is when my emotions were stirred.

It was like those times that I pretend I have something in my eye when I watch a sad movie. Fortunately, this time, my sunglasses protected my macho image. No one saw my tears.

Believe it or not, that reunion scene made this trip worthwhile.

My first thought was – what an absolute waste. Here's this old man who is seeing his daughter for the first time in three decades and who is meeting his teenage grandchildren for the first time.

If he had the courage, Frank could have been with his daughter when his grandchildren were first born, when the boys got their first hit in Little League and when they graduated from junior high school.

Then it hit me – I'm no better than Frank. In fact, I'm actually far worse because Frank supposedly had good reason for being an absentee father, but I don't.

At the rate I'm going, I will be the same as Frank in another 15 or so years – even though I may be physically present with my family, they won't know me and I won't know them.

I expect that like my father, stepping down from the pedestal of my lofty position will be a rude awakening. I'm also afraid it will be a severe test for me to make a transition to a second life since I'm not close with my family and have little outside interests. Even worse, I will be a complete stranger within my own house.

I don't want this to happen, but I'm not really sure how I can avoid what seems to be my destiny.

It may already be far too late for me to make meaningful changes, even if I am willing to do so; and I'm not sure I can effectively alter my personality at this stage in my life.

I have now read this note and decided that you deserve to know what I am thinking and how I'm feeling. It actually helped me to put my emotions down in words – I was troubled by this day, particularly when I saw Frank's reaction before and after he saw his family. But I wasn't sure why this scene brought me to such a low point.

Despite the emotion it stirred in me, I obviously couldn't be more delighted for Frank since this reunion was long overdue. I give full credit to Rocky for convincing Frank to take this bold step. Had it not been for Rocky, who knows when Frank would have had the courage to finally make that move.

I'm telling you all of this because I can finally admit to my fears. It's not that I have been hiding them from you or anyone else, but frankly, I didn't realize they existed until this trip.

So, if you're inclined to accept the mission, I'm literally on my knees as I type this note and asking for your help.

Understandably, you have essentially given up on me long ago, but maybe, just maybe, a little bit of your wisdom, support and direction (including a few well-deserved kicks in the ass) will finally make an impact.

Think of it this way: for once, I'm vulnerable. You can take advantage of me since I cannot effectively fight back. You can help mold the putty I've become.

Love you,
Pete

Fear – for me to even say the word about myself is unthinkable.

CHAPTER 22

"REALISTIC EXPECTATIONS"

BY PETER

April 19, 1999 – Los Angeles

I wasn't sure whether I should confess how I felt about what occurred today or leave things as they are with Kathy without making any further comments about my state of mind.

On the one hand, she may be a little more relieved to know that things are back to normal and that Rocky isn't receiving special treatment.

But this is why I'm also hesitating – I don't want her to know that things are the same –she might conclude that what she heard from me over the past couple of days was my typical crap.

Doesn't make sense, does it?

That clinched it; I'm so confused that I know I should make a full confession to Kathy.

Dear Kathy:

You won't believe how good it was to get your call this morning. I was just about to leave the room when the phone rang. I initially thought about ignoring the call, but then something told me that you were on the phone.

When I woke up this morning, I was embarrassed about the e-mail I sent you last night. If it were at all possible, I would have revised it by reporting only on the facts such as Rocky's "alleged" vendetta against the motel guy, our lunch at Santa Barbara and Frank's reunion.

Anyway, I'm glad you didn't take the e-mail the wrong way. You are probably right, my emotions stem from a combination of many things, including far too much driving and the lack of quality sleep.

Yes, I promise I'll talk about things with you when I return.

No, I don't think I need to visit a shrink.

You mentioned this morning that a woman psychologist is treating Kate. I know my callous insensitivity is again coming out, but you know I think that Kate has always been a dysfunctional person and I haven't seen any positive changes in her in the past few years. I can see why her first two husbands took a hike – she is just plain obnoxious.

But the "upgraded Pete" is a different person and receptive to all of your suggestions, so let's keep the shrink option open.

During breakfast, I gave Rocky a lecture about my responsibility to him and his father. I told him that he could not leave the hotel grounds while I'm away. And just to play it safe, I asked the manager to have security keep an eye on Rocky during my absence.

Since Rocky is well equipped with new walking shorts and swimming trunks, as well as sunscreen and sunglasses, I suggested that he hang around the pool area for part of the day.

During our breakfast, I leaned over and whispered that if he sticks around the pool long enough, he might get lucky with a young starlet or an abandoned trophy wife – but he didn't appreciate my sense of humor.

Well, Rocky apparently got lucky but I'll leave you in suspense about this juicy tale until later in this note.

Here is the boring part first.

I went to my meeting at our offices and in typical fashion, this first meeting with the Japanese representatives was cordial. I was warned by the president of our client to mind my manners; there was no need to play hardball at this early stage.

You would have been proud of me; I was more than obedient, but it wasn't easy at times to keep my mouth shut.

Just when it looked like I could escape after lunch with our foreign visitors, Jack called with another mini-crisis. Unfortunately, everything is dramatic with him these days. I'm not sure Jack is going to make it this time – he seems to be teetering on the edge of a cliff.

Anyway, Jack was in a panic because one of his deals was about to collapse. He was trying to maintain his composure, but it was clear he is desperate.

I try to help him in every way possible, but what he doesn't realize is that whenever he gets in such an emotional state, he becomes unbearable, particularly for the young associates and support staff in the firm. His alarm becomes theirs; and worse yet, he blames others for his faults.

He needs Kate's psychologist much more than I do. I'll talk with him when I return to New York. If you don't mind, I may even take him to the Nest for a "boy's weekend" in order to have a blunt conversation about his personal life and his career, what little may be left of it.

You probably know where this is heading – yes, another long night at the office, but this time in Century City.

I kept calling Rocky to give him updates because I still thought I could make it to the Dodgers game, but by seven o'clock, we were still a long way from finding a solution to Jack's dilemma.

I called Rocky for the last time early this evening and told him to have dinner without me at the hotel restaurant or in his room. As an alternative, I even offered to send an associate from the firm to have dinner with him wherever Rocky desired.

I was surprised at first because he seemed happy about missing the game.

This is where it gets interesting.

I'm sure he didn't tell me everything, but from what I can gather, he met another teenager (Mandy) at the pool this morning. Rocky assures me that she made the overture. Mandy is from Seattle and her parents are in Los Angeles on business. It seems that Mandy was also alone for the entire day, so they had lunch together.

Mandy was planning to join her parents for dinner with their business associates, but decided to stay at the hotel after she found out that Rocky might be available.

For Rocky, it was either another night of baseball with a relatively unknown 54-year old man who hates watching the game or an all-expenses-paid dinner at an expensive Beverly Hills hotel with a pretty (Rocky's description) girl named Mandy.

Let's see - lovely Mandy or a baseball game with boring Peter?

I'm sure it would have been a tough decision for Rocky, but thankfully, I made the choice for him. Actually, if he had to make this decision, I suspect that Rocky would have reluctantly joined me at the game – simply because he felt obligated to do so.

I was feeling horrible before I made the call and even worse after talking with him. It really hurt – the kid didn't even try to disguise his happiness about the cancellation.

Just kidding – I'm glad that he didn't eat alone.

I asked him to leave me a message about what he wants to do tomorrow on our free day.

When I arrived at the hotel, I was tempted to knock on his door, but it was past 11 o'clock – and I didn't think a bed check was necessary. So, I didn't bother him.

After opening the door to my room, I saw a hotel envelope on the floor. It was from Rocky – and the note said, "Viva Las Vegas." I suppose this means that instead of going to a place like Disneyland or Universal Studies, he wants to see Vegas.

I know this is a long way to drive, but I owe him this request for two reasons: first, I lost a bet at Pebble Beach, so Rocky is legitimately allowed to decide tomorrow's activities. And, even though he probably enjoyed spending the evening with Mandy much more than he would have with me, I also owe him for missing the Dodgers game.

We will leave early tomorrow, enjoy the afternoon and evening in Vegas and then take a flight to New York on Wednesday morning.

You should feel better knowing that Rocky was treated like the rest of my family tonight – he took a back seat to work.

I wonder whether I would have broken my engagement with Rocky if someone other than Jack asked for my help. I suspect you would disagree, but frankly, I'm not sure I would have canceled the baseball game unless it was a dire emergency for someone in the firm. So, maybe I'm making a little progress on my road to recovery from my work addiction.

I'll have fun teasing Rocky tomorrow about Mandy. If I squeeze out any more information, I'll let you know, but I doubt he will share any details with me about his fling. It just occurred to me, I hope that Michael spoke with Rocky about the "birds and bees" – I would hate to be responsible for any inappropriate behavior by Rocky during my watch. Knowing Rocky, he could probably give his dad information on this subject based on what he has learned on the Internet.

Love you,
Pete

You probably noticed that I didn't mention tonight's encounter with Rocky in the hotel lounge. It would have been difficult to explain two things – first, why I was drinking with a woman that I just met and second, Rocky's odd behavior. I suppose the best way to describe Rocky is to say that he seemed "goofy". I have no idea why he acted in this manner, but I suppose it has something to do with Mandy. If he had been with Amy tonight, I would have suspected that he smoked one of her joints or drank some of her brandy. Maybe he was just tired from all of the sun.

CHAPTER 23

"CHANCE ENCOUNTER"

BY ROCKY

April 20, 1999 – Beverly Hills

Dear Laura:

I just sent an e-mail to Dad telling him about my day, but I kept it short and left out the best parts. I was concerned that he might be worried about some things that happened.

Before you read any further, I want you to promise you won't reveal any of this information to Dad or anyone else.

I'm not in the habit of threatening people, but you know there are things you have done which you prefer that Dad never know. If you accidentally say anything to him about what you are about to read, then I can't be held responsible for what might happen to slip out of my mouth about some of your escapades.

Sorry to start this way, but I need your solemn promise.

If you agree to keep everything confidential, then read on.

I am writing this e-mail tonight from my hotel room in Beverly Hills.

As Dad may have told you, we came to Los Angeles because Pete was asked to attend a meeting at his offices near the hotel.

Before he went to work, Pete suggested that I spend part of the day around the pool.

After we ate breakfast, Pete left for his meeting and I stayed in my room, watching television and reading the paper.

You know that I read my horoscope every day, mostly to see if it gives me hints about betting or investing in the stock market. I usually ignore anything my horoscope says about my love life since it doesn't exist.

Today, my horoscope said:

"Lost article of another person will soon be located and you should return it to its owner. Blend idealism with ways of making money. Doors will open and you can enter if you so desire – all you have to do is ask. A new relationship will be hot and heavy. You could be in love. Libra plays a romantic role."

I took the first part of the horoscope to mean that I should invest in something that I believe in – so I used my laptop to buy a few shares in two companies that were mentioned in this morning's newspaper. One company recently gave shares of stock to every one of its employees, not just its executives, and the other is a paper products company that just won an award for its environmentally friendly approach to business.

The remainder of the horoscope didn't make sense to me, especially the part about a romantic role, so I ignored it.

After reading the paper, watching television and playing with my computer, I should have read one of the two books that I brought with me. But it was such a beautiful, sunny day, I found it hard to stay indoors. So, when the housecleaning lady came to my room, I went out to the pool.

I took my CD player, got a lounge chair and soaked in the rays.

Instead of eating lunch in the room as Pete had planned, I ate near the pool.

I was enjoying my hamburger when someone asked to borrow my CD player. I looked up and saw an unbelievably beautiful girl wearing a blue, two-piece bathing suit. You have to trust your little brother for once because I am not lying when I tell you that she looks a little like Winona Ryder, not quite as gorgeous, but pretty damn close.

You know how unusual I act with girls my age. Well, I did the same thing this time – I just stared at her and didn't respond to her question. She probably thought I was either deaf or a non-English speaking foreigner. As far as I was concerned, she could have taken the CD player and never have to return it. She could have asked me for all my money and I would have given it to her. She could have asked me to take my trunks off and jump in the pool, and I would have done as she requested.

I must have acted like a total imbecile because I just handed her the CD player without saying a word. She then pulled up the chair next to me and started talking. I couldn't concentrate on what she was saying – I just sat and stared.

At least I had the good sense to offer her some of my fries and went to the snack bar and got her a Coke.

After a while, I became more comfortable and I actually responded to her. But I kept on staring – she is unbelievable. I know I shouldn't say this to my sister, but she was bulging out of the top of her two-piece suit. Thankfully, since I had my sunglasses on, she had no idea that my eyes were also bulging.

It turns out that her name is Mandy (now I suddenly love the song of that name by Barry Manilow). She is in Beverly Hills with her parents, who are here from Seattle on a business trip. Her parents own a chain of women's clothing stores in Seattle malls and they often come to the Los Angeles garment district to buy the latest fashions.

Mandy usually stays home when her parents travel for business, but I guess her grandmother, who typically watches her, is on a cruise with her seniors group.

After lunch, I violated Pete's instructions by leaving the hotel with Mandy.

We walked around Beverly Hills for a couple of hours.

Mandy is a gutsy girl – we went in very expensive stores and she told the salespeople that her mother gave her the credit card to buy whatever she wants for a family wedding. She flashed around the hotel key to let the salespeople know she has big bucks.

Many of the dresses she tried on are so expensive that they didn't even have price tags. One dress cost $6,500 – can you believe it? You can feed a family of three for a year for that kind of money. That's obscene!

My second violation of the day was when I told Mandy a big lie – she is 16, so I couldn't tell her I am 14. I did what any other guy would have under these circumstances – I lied.

Your little brother just turned 17. Not only that, but I am in Los Angeles with my agent, who is meeting with a major studio that is interested in buying the rights for one of my screenplays. I thought about telling her the true story about my trip to the West Coast, but she probably would have asked a bunch of questions about my condition. If she knew my real age and my medical stats, she would have dropped me in two seconds.

I have no idea why I told her these particular things, but I figure that everyone tells falsehoods in Hollywood. I'm sure what I said is considered a small stretch compared to what the slimy business guys lie about in this town.

It will also interest you to know that the reason I am on the smallish side is because our grandmother was a "little person" who worked in a circus before she married our grandfather. I also told her that grandmother was one of 12 little people who jumped out of a small car in the opening act. Since I was on a roll, I went on by telling her that our dear grandmother was later promoted to be the "human cannonball", and was shot from a cannon as part of the grand finale.

Probably not very creative, but I thought it was a pretty good story under the circumstances. At least I think she believed me because she kept saying, "Wow". Of course she could have been using that word because she never heard so much fiction from one person in her life.

I was lucky in the afternoon because when I got back to the hotel after walking around, I heard the phone ringing just as I was opening the door to my room. It was Pete, who had called a couple of times before and even had hotel people look for me at the pool area.

I told him I fell asleep in the lobby while reading my Algebra book. I couldn't stop lying.

He felt bad because he had to work longer than expected, but he still thought he would be free to go to the Dodger game. Little did he know that I was wishing he wouldn't manage to free himself from work, because all my thoughts were focused on Mandy.

Then things really turned in my favor.

First, Mandy said that if I didn't go to the game, we could have dinner together at the hotel and watch a movie in one of our rooms.

Then Pete called again to apologize – he was asked to help a close friend with a project and he couldn't leave in time for the Dodger game. He was planning to send a young associate from the firm to take me to dinner, so I finally had to tell him about Mandy. He had to give me a hard time by singing something like, "Rocky has a girl friend." Nice man, but sometimes, he really gets on my nerves. He sounded like a kindergartener.

Anyway, Pete said that I could take Mandy to the dining room of the hotel and sign my name on the check.

Pete also told me to leave him a message in his room telling him what I would like to do tomorrow, the last day our trip. He owes me "big time" because he lost a bet at Pebble Beach and I think he also feels guilty about missing the Dodgers game.

Remember what my horoscope said – that doors would open; all I have to do is ask.

I originally planned to ask Pete to take me to see the sights in Hollywood, but now I decided to go for broke. I delivered a message to his room that said, "Viva Las Vegas." After I slipped the note under the door, it occurred to me that given his lack of creative thinking, he might not understand what I meant. I think there was an Elvis Presley movie with that name. He might conclude that I want to see this movie.

If he can't figure it out, I'll help him tomorrow. I know he may say no, but I figure there's no harm in asking. You never know how the door may open.

Back to Mandy - here's what we did instead of eating in the hotel dining room. We ordered a dinner through room service, I had a steak and she took the lobster. Then we had the hotel specialty, a chocolate mocha dessert that you would have absolutely killed for – it was sooooo very rich.

Since Mandy's parents were planning to be out until late, we ate in her room, or should I say her parents' suite. Because her parents entertain business people at the hotel, they usually get a suite. Mandy has an adjoining room.

I charged the dinner to my room as Pete had suggested, which strengthened my credibility about being a screenwriter. I gave the waiter a $40 tip, which was also charged. I doubt that Pete will be pissed because of his guilt over leaving me alone.

Before watching a movie, Mandy asked whether I'd like a margarita.

I was pretty sure she meant some kind of drink, but I really wasn't certain. I was trying to remember the words to the Jimmy Buffett song, "**Margaritaville**", but it was no help.

Before I could answer her, she got up and went to a bar area – there were a few bottles of liquor and mixers. I recognized the Bloody Mary mix, but there was another mix that was kind of yellow/green in color.

Mandy said that her mother's favorite drink is a margarita so she always asks the hotel to have a blender, Tequila, salt and mix in her suite. When they entertain other business people, Mandy's mother whips up a bunch of these drinks for their guests. I guess that Mandy became an expert by watching her mother because she poured Tequila, mix and ice in the blender like a regular bartender.

While the concoction was being blended, Mandy poured salt on a paper towel, rubbed the rim of two glasses with a lime and then put the glasses upside down on the salt.

Maybe it was the warm weather or because I was sitting around the pool for a couple of hours, but I was awfully thirsty all day. When she gave me the first glass, I took a small sip. It tasted pretty good and very refreshing, so I quickly drank the rest of the glass and she did the same thing.

Mandy filled our glasses again with the remaining mixture from the blender.

After we finished our second drink, she made two more for each of us.

I don't know if she has done this before, but she seemed to know exactly what to do to bury her tracks so her parents would never know.

She poured water into the Tequila bottle and did the same with the mix. The color of the mix changed a little, but not much. She threw away the paper towel, brushed the remaining salt from the bar area, cleaned the blender and dried it with a hand towel.

Mandy said her parents would never know what happened tonight because they are all leaving early in the morning – so they wouldn't be making any more drinks.

After four drinks, everything became fuzzy. It is hard to explain exactly how I felt, but I'm sure you have more than a vague idea. I was talking, but it seemed that my voice was far away. We laughed a lot, but if you paid me a million bucks, I couldn't remember what was so funny. We started to watch a movie, but trust me, I have no idea what we watched. For all I know, it could have been a porno movie on the pay hotel channel.

At around 11 o'clock, Mandy said her parents would soon return to the hotel.

In other words, this was my cue to leave. I guess my condition was obvious, so she was worried that they would see me staggering and talking funny.

From what I could tell, she was acting fairly normal. The drinks didn't seem to affect her as much as they did me. She must be used to drinking.

As I was leaving her room, we exchanged telephone numbers and e-mail addresses.

She then gave me the thrill of a lifetime – she hugged me, and planted a kiss t on my cheeks. I wish I wasn't numb so I could remember the feeling forever. After she finished, I just stood there – I froze and couldn't move. She finally had to shake me to get my attention.

You know what's really weird about all of this experience – Mandy's birthday is October 15 – she is a Libra. That was one hell of a horoscope!!

After leaving her room, I had to pass through the lobby of the hotel to get to my room.

I was surprised to see Pete sitting in the lobby, but he wasn't alone. A younger woman was with him and they had drinks on the table. At first I thought she looked like a hooker. But then it occurred to me that I don't know what a hooker looks like and even if I did, my condition prevented me from thinking clearly.

At first, I tried to avoid him – I was afraid he would see me in a compromising condition. Actually both of us were in an awkward situation. So, I quickly walked past the lobby to avoid making eye contact with him. I'm sure he didn't see me.

When I got to the room, I kept thinking about Pete. I was hoping he wasn't playing around on his wife because Kathy seems like such a nice lady.

I brushed my teeth and gargled with a small bottle of green mouthwash that was in the bathroom. I was trying to wipe out the smell of alcohol.

I waited for another 20 minutes and returned to the lobby. Pete and the woman were still talking – they seemed to be enjoying themselves because there was lots of laughter. He was what you girls would call "charming" – he had a silly grin on his face and continued to stare into the woman's eyes as he spoke with her. I hadn't seen him act this way during our entire trip. Talk about a goofy look.

Even though I will admit that I was probably only functioning at 30% of my brainpower, I thought about the situation for a while. I had two choices – either to walk away and pretend I never saw anything or to torpedo his plans with this pretty young woman. I decided that I had an obligation to him and his wife, so I made my move – which was dangerous considering my condition.

I went up to Pete – he saw me and I could tell he was embarrassed. He said something like, "Rocky, why are you still up?"

I didn't answer his question, but instead, I said, "Mom is wondering when you're coming back to the room."

Naturally, he said, "What the hell are you talking about?"

I was saved from answering, because the woman quickly got up, took her purse and said that it was getting late – she needed to be up early for a meeting. She said goodbye and left.

Pete asked me to sit down and thankfully, I didn't fall off the chair while he was speaking.

I'm not really sure what he said, but I think he told me that he wanted to set the record straight. According to Pete, he was simply enjoying a beer in the lobby when he noticed the woman reading a book by his favorite author. They started talking about the author and he offered to buy her a drink.

He assured me that it was an innocent encounter – he may have done a lot of bad things in his life, but he has never cheated on Kathy.

Pete seemed more than a little miffed and I guess he had every right to be upset.

He said other things, but I was so bombed that I heard words, but their meaning didn't sink in. I saw his mouth moving, but nothing seemed to penetrate my head.

I was embarrassed – I was tempted to blame my temporary lunacy on the margaritas, but at least I had the good sense not to tell him I was drunk. I doubt he would have been understanding.

We said goodnight and when I got to my room, the last thing I remember is falling into bed without changing my clothes.

As you can see, I am writing this note at a little past six in the morning.

You won't believe how hard it is to type on my laptop because everything is a blur, but I just had to tell someone about my experience.

Right now, I feel like I went to hell and back. I already threw up twice, but I would do it all over again if it meant getting another kiss from Mandy. It was worth the torture.

In a way, I wish I hadn't suggested Las Vegas. I'm not sure I can stand a long drive – my stomach is still rolling and my head hurts. I looked in the mirror and my eyes are beet red.

Maybe I can sleep for another hour before breakfast, although the thought of food sounds awful right now.

Love you,
Rocky

Incidentally, I told Mandy that Pete and I are keeping a journal of our experiences and thoughts that Ned may publish. I mentioned this to her in case she wanted me to change her name to protect her innocence. She not only wants me to use her first name, but also hoped that I will refer to her last name. In all fairness, however, her consent was given after the third drink, so she may not have been completely coherent at the time.

CHAPTER 24

"ROLLING THE DICE"

BY PETER

April 20, 1999 – Beverly Hills to Las Vegas

I started the day thinking that it might be an awkward day with Rocky, at least at the beginning. To give him the benefit of the doubt, I'm sure his antics last night in the lobby were his way of protecting me from my own devices, or maybe he was thinking about Kathy.

I don't care what the woman thought – I certainly didn't have any intentions of taking it any further than talking in the lobby and I doubt she did either.

What was upsetting was his lack of confidence in my character. In fairness, he doesn't know me very well – also, since he watches so many movies and television shows, he must think that every husband away from home must be on the prowl for some action.

The comical part was the way he acted – he looked so tired, probably from too much sun, that he could barely speak and he was obviously having a hard time keeping his eyes open. It was very strange behavior.

I don't plan to bring up the incident – I hope he also pretends that it never happened.

To my surprise, I actually look forward to going to Las Vegas; I am told that the city has totally changed since my last visit, which was in 1993.

The question was whether we should drive or fly.

Part of me wanted to continue the trip by car. Even though I was a little tired of driving, I must admit the Mustang is a fun car to drive.

The other choice would be to drop the car off at the airport and fly to Vegas.

After I packed, I checked my e-mails. I skipped the work-related messages and went directly to one from Kathy.

Dear Pete:

You are right – even though Rocky probably enjoyed himself more with Mandy than he would have with you at a Dodgers game, you still owe him for the bet you lost at Pebble Beach.

Actually, to be honest, I hope you continue to Las Vegas because this is another place that I want to see when we take a two-week (you heard me, TWO WEEKS) vacation to the West Coast. I already know what I want to see and you won't be backing out of this one for any work-related reasons.

I know that when you sent me the e-mail after Frank's reunion with his daughter – you did so in a moment of relative weakness. But your message came through loud and clear; you want me to help you focus on the important things in life.

Well, I have accepted this challenge – I am now taking more control over your actions because as you said, you are vulnerable. If I don't act now, I may never have another chance.

After I got your e-mail about Las Vegas, I first called Michael Brooks to ask whether he objected to extending Rocky's trip.

He doesn't – just as long as Rocky isn't a burden to you.

I told Michael that on the contrary, Rocky is having a positive influence on you (naturally, I didn't mention what happened to the two outlaws at the second Giants game).

So, you can tell Rocky that this is settled. He has his father's blessings.

But I didn't stop there. I then contacted Jack to find out whether they can spare you away from the office for a few more days. He called me back to tell me that your calendar was cleared and Jack has no objection if you remain on your trip for the remainder of the week, but on the following condition: That you call him at least once each day and keep your cell phone operating in case he needs you in an emergency.

You are probably asking why you will need another few days away from the office.

*Because "Mr. Changed Man", you **will** be visiting your son at Park City, Utah to clear the air about your relationship.*

I can't stand to have my husband and only son totally estranged from each other – this isn't right, particularly given the foolish reason why you two aren't speaking with each other. I'm not going to be in the middle any longer between the two of you. You are going to do whatever it takes to get back your son.

Josh is a good kid – if he doesn't want to go to college, so what? It isn't the end of the world. And by the way, it's his life, not yours.

If you had the courage to tell your father what you really wanted to do in your life, you might not have been as miserable as you have during your working career. I am still hoping that Josh will see the light on his own, but if he doesn't, then so be it –he is old enough to make his own decisions and neither you nor I can dictate his future.

Believe me, I am not taking sides in this fight – I told Josh the same thing on the phone today.

Josh expects you in Park City later this week. Was he thrilled? Not on your life, because he thinks you will again try to put the squeeze on him about college.

Just so you know, I already checked on flights from Las Vegas to Kennedy. If you or Rocky prefer that he return to New York directly from Las Vegas, I will pick Rocky up at Kennedy.

Whether you drive or fly from Las Vegas is entirely up to you. The "easy rider" approach seems to be favorably changing your mood, so I suggest that you continue to drive to Park City. By the way, I checked the mileage on the Internet – the distance is 420 miles and Josh suggested that you stop half way, particularly for Rocky's sake.

After Park City, you will be getting on a plane in Salt Lake City and flying east, but not immediately to New York. Your next will stop will be Chicago for that Saturday night to visit Maggie.

This is another relationship you have totally screwed up. This time I am taking sides – it is Maggie's. Yes, she can be very difficult, but without making excuses for her, I know that her marriage has been a major problem. You were the first to say that John is a very odd man. Add to her problems an only child who has become a juvenile delinquent and you have a messed-up woman who needs full support from her older brother.

You are going to mend your relationship with Maggie – not for me, but for you, Maggie and most importantly, for your mother.

I already called Maggie and she is expecting you some time Saturday afternoon, possibly with Rocky at your side. I must warn you that Maggie was less than pleased about the visit – in fact, she readily admitted to feeling apprehensive because she knows that you and John can't stand each other. So, please, keep your mouth shut, regardless of what John may do to irritate you. Otherwise, you will place Maggie in an even more difficult situation.

*Notice I have said that you **will** mend your relationships with Josh and Maggie – not that you will try to do so. So live up to your reputation as the "miracle worker" or whatever the kiss-up associates call you at the firm.*

Solving these minor domestic problems should be a snap for a guy who handles complex issue in billion dollar deals. I have every confidence that you will be successful.

By the way, Michael again said that he doesn't mind if Rocky stays with you in Chicago as well. This is entirely up to you and Rocky.

If you think that I sound feisty and a little belligerent – well, you're damn right I am. You asked me to battle on your behalf; now let's see if you have the guts to do the same.

If your massive ego and pride prevent you from groveling a little to regain your family, then there is absolutely no hope for you.

I don't want to grow old by constantly defending your uncompromising behavior and acting as an intermediary between you and family members. As much as I love you, I won't do this any longer for you.

Pete, you don't have any excuses and there are no other choices for you. Just follow the route I outlined. Your office has already tentatively reserved seats for you and Rocky for the remainder of your trip. They are expecting your call for confirmation.

Don't let me, Josh or Maggie down.

If nothing else, think of yourself as a role-model for Rocky. If he sees you making an effort to improve your family life, he may get the courage to fight his medical battle.

I look forward to hearing more about your trip when you get home on Sunday.

Love,
Kathy

My dear wife was right – there was no other choice. I hate to be placed in a situation in which I have little or no room to maneuver. Kathy has effectively foreclosed my options – usually, I'm the one who corners people so they have no room to escape. I had the impression from Kathy that if I objected to anything, she would have hung up the phone on me. It wasn't worth the risk of debating with her.

I called my office to confirm the schedule. My assistant was surprised by my call because she had the impression that I had asked Kathy to call on my behalf. At one point during the conversation, it was clear that she was concerned that Kathy and I are having domestic problems. I assured her that everything is all right at home but I am needed to help with other family problems. I couldn't very well tell her that my "commander" had instructed me to agree on an unconditional truce with two of my immediate family members.

I can't remember the last time that I went into "negotiations" with less leverage than now.

CHAPTER 25

"THE DAY AFTER"

BY ROCKY

April 20, 1999 – Beverly Hills to Las Vegas

This e-mail was waiting for me when I logged onto my laptop in Las Vegas.

Dear Rocky:
Thanks for your note from Beverly Hills. Here you left New York as a geeky teenager and you're now hobnobbing with your movie friends in La-La Land. I can't wait to see your screenplay made into a movie. Can I sit next to you when your name is called to accept an Oscar? Wow – my little brother is now a big-time moviemaker. Okay, enough of the shit, but I couldn't resist. At least I didn't say anything about our little "cannonball" grandmother.
First, I hope you took a picture of Mandy. I can't believe your description of her – in fact, based on what you said, I have serious doubts that you even looked at her face. I have a feeling that you're so infatuated by this little wench that you can't even objectively describe her.
Second, I have sympathy for how you're feeling. I never told you or Dad the reason I was so sick at my high school graduation. I'm sure you will never forget the pictures you took of me after I passed out on the football field following the ceremony.
You probably may not remember that I spent the prior night with Liz at her house – while her parents were out, we did virtually the same thing as you and Mandy did. No, we didn't kiss, but we experimented with a bunch of drinks – this was our fatal mistake; we should have stayed with one kind of alcohol.
I didn't think it was humanly possible for anyone to puke as much as Liz and I did that night. We each must have lost at least five pounds that night.
If you really want to feel miserable, try mixing a bunch of different drinks in one session. It was a good lesson for Liz and me – now when I

see some of my sorority sisters doing this, I know they will be in big trouble. I don't even try to convince them anymore – you have to personally feel the pain to understand.

Now you have another secret you can hold against me.

By the way, you should never fear that I would divulge any of our confidential discussions with Dad or anyone else. We have always been tight and you know I've always been very open with you – much more than in the average big sister-younger brother relationship.

Don't worry about breaking up the session between Pete and the secret woman. Even if he wasn't planning anything inappropriate, I'm sure he appreciates your gesture. You were only thinking of him and his wife. I doubt I would have had the guts to do the same thing, so I give you full credit for your bravery, especially given your diminished capacity.

I have talked with Dad several times while you have been away. I know this was not an easy trip for you, but I'm glad you went – I gather from your note that you are enjoying the experience.

Dad was worried about you at first, but he now seems more at ease, although he misses you terribly. I know he doesn't always communicate much but you should always know that he loves us a great deal. I sometimes worry about Dad because other than his work and the two of us, very little is of interest to him. I know he wants to retire early, but I'm not sure how he will remain active with all of that spare time. We need to help him – maybe we can fix him up on a blind date.

I'm late for a class that I can't afford to miss. I know you have definitely decided against considering college, but do your big sister a huge favor and keep your mind open. I really think you would enjoy college life, especially now that I know you have such an interest in pretty girls.

Let me know how your day went. I am anxious to hear if you actually went to Las Vegas.

Kisses from your big sister,
L

Dear Laura:

Yes, I took a few pictures of Mandy and I asked a person at the pool to take a picture of us together. You can be sure that I'll enlarge this picture and mount it on my wall.

Yes about "Viva Las Vegas", but I wasn't very good company for Pete during the drive. There was no "viva" in me. I told him I felt awful and thought it must have been something I ate last night or maybe that I stayed in the sun too long yesterday afternoon.

He was in a minor panic and thought that my sudden illness was due to my condition. He wanted to take me to an emergency hospital, but I convinced him that this wasn't necessary.

I'm so glad I have sunglasses. The sun would have been complete torture to my tender eyes without the glasses. I was also worried that Pete would ask why they are so bloodshot.

I slept for about two hours along the way, but I'm still tired from last night.

Pete was kind enough not to even mention the incident last night at the lounge. I was worried that he may still be irritated with me – but if he is, he isn't showing it. I hope he understands that I didn't do it to be cute – it was really all for his benefit.

If he talks to anyone else during this trip, I can assure you that I won't get involved.

During the drive through the desert, Pete was kidding me about Mandy; he said that he has a feeling she will be the one for me. That in a matter of a few years, he expects to be dancing with Mandy at our wedding reception. Then a few years later, he sees himself attending the baptism for our first child.

When I told him I don't plan to marry and I will never have kids, he thought it was the typical response from a teenage boy - "No way! You'll ever find me married" kind of thing.

I wasn't really in the mood to joke around, especially about this subject and not with my splitting head. After taking it for a while longer, I finally lost it and reacted in a childish manner, which I now regret.

I told Pete about my medical condition, not in a calm way, but I shouted this revelation to him while he was driving at 80 miles an hour through the desert. I was planning to tell him anyway, but under totally different circumstances.

Now that I think about it, we were lucky that he didn't drive the Mustang off the road.

As you can expect, he was shocked – for once he was at a loss for words. A short time later, he pulled the car off the road, got out and walked around in the desert for a while. Since I hate snakes, I stayed in the car.

I guess it was appropriate that we were listening to one of my favorite songs when I told him; it was a blues song by B.B. King. As B.B. would have said at that moment – "the thrill is gone."

Pete said this was a "surreal" day – I don't know exactly what he meant, but he told me earlier that Kathy had given him an ultimatum of some kind in an e-mail he received from her this morning. So, I only added to Pete's problems.

Because of what Kathy said, Pete will be traveling to see their son in the mountains near Salt Lake City after our visit to Las Vegas. He will then fly to Chicago to see his sister. It's a long story as to why he is making these visits, but it's fair to say that he will be on peace missions.

Pete told us (his youngest sister Amy, a friend named Frank and me) a few days ago that he no longer speaks with his son or Maggie, his other sister. I bet Kathy told him that he needs to patch up his differences with both of them.

I think I will join him, but right now, I'm not in a frame of mind to decide anything.

Pete asked a few questions about my condition while we were on the road, but most of the time, we both just listened to music. I actually felt sorry for him – I should have eased into the subject of my condition at another time instead of telling him in an angry moment.

I have no idea what Pete may be thinking about my situation. It could be one of several things – he may be nervous about taking care of me for the remainder of the trip or he may feel sorry for me. The other possibility is that he is already on the phone with his office discussing a big deal and I am the last thing on his mind. Of all these choices, I would bet a million dollars that he cares and feels bad.

I'm thinking I may have spoiled the trip for Pete. Las Vegas is everything I had expected and much more and we should be out on the town enjoying the sights. But we both feel crappy, for different reasons. I'm not sure whether my condition is due to the drinking binge or because of my feelings about Pete. I think it's a combination of both.

Pete offered to take me to dinner tonight, but I declined. I just don't feel like eating much, so I ordered soup and toast in my room, along with two bottles of ginger ale.

By the way, remember that you gave me a computer program to learn Spanish? It came in handy today because I was able to talk with a very nice hotel maid who cleaned the room this afternoon and again this evening.

Her name is Maria and she is from Mexico. She had been a hairdresser before she immigrated and she hopes to do the same thing in the U.S. – but it will take her another year to save enough money to attend a hairdresser's school in California. Her sister finished the same school recently and Maria wants to move to California to live with her sister while she attends school.

It may be my down mood, but I think I may try to help her. The second time she came to my room, she turned down the bed. After she finished, she stayed with me for a few minutes to make sure I was feeling better. She was genuinely concerned about me.

The funny thing is that even though I'm not feeling well, this is only temporary and I should be better tomorrow. I'm actually more concerned about Pete. I know he must be in great pain.

At first, I honestly thought he was a conceited jerk who doesn't care about anyone but himself and his business success. Now, he seems much different to me.

Don't get me wrong; I know that a person doesn't suddenly change his personality in one week, but I wonder whether some people are really warm and decent yet we only see their cold and rough exterior.

Maybe some people are scared to show their sensitive side because they may think it is a sign of weakness – especially people who act tough in their business life.

Some people think that they have to modify their style in order to survive in a personal relationship or at their occupation.

Think about some of the most difficult teachers you have ever had – they may have been more understanding in their early years, but after a decade or more of disappointment with uncooperative kids, they just give up.

The young cop who let you off the hook for jaywalking might become like the rude prick that gave Dad a speeding ticket while we were in Long Island. An individual's environment and experiences have a great impact on their personality. In our case, we were lucky to have been raised in a loving home, one in which our parents never hid their love for each other or their caring spirit for those in need. You and I would probably be quite different today if our parents were nasty people who didn't have a soft heart.

My point is that maybe, just maybe, Pete is really a good guy down deep inside, but after years in a brutal business, he has turned into a heartless person whose only desire is to win – regardless of the toll it takes on him and his family. The question is whether people like this can ever dig deep down to regain their soul. Unfortunately, it sometimes takes a tragic event for them to make changes. I hope this isn't necessary in Pete's case.

After seeing Pete in Santa Cruz, at Frank's reunion and again today when I told him about my problem, I really think that he is a decent person, but he no longer remembers how to act like caring person. It seems that he is struggling within himself – trying to find out who he really is.

To me, Pete is a warrior who has fought for such a long time that he has no memory of a peaceful life. He is either too scared to take his shield off or maybe, the shield has become attached to his body.

Now I know I'm really sick – usually, I'm the cynical guy who often suspects the motivation of others and you're the warm and fuzzy person who finds the good in people.

It must be beyond my bedtime, as I'm no longer making any sense. I should definitely get some sleep before I float to a "peaceful place" , as you would say based on the metaphysical crap you have learned from your yoga instructor.

Remind me never to get drunk again – you feel pretty good for a while, but other than the kiss from Mandy, it wasn't worth all this discomfort. Worse yet, I have become philosophical. Actually, I prefer to puke rather than get into heavy discussions about the meaning of life.

By the way, I'm way too tired to send an e-mail to Dad; please do me a favor and send him a note telling him I told Pete about my condition. I also told Pete he could share my information with Kathy. I don't want him to be surprised if he receives a call from either of them.

Love you,
Rocky

What if I'm wrong about Pete – maybe he really isn't having any difficulty dealing with my condition. He could be at the casino having the time of his life and I may be the furthest thing from his mind. I doubt this is true, but he is difficult to read at times. Even though I don't want him to worry about me, I would be awfully disappointed if he is totally unaffected by what he heard today.

I have to admit that I'm inconsistent about how I would like people to deal with my condition. On the one hand, I want them to care, but I don't want them to worry or feel sorry for me. Once they know about my condition, I would like them to keep it in mind and not ignore it, but on the other hand, I don't want them to dwell on it. Now that I mention this, I can better understand how difficult it is for people to deal with me after they have knowledge of my illness. They don't know how to act because I'm not even sure how I want them to handle the situation.

What it comes down to is that it's never easy for ill people or those around them. I just hope that when things get bad for me, I have the strength and patience to comfort those who are dear to me. They will need far more help than me.

By the way, I have told everyone that I have mentioned during my reports about the possibility that Ned might publish this chronicle. All have agreed to have their names included and some, like Mandy, are thrilled about the concept. Amy didn't have any problem because she hopes her story might help others who have struggled and at the same time, our story will be free advertising for her inn. Frank is delighted at the thought of having his name in print, particularly since it isn't in a crime report. However, Maria expressed reluctance for reasons she didn't share, so I changed her name for my report.

CHAPTER 26

"THE BLUES"

BY PETER

April 20, 1999 – Beverly Hills to Las Vegas

I didn't want to talk with anyone – but I wanted to vent. It was an acutely painful day for both of us.

Rocky understandably didn't want to eat out tonight – I just hope that he's not suffering something major – I just hope he is experiencing minor discomfort because of something he ate. Even with that, I don't know if his system can handle the complications. He is already frail – Rocky can't afford so little food for the better part of the day.

I thought about calling Michael – but what would I say that wouldn't unnecessarily alarm him?

I called Ned to tell him that I wanted to stop playing his game. I had more than enough of this pouring out my heart. I was emotionally and physically drained. I was also slightly embarrassed because I was losing my sense of balance, and even more importantly, I was no longer thinking clearly.

Ned listened quietly as I unloaded and then calmly made two points. First, I had committed to this project and even though the situation has become a more difficult melodrama than any of us first expected, Rocky has not asked to be released from his obligations. Second, that I should be patient because in the end, he still believes our chronicle will help not only Rocky and me, but also its readers. They were admittedly persuasive counter arguments, but I still wasn't completely convinced.

We agreed that if at the end, Rocky and I decided against the project, it would be dropped.

After downing the tiny Scotch bottles from my mini bar, I went to the casino, hoping that the excitement at the gaming tables would distract me, but it didn't work. I played Blackjack for a while, but it was difficult to concentrate. I suspect the people at my table couldn't understand why I was taking another card when I already had 18 and the dealer showed a five-card.

Playing craps was no better – I was making bets that were against the rules. The pit guys were not pleased, nor were the other people on the table. An elderly lady, who was rolling the dice when I made an inappropriate bet, suggested that I get my head out of my ass.

I moved to the dollar slot machines; totally mindless entertainment – just slide money into the machine and keep pressing the button. With the aid of many, and I mean many, watered drinks served by a scantly clad barmaid, I sat on the stool and played the same slot machine for a couple of hours.

On several occasions, bells rang and lights flashed, but my machine didn't deliver any money. I didn't realize until I had been there for some time that these machines give you credit for your winnings instead of an immediate payout. But it didn't really matter. It was a way to pass the time and not think about what had happened earlier today with Rocky.

With the unpleasant combination of a brutal headache, loud noises and people smoking around me, I decided to call it a night at the casino.

I offered a senior man with a cane my machine and all of the earned credits. I have no idea how much I left in the machine, but I couldn't give a crap.

I went outside and walked on the "Strip" for the better part of an hour. I would have been dangerous behind the wheel of a car and in my condition, I probably wasn't even safe walking, particularly with the heavy traffic.

The mix of my spinning head with the lights, traffic, crowds, noise and spectacular presentations in front of major hotels made the night even more bizarre. I have never taken any hallucinatory drugs, but I bet this is what it feels like – everything is obscure and all of the sounds are elevated.

Since I was feeling even worse trying to drown out my emotions in the casino and on the street, I retreated to the solitude of my room and sent this e-mail to Kathy.

Dear Kathy:

Before I talk to you about something that occurred today with Rocky, I want to thank you for everything you said in your e-mail and all that you have done to firm up my schedule for the rest of this week.

You are right – it is entirely up to me at this point. You've done your part.

You are also correct in saying that "trying" is not good enough; if I don't regain these relationships, then I'm truly a failure with my family.

What worries me is how I will react when I see Josh and Maggie. You know that I am often my own worst enemy – I may not be able to control myself with them. Maybe Rocky's presence will serve as a constant reminder for me to behave myself and control my emotions.

If I don't handle the situation well– then there is little hope for me.

By the way, Rocky wasn't feeling well today, so he is not sure whether he wants to continue on the trip to Utah and Chicago He will let me know tomorrow morning. If he decides to fly back, I will take him to the airport and wait until he gets on the plane to New York. I will let you know his decision either way.

The reason I'm sending you this e-mail so late at night is because I needed to talk with you. Since it is the middle of the night in New York, I will not disturb you with a call. Besides, I doubt I would make any sense in a telephone conversation, for various reasons.

Rocky told me today about his medical condition and said I could share this information with you. Since he finally told me, I felt it was appropriate to read the doctor's letter that Michael had given me in a sealed envelope.

Although much of the letter is written in complicated medical jargon, I gather that after the birth of Rocky's older sister, his mother (you remember that Michael called her Evelyn) was unable to conceive. After undergoing medical tests, it was determined that Evelyn had developed a relatively minor condition that was treatable through surgery.

Even though the surgery was not considered major, Evelyn developed complications and lost a significant amount of blood. As a result, she required a blood transfusion. Unfortunately, the surgery occurred before donated blood was screened for HIV and AIDS. The blood Evelyn received was contaminated - this is what killed her and now threatens Rocky.

No one knows if the infection was spread to Rocky during the pregnancy or it was transmitted during breast-feeding. The point is he has been infected since he was a baby.

According to the doctor's letter, there is a silver lining for Rocky, at least until now. The letter says that Rocky is "asymptomatic" – which I guess means that there may be a very slow deterioration of his immune system, but nothing that is noticeable.

The letter also mentions that someone Rocky's age would have normally shown signs of the disease long before this age. So whether it is some of the medication that Rocky has been given or his genetic makeup, Rocky has essentially been spared up till now.

No wonder the kid won't plan for his future. I wouldn't either – in fact, he handles his situation far better than I could if I were in his place. I would have given up long ago and probably become a lonely, bitter man.

As Rocky said today – he is a ticking time bomb. The only question is not if, but when, the bomb will go off.

Here I was showing him college campuses when he has no idea whether he will even be around to see the new millennium, let alone think about attending college.

I doubt that I can feel any lower than I do at this moment. Even though we have only been together for one week, I already feel close to Rocky.

When I took Rocky up to his room this afternoon, he made one thing very clear to me. He doesn't want me to feel sorry for him or to treat him any differently. He said that it would upset him if I do either.

Kathy, I'm not sure I can act the same with Rocky because things are not the same after what he told me today. I simply can't ignore the horrible reality of this situation.

Isn't it amazing what has happened in a matter of a few short days?

You would think that with my "can do" spirit, I could convert virtually anything from a negative to a positive. But right now, I feel totally dejected; I am just so sorry for Rocky and even more for Michael. He already lost his wife and he may soon lose his son. I don't know how to help either of them- I'm frustrated and feel totally useless.

I am also ashamed because I made a big deal out of this trip, even though it only meant that I would be away from the office for a few meaningless days.

What the hell are a few days compared to what Rocky is facing? The worst part for him must be constantly facing the inevitable.

Here I wake up in the mornings and think about the projects that I will face that day. And what about Michael – whenever Rocky experiences what might otherwise be a minor medical problem, Michael must think that his nightmare is about to be repeated.

And Rocky, the poor kid must wake up every day with the thought that his condition will inevitably deteriorate.

I hope Rocky continues on this trip with me. I need him for moral support and at the same time, maybe I can find a way to assist him and Michael.

I am so sorry for everything, Kathy – you deserved better. I have made your life unbearable at times and now, I am giving you even more heartache.

There is something else I need to share with you. While walking in a daze tonight, I asked myself this question – if through some magical transfer I could trade places with Rocky, would I do so? I have to honestly say that I'm not certain I would, even if it would be mean full recovery for him. What a hypocrite – I say I would dearly love to find a way to help Rocky, and Michael, but I would not go as far as sacrificing my life for their benefit. I don't know if I'm a coward, selfish or just realistic. If you or the kids were in such a situation, you know I wouldn't hesitate to give up my life for any of you, even if we couldn't be absolutely sure that your disease would disappear by my sacrificing my life.

I want your advice about how I should handle things with Rocky. Should I make reference to his illness or pretend it doesn't exist? Should I ask him for more details? Should I treat him any differently now that I know?

I'm at a complete loss about how to deal with Rocky for the rest of the trip and I feel awkward asking him.

It's funny how life works – I could have easily missed the foundation dinner because of my intense negotiations that evening or not volunteered for the trip with Rocky had I known the true conditions of doing so. But despite the horrible news I heard today, this is a journey that was long overdue. I clearly needed to regain my perspective and sadly, it took Rocky's plight to do this.

Pete

CHAPTER 27

"FRESH START"

BY ROCKY

April 21, 1999 – Las Vegas to Utah

If I were asked to rank yesterday, with 10 being best, I would say it rated a two. It started out bad and got worse as the day went on. It was so crappy that I don't want to even discuss it.

The good news is that I feel much better today, but I wish I could say the same about Pete.

I knocked on his door at a little after eight this morning. I was hungry because I barely ate yesterday and I couldn't wait to load up at the breakfast buffet.

Pete looked the way I felt yesterday morning – he must have slept in the same shirt and pants that he wore last night and he could barely open his eyes.

Knowing him for just a few days, I can tell already that he wouldn't appreciate being called a sensitive person. So, even though I knew that our conversation yesterday bothered him, I pretended that his "illness" was due to something else. I told him that whatever "bug" I had must have been contagious. But judging from his looks, this particular bug came in a bottle. I hope for his sake that he drank something other than Tequila because that stuff is murder.

Pete tried to make the best of things by claiming that he worked through the night on an emergency office project, but his face told me something different. He had a rough night – there was no disguising the fact that he was feeling down, both physically and emotionally. He asked me to return to my room and said he would pick me up after he showered.

He must have taken a long shower because he didn't knock on my door until after nine, but he still looked like hell – he either forgot to shave or didn't care how he looked, but at least he changed from his rumpled clothes.

We got into the buffet quickly, but I could tell that Pete wasn't eager to look at food, let alone eat. Based on my experience yesterday, I sympathized.

After I had eggs and ham, I went for waffles and bread pudding. When I returned to the table, Pete was still nursing his coffee and plain wheat toast.

I told him that it's a crime for him to spend over 10 bucks for a cup of coffee and a piece of toast, but I know that the price of breakfast was the least of his concerns.

Then I had to come out with it – I said: "Listen, I'm going to continue on the trip with you for two reasons: first, I'd like to see Utah and Chicago and second, I think you may need me to push you along for the next few days. It seems as if you've lost your confidence.

"You set the ground rules on the plane on the first day; I'm setting a few of my own for the rest of the journey.

"I don't want any pity from you. That's the worst thing you can do for me. But I also don't want you to ignore the situation. I have HIV and there is nothing that you or I can do about it.

"We've got five more days on this trip and you're not going to spoil it for me by being sad the entire time. When you return to New York, you can do whatever you want, but you have a mission to accomplish with your son and sister and I'm going to help you so you won't chicken out.

"One more thing. Dad thinks I have a death wish. Well, nothing could be further from the truth. You want my secret for the day – here it is, I'm afraid of dying; but I know it's going to happen sooner than later, so why fight it. I wonder - if you were in my shoes, how would you handle the situation? Would you honestly think that you could conquer this disease?

"Don't judge me unless you're staring at the same gun that I face every single second. For example, would you want to tour college campuses if you were my age with HIV?

So don't feel sorry for me – I know exactly what I'm up against. And please, don't feel sorry for yourself. It doesn't become you.

Let's just pretend we are a couple of free spirits – the only difference is that you'll be swimming the English Channel for the next few days and I'll be riding in a boat next to you to make sure that you say afloat."

The look on his face was priceless – here he was, feeling low and sick, and this punk kid is giving him a lecture. This had to be like a bad dream for Pete. He probably wishes he could be instantly vaporized and transported to his New York office to do his deals and push people around.

After a long pause, Pete simply said – "Fair enough."

Pete mentioned that during his low point yesterday, he considered abandoning his daily reports because they were becoming too emotionally difficult. He was convinced to continue in part because I wasn't going to drop out. I didn't dare tell him that I felt the same way, but I didn't have the guts to call Ned. So, we are now both committed to seeing this through until the end.

He also said that he is eager to continue with the trip. He is an action-oriented person and he hates to sit around waiting for something to happen. Then he said something totally unexpected. "Thanks for staying with me. I need your courage to prop me up."

Based on his reputation, the sincerity of his last statement could be questioned, but it didn't matter to me. I just wanted to get back in the car and on the road. I was determined to forget about the prior day, to have a good time for the rest of the trip and to help Pete through this tough time.

In order to ease the tension, I played a few games of Keno while we were still eating. In the end, I recovered my investment. I also gave Pete my formula for blackjack and I gave him $100 to play for me based on this formula. I gave him these instructions: Play until he gets up to $200 or loses the $100. If he reaches $200, he should walk to the nearest craps table and put $80 on the "pass" line for one bet only.

While Pete was gambling with my money, I used the business office to print a document that I had typed this morning on my laptop. It was a note to Maria, the housekeeper. I put the note in a sealed envelope and asked the housekeeping supervisor to give it to her when he arrives at work.

Here is what I said:

Maria:
I am the New York kid from room 1216.
First, I want to thank you for checking on me yesterday – it was sweet of you to think about me. I'm feeling much better this morning.
When we talked yesterday, you told me that it is your dream to become a hairdresser and you are saving money to attend a school in California. I think you said that you need $3,000 for the tuition.
I have a proposal for you.

I am willing to give you a loan for this amount, but with the promise that you will repay me $3,500.

Don't worry whether it will take you two years, three years or more to pay off the loan after you graduate, but you have to promise me that I will receive the full amount.

If you accept my proposal, you must make another promise. If possible, you will give one free haircut each week to a person who cannot afford one until you have completely repaid me.

Just so you know, I'm not rich and my father works very hard to make a living for us. Also, I will eventually need the money to pay my medical expenses for a condition that will take my life, probably within a few years.

Yes, I'm telling you this because I want you to feel guilty if you don't repay me.

If you accept this proposal, please sign the bottom of this letter and return it to me in the enclosed addressed envelope.

Whatever you do, good luck.

Your friend,
Rocky Brooks

I met Pete in the hotel lobby and he handed me $280. He said my system worked when he followed my directions. After he won at blackjack, he went to the craps table and bet $80. A guy with a big cowboy hat made his number on the fourth roll. I will never know whether Pete told the truth or he supplemented my winnings. I hope he didn't do me a favor because I know better than anyone that life is a game of chance.

I kept a copy of the letter and showed it to Pete while he was filling our gas tank before we left Vegas.

He made me two bets: the first for $10 that she wouldn't return a signed letter and the second bet was $2 with 50 to 1 odds that if she returned the letter, she wouldn't repay me one penny.

It was actually refreshing to see Pete back to his old cynical self instead of continuing to feel sad.

If I won both bets, Pete would pay me $110 - $10 for returning a signed letter and $100 if Maria paid anything.

If I won the first bet, but lost the second, I would still be $8 ahead – he would pay $10 for the first and I would only have to pay $2 for the second.

Actually, let me recalculate - if I won the first bet but lost the second, I would actually be $2,992 down - $8 ahead from Pete from our bets and down a loss of $3,000 from my loan to Maria.

After drinking a large cup of coffee, Pete seemed to feel better. Maybe my lecture during breakfast also had something to do with his changed attitude.

During the next couple of hours, we drove through the Southeastern part of Nevada, then for a couple of miles through the Northwestern tip of Arizona and finally into Utah.

My portable CD player came in handy on this part of the trip – Pete cranked the volume up and we listened to rock and roll classics. Since Pete wouldn't stop singing, I joined him; at least I was better than Frank. We reached an agreement that some day, we would give a duet concert dedicated to our family members – we would sing all their favorite songs.

Shortly after we entered Utah, Pete said he had a splitting headache. Again, I knew how he felt because of my condition yesterday. He pulled over to the side of the road and took a walk to stretch. When he got back in the car, he held his head with both hands and said he would take a short nap before continuing with the drive.

I offered an alternative – I would drive for a short time while he rests. As you would expect, the immediate reaction was negative for a variety of reasons, all of which made sense. But I continued to push because he was in a weak position for argument.

So, even though I don't have a license and have never been behind the wheel, he finally said I could drive slowly, not more than 30 miles an hour while he rested for a few minutes. For the first few miles, he gave me a hands-on lesson in the fine art of driving. Compared to my video racing games, this was like driving a car at Disney World; it was a snap, especially at this speed and with few cars on the road.

He didn't say anything for a few minutes and when I glanced over at him, his head was back and he was quietly snoring. I just continued to drive and as I became more comfortable, my speed gradually increased to 45 miles an hour. Then out of nowhere, a speeding Camaro convertible approached me from the rear. I could see from my mirror that there were two youngish women in the car, their long hair flying in the wind. I felt cool, cruising along wearing my golf hat and sunglasses and sitting high on top of my backpack. I bet I looked like an actor in my hot, red Mustang.

As the Camaro got closer, the girls began waving and flashing their headlights. I waved them to pass, and as they did, the passenger got up from her seat, pulled down her shorts and "mooned" me. As she did, the driver honked the horn a few times. This startled Pete out of his nap and when he looked up, he saw a Camaro passing us with a bare ass hanging out of the passenger's side. Pete looked at the speedometer and saw I was traveling at more than 65 miles an hour, which prompted him to scream, "Holy shit! What the hell are you doing? Slow down and pull over."

I have a feeling that I won't be driving any more on this trip.

A short time later, we arrived at Cedar City, a small community in the southern part of Utah. While we were having lunch at a local café, Pete said that if I didn't mind continuing, we would drive straight through Utah and stop in Provo for the evening. He estimated it would take us about four hours to get there. If he or I got tired before Provo, we could find a motel along the way.

After lunch, I went to the bathroom in the back of the café. While I was washing my hands, I noticed something on the floor near the toilet – it was a black wallet.

When I looked inside, I could see a few $20 bills, credit cards, a driver's license and a bunch of photos. The license showed a picture of an older man – his name is Clifton Pass. He was born in 1931. The license gave a Cedar City address.

I took the wallet to the waitress and she immediately recognized the picture. She yelled to the cook through the pass-through opening to the kitchen: "Cliff lost his wallet again."

I explained what happened to Pete – he suggested that we leave the wallet with the waitress; she could contact the owner. This was fine until I remembered Monday's horoscope.

The horoscope said four things:

1. Invest in things that are idealistic.
2. Doors will open if I ask.
3. I would be involved with a Libra woman.
4. I would find a lost item – I am to return it to its owner.

The two stocks that I bought that morning were up.

My door to Vegas was opened after I asked.

I experienced my first romantic encounter with Mandy, the Libra woman.

And now, I found the wallet.

I explained this to Pete and the waitress. She didn't seem to care – but she probably thought I was hoping for a fat reward from Cliff. When Pete was told that Cliff's house was no more than ten minutes away, he stopped objecting.

It wasn't hard to find Cliff's house – the cook wrote out specific directions for us and it's hard to get lost in such a small town.

Pete rang the front doorbell, which was answered by an elderly woman who was drying her hands with a towel. She was probably cooking or washing dishes. She was friendly, but I think she thought we were there to sell something or ask for donations. I held the wallet in my right hand and before I could give her an explanation – her eyes lit up and she had a big smile on her face. She opened the screen door, pulled me inside the house and pointed through the living room window to a man sitting in a rocking chair in the backyard.

She led me to the back door and asked me to take the wallet to the man. When I first approached him, I thought he was sleeping, but then I could see that his eyes were looking towards the ground.

Just like his wife, I didn't have a chance to explain where I found the wallet – the second he saw the wallet, he grinned, put his hands together and looked up – he then said, "Thank you."

After I told them where I found the wallet and introductions were made on both sides, Pete accepted their invitation to stay for dessert: homemade peach cobbler with whipped cream. This was a nice gesture by Pete because I know he was determined to hit the road.

They are a nice couple – as I told Pete later, she reminds me of Jessica Tandy in "***Driving Miss Daisy***" and Cliff is like Henry Fonda in the movie "***On Golden Pond***."

In a matter of a few minutes, Mrs. Pass gave us their family history.

Cliff worked in the aerospace field for over 30 years in the Los Angeles area. After he retired, they moved to a senior citizen's golf community near Palm Springs. Instead of peacefully enjoying their golden years, this is when their troubles began.

Their only child, who was always trying to make a fast buck, took a job with a firm that specialized in selling stock in small start-up companies, before the companies went public.

Their son claimed that he had come across a "sure thing", and he pressured his parents to use a portion of their retirement funds to buy shares in this company. He told his parents that it was a medical laboratory that was on the verge of a major discovery – something that would help cure people suffering from diabetes.

Pete knew what they were talking about – but he was surprised they would qualify for such a risky investment. He said that private investors in such deals have to demonstrate they are investment savvy and can afford to lose their investment if things turn sour.

Well, it turns out that their son was so anxious to get them into this deal that he lied on the application papers by saying that his parents had a small fortune and an extensive knowledge about this type of investment.

As if this wasn't bad enough, their son also convinced other seniors who lived in the desert community to invest in this company. In order to show support for their son, Mr. and Mrs. Pass invested more than one-third of their retirement funds in this company.

Within a short time after they made their investment, governmental authorities charged the president of the medical company with lying about his claims of a major discovery. The company ended up in bankruptcy and the investors lost everything.

Mr. and Mrs. Pass were not only financially strapped, but they were also embarrassed to live with the other investors in the small retirement community.

So, they sold their house in the desert, paid their debts and moved to Cedar City with a much smaller retirement nest egg.

Once in a while, they receive a note from their son, who is now selling real estate to Americans in a coastal tourist community near Ensenada, Mexico, which is located south of San Diego.

Cliff thinks that their son was forced to leave the U.S. because he got into trouble, probably with the tax authorities.

The worst part for them is not losing their retirement, but their inability to see their two grandchildren; their former daughter-in-law was so upset with their son that she doesn't allow Mr. and Mrs. Pass to communicate with their grandchildren.

Cliff now works a few hours each week as a maintenance person at a nearby elementary school. Mrs. Pass spends a lot of her time volunteering at their church.

When Cliff went to get coffee from the kitchen, Mrs. Pass said that he has not been the same since the investment fiasco. She said he has become forgetful – he either loses things or often forgets where he is going when he is driving.

Earlier in the day, he deposited their social security check and kept $100 for their monthly cash purchases. She was afraid they had lost the money along with the other stuff in his wallet.

By the time we finished dessert, it was already after four in the afternoon. Pete decided that we should stay in Cedar City for the evening and start early tomorrow for the remainder of our drive to Park City.

Cliff and Mrs. Pass wouldn't allow us to stay in a motel. They insisted that Pete use their spare bedroom and that I sleep in the living room – their sofa has a pullout bed.

Pete said we would accept only if we could take them out for dinner. They agreed.

During dinner, we got the full scoop on Cedar City. It has slightly more than 20,000 residents and it is known as the gateway to Bryce Canyon and Zion National Parks. The town is the home of Southern Utah University and it hosts a Shakespearean festival each year.

The odd thing is that even though they have had more than their share of problems and they struggle financially, Mr. and Mrs. Pass seem happy, and they love their new community and cozy little home. Cliff said that other than missing seeing their son and grandchildren, he wouldn't trade his life with anyone. I'm sure Pete must think that Cliff is senile, but I believe Cliff knows exactly what he is saying.

After dinner, we were invited to join Cliff and Emily at their weekly Bingo game at their church. The first four games were the typical "one-line" pattern. The next game was called "four corners" and while Emily was explaining the rules for this game, Cliff and Pete were engaged in a discussion about something else.

It seemed like 10 or 12 numbers were called when Pete jumped up and yelled, "Bingo", which resulted in surprised looks by our fellow players followed by applause. Well, unfortunately for Pete, when he took his card to the front, he was reprimanded for not listening to the instructions. He had a "one-line" rather than a "four-corner" card. After this was announced, his face turned beet red and poor Emily and Cliff were embarrassed, too.

To his credit, Pete didn't slink back to his seat. He quickly recovered and apologized for not paying attention and announced that he would add $50 to the prize for the next four games. He changed from a big city jerk to a local hero in a few seconds in front of this church group in Cedar City. I'm not sure what Pete would do if he didn't have money and power to back him whenever he screws up.

When we returned to the Pass home, as Emily was preparing the sofa for me, Cliff took me aside and said they wanted to give me a $40 reward for returning the wallet. I politely turned Cliff down, but asked him to do me a favor: to use the money to treat themselves to a nice dinner for their next anniversary.

Cliff and I shook hands.

As I was lying on the sofa bed, I couldn't help but feel sorry for Mr. and Mrs. Pass because I thought of Frank's face when he saw his grandchildren. Unfortunately, they may not ever be allowed to have a similar opportunity. It is sad not only for them, but for their grandchildren as well.

The other thing that came to mind was their son – I can't imagine how he must feel. I couldn't live with myself if I lost a good chunk of Dad's retirement fund.

At the same time, I was pissed off with their son, even though I don't even know the guy. What a complete jerk! He should be forced to pay them back every penny they lost– even if it means that he can't live a normal life for years. If I could, I would go to Mexico and arrange for someone to scare the hell out of this guy until he agrees to make up their losses; I would make him "an offer he can't refuse."

What's wrong with me? I've become a vigilante – next thing you know, I will be joining a para-military militia in the woods of Idaho. I have to stop believing some of the crazy movies that I often watch. I can see why people get so absorbed in movies – but the scary thing is that many of them act out what they see.

Every once in a while, I must admit that I feel sorry for myself – this doesn't happen very often because I don't allow it. But as I reflect on the day, I was actually proud of myself for lecturing Pete to get his attention. I was also happy that I found Cliff's wallet – it's hard to believe, but probably more than half of the population would have kept the wallet, or at least the money.

When you grow up knowing that your time on earth is going to be much shorter than others, you develop a different perspective. You would think that a short-timer's bitterness would result in a "me first" attitude, but the contrary is true. You have a short time and you feel that you should help others in need as much as possible.

This is when I become sad about my situation. I'm not being egotistical, but I really think that I could be of assistance to people. Unfortunately, I don't have very much time to accomplish as much as I would like.

Ned should know that I told Mr. and Mrs. Pass about the journal that Pete and I are keeping. I asked whether they prefer that we change their names so they wouldn't be bothered by anyone if our journal is ever published. To my surprise, they are flattered that we would mention them in the story. In fact, Mr. Pass said that he hopes their former neighbors in the retirement community will read the story. He wants them to know how sorry he is that they lost money as a result of their son's investment recommendation.

CHAPTER 28

"RUDE AWAKENING"

BY PETER

April 21, 1999 - Las Vegas to Cedar City, Utah

I don't know where to start in describing this unusual day. But who I am kidding, every day on this trip has been strange for one reason or another.

A knock on my hotel room door woke me up at a little after eight this morning. I looked around the room – and it was a very odd sensation because I didn't recognize anything. I knew I was in a hotel room, but it took me a couple of minutes to remember that it is Las Vegas. As I walked to the door, I thought for a moment that I had a nightmare about Rocky's medical condition. After I saw him, however, I realized it wasn't a dream.

I tried to smile, but the best I could manage was a half grin. Rocky, on the other hand, was a changed man and completely recovered from his stomach pains of yesterday.

It's funny how he started out yesterday in a miserable mood and I was fairly jovial, but by the end of the day, we were both in the pits. It was only a question of who was lower. Unfortunately, I think I took the prize.

Now, he was smiling and charged up for an exciting new day, whereas I felt awful, from head to toe. My heart was also heavy because as much as I've tried, I can't be optimistic about Rocky's prognosis.

When I noticed that Rocky was looking at my wrinkled pants, I told him that I worked late last night on an emergency project and fell asleep before changing. This was actually true because I had an emergency project, meaning my goal of drinking myself into oblivion, and I marginally succeeded by falling asleep without changing due to a dazed stupor.

I asked Rocky to wait in his room until I prepared myself for the day. He asked me not to take long because he was hungry.

A long shower helped – but since I didn't expect to see Josh until tomorrow, there was no need to shave. In fact, if it weren't for the visit with Maggie on the trip, I wouldn't bother to shave until next Monday morning.

I was glad to see that Rocky's appetite had returned with a vengeance, but I could barely manage toast and coffee for myself. It made me sick to look at all of the food that people piled on their plates at this Vegas breakfast buffet. Most get more than their money's worth – I saw one guy polish off fried eggs with ham and then he returned to the table with scrambled eggs with sausage. His last course was a stack of pancakes and bacon.

While Rocky was eating his large breakfast and I was nursing my headache, he demonstrated his formula for blackjack. I ordinarily would have followed him, but this morning, it was like teaching Einstein's theory of relativity to the homecoming king the morning after the prom. After a while, I didn't even try to listen because it meant nothing to me. Little did I know that I would be tested because after concluding his seminar, Rocky handed me $100 and pointed me to the blackjack table. My instructions were to take some of the winnings to the craps table and make one bet on the "pass" line.

I don't mind losing my money, but I certainly didn't want to lose any of Rocky's. I tried to pay attention, but everything was still fuzzy; I know that I violated Rocky's instructions by taking cards when I shouldn't have, but thankfully, the dealer "busted" four straight times. After a while, I was up to $200, so I took the money and shuffled to the craps table to wait for the appropriate time to place my bet of $80 on the "pass" line. The roller crapped out on his third try.

Because I was still feeling guilty about the way I handled myself yesterday, I lied to Rocky by telling him that everything went according to plan and I handed him $280. I don't know whether he believed me, but I wanted him to start the day off with a bang.

Rocky continues to amaze me – he told me about a hotel housekeeping person he met twice, for probably a total of no more than 20 minutes, and he not only knows her life story and ambitions, but now, he's decided to loan her money for tuition to become a hairdresser.

The poor kid is going to be awfully disappointed because he'll never hear from her after she takes his money. He'll learn soon enough, but I hope not too quickly. It's refreshing to see someone who still has even a small degree of trust in his fellow man.

This morning, Rocky gave me a brutally honest lecture. You could say that he slapped me around a bit, which I frankly deserved. One thing is for sure, no one is holding back with me – Rocky and Kathy are punching me right between the eyes with lethal jabs. They see that I'm drained and my knees are wobbly; but oddly enough, they're not going for a knockout punch. My spirits are so dismally low that I'm barely putting my hands up to block their punches – I seem to have temporarily lost my capacity to fight back.

I truly believe that Rocky and Kathy are trying to get me out of my funk; they may figure that sympathy won't work, so they are taking a "tough love" approach. They are slapping me around until I regain my spirit.

I can't believe that either of them enjoys kicking me while I'm down, but in Kathy's case, she may finally be getting a minor degree of revenge for her stored up hostility. In Rocky's case, he must be harboring bitterness, so he's taking it out on me. As odd as it sounds, I don't mind being pushed around now because I deserve the punishment.

Rocky's words had an impact; hell, what do I have to feel sorry about compared with him? I seriously doubt that my attitude would be any better if I faced his problems. I'm not only a coward, but also a malcontent compared with Rocky.

I wasn't surprised to hear that he has his fears; otherwise, he wouldn't be human. The real irony is that we both fear the unknown, but in radically different respects. I fear living and he fears dying.

Typically, people in my line of business don't work until a ripe old age; they either pack it in early or change professions. I'm considered a dinosaur in the investment banking business.

The primary reason I continue is my trepidation about the future – in other words, my pure unadulterated fear. I don't want to be like Father in retirement– a depressed individual in an empty shell. Like him, I can't draw on my family relationship because it is virtually non-existent. I will undoubtedly fall in an awkward manner from a 60-story high rise, as "hot shot" in the banking world, to a retirement "cottage" in the country, as a reclusive common citizen. There will no longer be a line of ambitious "gophers" ready to handle all of my little missions.

The thought of changing professions is equally repulsive. I can't stand the thought of having to prove myself again in a different uniform. I would be a high-priced commodity, which would mean that I would need to deliver big dividends in a short time. I just don't want this kind of pressure and worse yet, I'm afraid that people will finally see through me. My bluster may not work in another profession and I could easily fail. That is a word in my memory banks that only applies to others, usually my opposition, but never to me.

My other fear is that I'll be lonely. Kathy has rightfully carved out her own life and I doubt she would want me involved in her activities. For all intents and purposes, the kids are gone. People from the office won't make time to see me for social gatherings and I don't have a close circle of friends outside the business world. And with my social skills, making new friends won't be easy.

When I shared this with Rocky, I was hoping he would be somewhat understanding and have a slight degree of empathy. But nothing could be further from the truth because he really let me have it. He said that if a man with my brains and resources couldn't find something useful to do when I stopped working, then the first thing I should do on Monday is break the window in my office and jump out head first.

As far as my family relationship is concerned, Rocky fairly accurately repeated what Kathy said in her e-mail – the situation is in the palm of my hand. I have control over my own destiny. It's my choice and for once, I can't place the blame on anyone else.

One thing is for sure, Rocky and Kathy have independently reached the same conclusion – they're not going to put up with any crap from me.

Josh was miles ahead of them – he made this same decision long ago.

If I'm not careful, Jennie will soon be in step with the rest of the pack. She is not yet tainted to that degree, so there is still an opportunity to salvage that situation.

Anyway, back to the events of the day. At one point during our drive, I felt terrible – as if my head was about to split open. I pulled over to the shoulder and told Rocky that I would take a short nap. He came up with an alternative plan – in order for us to continue without losing much time, he would drive at a slow rate of speed while I rested for a short time. This was a crazy idea and I was even crazier for agreeing, but the road was virtually deserted and I frankly wasn't thinking clearly.

After watching Rocky drive for a while, I dozed off. I awoke suddenly when I heard a loud noise, which I assume was the horn of a passing car. I thought I was dreaming because the next thing I saw was a girl's pale ass smiling at me. Then I realized what was happening.

I must have been out of my mind to allow Rocky to drive. No license, no experience and no insurance. What if a cop had stopped us? Imagine trying to explain that situation to Michael and Kathy.

One thing I have noticed while on this trip: somehow, things seem to happen for a reason. Events also occur when it is most timely for them to do so. Rocky's adventure behind the wheel was timely and the day I was brooding about Rocky's health and my life, we ran across Cliff and Emily Pass in the small Utah town of Cedar City.

How we became acquainted is a story in itself; let's just say that Rocky and I were meant to eat in a family style café in Cedar City – this eventually led us to meet the Pass family.

Here is an elderly couple that should be totally despondent about their lives, but for some reason, whether it's their faith or inner strength, they have more than adequately adapted to an adverse situation.

The Pass family and Rocky cherish what little they have; compared to them, I have it all, but I don't appreciate anything.

I have totally lost all sense of reality. The speed of the treadmill has constantly increased and the elevation has been so heightened that I simply can't remember what it feels like to walk slowly on level ground and see the sights.

I don't know if I have the determination it takes to recover. Worse yet, the more I see of myself, the more I am ashamed of what I have become. The interesting thing is that for many years, I was actually proud of the conversion I made personally because of the success it brought me in my business.

In the end, I probably would have reached the same level of success had I been true to myself. If, on the other hand, I wouldn't have reached this success based on my former personality, then someone could say that at least I didn't sell out. But the truth be known, I have to admit that I like the material things that came along with the success.

The most difficult question would be if someone rewinds my life – takes me back to the age of nineteen and I am given a choice about the future:

1. The first choice is Curtain A – I could be a drama teacher at a small college in the East Coast – two kids and a loving wife – but constantly struggling to meet our financial obligations. No second house and long-term loans for the kids' college education. Two

cars, one six years old with bald tires and the other only a few miles away from being junked. I wear one of my three sports jackets to class and Kathy works part-time at a gift store in order for us to afford yearly one-week vacations.
2. The second choice is Curtain B – which is my life as of today.

One would hope that I would select Curtain A, but to be very honest, I'm not so sure. Don't get me wrong, I might select Curtain A, but it isn't an automatic decision by any means.

I need to create Curtain C, which is a blend of the other two.

CHAPTER 29

"BITING MY TONGUE"

BY PETER

April 22, 1999 – Cedar City to Park City, Utah

Dear Kathy:
Today started out far better than yesterday.
A flurry of emotion, that was all negative, hit me hard after I learned about Rocky's medical condition. I still can't accept that he has HIV and may die from this condition.
Anyway, I was in the abyss that evening and I felt no better yesterday morning, until we cleared the air. I guess I shouldn't say "we", it was actually Rocky who took a page out of your book and set me straight on a few things.
We had a fascinating drive in the morning and saw some interesting sights. After we ate lunch, we met an elderly couple (Cliff and Emily Pass) in Cedar City, which is a small town in Southern Utah, about 170 miles from Las Vegas.
I will explain how we ended up sleeping in their home when we see each other – yes, another unexpected detour into my subconscious journey.
Even though we have only been away for 10 days, I feel like we have been traveling for months and sometimes, I feel like we are in an imaginary world. Every stop along the way has been eventful and each experience has special meaning. This was all meant to be.
This is probably going to scare you, but as I was laying in bed last night, I asked myself a few rather odd questions, like: Is this really happening? Am I awake? Does Rocky really exist? Just to set your mind at ease, this silent dialogue was without the benefit of any drugs or alcohol. Actually, it may make you even more uncomfortable to know that I wasn't under the influence of anything other than my own reality.
If nothing else, I know what I can do in my next career – I'll hire young people like Rocky to accompany lost adults like myself – they can

tour the country for a self-actualization journey. People would pay thousands to get an insight into their inner selves.

That's enough – I'm going off the deep end again, but this time, I'm smiling. Kathy, if I take this journey and myself too seriously, I may drive myself crazy.

I better lighten up before I see Josh. Otherwise, he may think I've flown far too many times in pressurized cabins or that I've finally overloaded my personal hard drive with all of the barefaced lies that have become necessary tools in my profession.

Returning to the Pass family - suffice it to say that they could not have been more hospitable to two roaming strangers. I can't imagine anyone in our fair city allowing complete strangers to sleep in their house.

The Pass accommodations were fine; I slept in the guest bedroom and Rocky on a sofa bed in the living room. The only problem was their dogs – they have three, two large ones and a small one.

I forgot to close the bedroom door before I went to sleep and during the night, the two larger dogs jumped in bed with me. I tried to shove them off, but they wouldn't budge. I was afraid that if I pissed them off, they would growl, just like your "sweet" little dog. I know she hates me, but I still don't know why. I swear that she knows what I'm saying whenever I make a sarcastic remark about her.

When I got up this morning, the dogs were gone, along with my left shoe. After unsuccessfully searching for it around the bedroom, I went to the living room and found one of the dogs chewing on my shoe, but unfortunately, it was too late. There was no chance for its survival. Thankfully, I still have my dress shoes.

Emily got up early this morning and prepared a hearty breakfast – you name it, she made it. It really is a wonder that Cliff isn't obese or hasn't had quadruple by-pass surgery given the cholesterol-laden food he eats.

We were back on the road just after nine; there was no fear that we would run out of food - Emily prepared a bag full of goodies, including sandwiches, chips, homemade oatmeal cookies, apples, candy bars and sodas.

Since we only made two short stops, we reached Park City late this afternoon. It is a beautiful area and while there is lots of snow, the roads are clear. It isn't difficult to see why Josh likes this area.

There was a message from Josh when we checked in saying that he would meet us for dinner at around seven in the lobby. Much to my surprise, the kid was actually fairly prompt - so at least there is already one favorable change in his character.

I will admit this – he is one handsome guy. Thankfully for him, he resembles your side of the family. Imagine if he looked liked me and didn't have a quality education – there would be two strikes against the poor kid.

We went to a pizza place and it was far too loud for a meaningful discussion, but I didn't complain. I just sat and enjoyed my food and beer.

During dinner, Josh told me about his plans for after the ski season - you are going to love this one - he and his buddy will be joining a crew to repair mountain roads. He is excited about becoming a flagman to direct traffic. You know what I am talking about - he will hold up a flag and a go/stop sign – this is what your son considers a thrilling opportunity with upward mobility. I suppose that if he excels at this task, he may be promoted next summer to the lofty position of filling potholes.

I must confess that at one point I started to ask him about the possibility of returning to school and he blew me off with a "maybe" kind of answer.

Thankfully, Rocky was here to save the day because as I was just about to pounce on Josh, Rocky kicked my shin under the table, which was my signal to "back off."

You would have been semi-proud of me for my half restraint.

I'm sure I will do even better tomorrow, but believe me, it was brutal to maintain a calm demeanor – I think your son enjoyed every moment of my torture. Based on the pressure you are putting on me, he knows that I have no bargaining power. Josh clearly knows that I am helpless and unarmed in this mission to restore peace. I am carrying a white flag and ready to unconditionally surrender to the enemy.

It is like someone goading a kid into a fight, but he has to stand there and take the verbal abuse because he promised his mother he would behave himself.

Please don't misunderstand what I am saying – I'm not complaining, but think about it for a moment. I have my hands tied behind my back and you have used one of your expensive scarves to muzzle me.

There is a clear conspiracy between you and Rocky to test my limits on this trip. So far, I have even surprised myself. Now Josh is in the act and soon, Maggie will follow. However, I have the patience and perseverance to prevail. Mark my words – don't bet against me.

After dinner, we agreed that he would pick Rocky up tomorrow morning and get him free ski lessons. We don't have to worry about the ski clothes because Josh will borrow some from his roommate, who is apparently about Rocky's size.

I will do some work tomorrow from my room, walk around the area and Josh will bring Rocky back late in the afternoon so we can have dinner together.

When we first saw each other tonight, Josh shook my hand. At the end of the evening, he gave me a hug.

So, progress was indeed made.

If we decide to visit him next summer, maybe we can surprise him by driving near his highway crew; wouldn't it be fun to see him holding a flag?

Just trying to keep a sense of humor.

Love,
Pete

CHAPTER 30

"THE REFEREE"

BY ROCKY

April 22, 1999 – Cedar City to Park City

Dear Dad and Laura:

We had a great day, even though we were in the car most of the time.

I am so glad that I brought my CD player – we have been using it constantly. We're lucky because we like the same kind of music.

We started the day at the home of new friends in a small town called Cedar City – Dad, relax, these people are in their sixties and couldn't have been nicer. Yesterday, while we were in a café, I spotted a wallet. We returned it to the owner – his name is Cliff Pass. One thing led to another and we ended up staying with them for the night.

By the way, Mr. and Mrs. Pass rescued three dogs from a local shelter after they moved to Cedar City. Two of the dogs are large, a shepherd mix and a yellow lab. The third dog is a fluffy little white guy – kind of like a poodle mix. The two big dogs settled in the guest bedroom with Pete and the little guy slept with me on the sofa bed.

Dad, you are always saying that I should have a better outlook on my future. Well, one way to show this positive attitude is to get something that will hopefully remain with me for a long time. When I get back, let's talk about a small dog – he would offer everything that you want for me, companionship, responsibility and an opportunity to walk a few times each day.

Don't dismiss this suggestion until we talk– I really think it's a brilliant idea.

Okay, Laura – I've found you a boyfriend. His name is Josh – he is Pete's son. Josh is a few years older than you; he's handsome, funny and a jock, but a smart and gentle one. Josh works as a ski instructor in Park City.

Dad, I know that Kathy told you why Pete decided to travel to Park City. For Laura's information, Pete and Josh have not spoken to each other for a while. Their feud started when Josh dropped out of college after his second year.

I think Pete understands that he and his son have to make up – or maybe Pete feels pressure from Kathy because of an ultimatum she gave him; which is the word that Pete used with me when he described an e-mail from Kathy. She must have really let him have it, because it made such an impact on him and he has been on his best behavior with Josh.

After arriving in Park City, we met Josh in the lobby of the hotel and then went to a pizza restaurant. Even though Josh doesn't know me from a hole in the wall, he immediately became a friend.

While Pete was in the bathroom of the restaurant, Josh told me that he was going to "jerk his father's chain." I don't know what he meant, but whatever it is, he laughed when he said it, so it can't be all that bad. I didn't have the chance to ask Josh what he had in mind before Pete returned to our table.

During dinner, Josh said that after the ski season, he and his friend are going to join a crew that will be repairing mountain roads. They would do odd jobs, but most of the time, they will be flagmen to direct traffic while the crew is working on the road. He told Pete that he is very excited about this new challenge.

It was almost cruel because Josh was really on a roll, exaggerating the story the more he saw his father squirming in his seat.

At one point, Josh said that he may move to Alaska with a friend for a few years; but he didn't want Pete to mention this to Kathy until he finalized his plans. He said there was no need to worry her unless he decides to go.

Pete was comical – casually sipping his beer and looking away from Josh. Most of the time, he would say things like "sounds great" or "sure, whatever you want to do", but I'm certain that this conversation was eating him up inside.

Just when I thought Pete was going to explode, I changed the subject by asking Josh questions about skiing. He saw I was interested and offered to give me a private lesson tomorrow since it is his day off. I think I may do it.

After that discussion, Pete couldn't contain himself any longer – he asked Josh whether he has considered returning to college, to which Josh gave a simple answer – "I may sometime in my life."

When I saw that Pete wasn't satisfied with the answer, I kicked him under the table. I then yawned and said I was really tired from the ride – Pete looked at me and I'm sure he got the hint because he didn't ask Josh anything else.

I bet he is so frustrated right now that he is either drinking at the bar downstairs or sending an e-mail to Kathy.

Poor Pete – as if he hasn't had enough sleepless nights on this journey – now, he will again be tossing and turning while thinking about Josh and his plans.

Speaking of that, I'm tired.
Dad, see you on Sunday.

Love to both of you from Utah,
Rocky

There is something I needed to tell Laura privately in a separate e-mail.

Dear Laura:
Guess who was grounded by her parents? Yes, little Miss Mandy.
I guess they were supposed to leave the hotel at nine the morning after our margarita party. The clock radio went off at eight, but Mandy was so tired that she turned it off and went right back to sleep.
By the time her dad knocked on the door, it was well after nine and she was still sleeping. So, they missed their return flight to Seattle.
I think about her all the time. I thought she would never communicate with me – I was happy to hear from her, even though she got into trouble.
The good news for her is that they don't suspect anything – they think she just overslept.
I would never tell her, but I was actually glad to hear that she also struggled the following morning. Now I don't feel like such a wimp for being a basket case the day after our drinking session.
I meant what I said about Josh – you can't help but like him. He looks a little like Kevin Bacon, except that his hair is shorter and darker. And he is a nice guy with a great sense of humor. I can't wait till tomorrow when I see him in action again, tormenting Pete.

Love,
Rocky

CHAPTER 31

"YOUR SON"

BY PETER

April 23, 1999 – Park City

Dear Kathy:

It is a little after 10 in the evening in lovely downtown Park City.

I will confess that even though I tried to work for the better part of the morning, I wasn't able to concentrate. This should make you and Josh happy.

I am having an awfully hard time accepting the fact that Josh will go through life doing odd jobs as they come his way. I know he is capable of much better things.

You're probably thinking that I'm an insufferable snob –and that I'm embarrassed to tell our acquaintances that my kid is a college drop-out and works as a flag man in the Utah. I plead guilty on both counts. But it's more than just how I feel– I would hate to see my kid struggle all his life. It's perfectly fine if he wants to take a couple of years off to travel or ski, but not forever – at some point, he needs to settle down and get an education.

After talking with Jack and others in the office this morning, I took a stroll through town and had lunch at a good Chinese restaurant. Actually, you would be pleasantly surprised at the caliber of food in Park City – although I have only eaten pizza and Chinese, the menus posted on shop windows are intriguing.

I also got information about the annual Sundance Film Festival. Maybe we'll come next January – I could watch off-beat, low-budget movies and you can wash and iron the flags that Josh will use to direct traffic as part of the road crew.

Just a little joke – I've got to laugh, otherwise, I will drive myself crazy.

Josh was kind enough to take Rocky for ski lessons. He invited me, but with my luck on this trip, I would probably break my neck. Worse yet, maybe our dear son would take me to an off-limits slope and watch me fly over a cliff.

Kidding again.

Josh dropped Rocky off a little after three this afternoon and the poor kid was exhausted. I guess the combination of the altitude, exercise and his lack of stamina tired Rocky. He immediately went to his room for a nap.

Josh picked us up again at five. Two friends, both fellow ski instructors, joined him; a young woman from Colorado named Tina and a surfer-type guy from California – his name is Gary.

It seems that little Rocky has an eye for the girls – he kept talking with Tina while we were in the car and during dinner. I have a feeling that he didn't mind being squeezed next to Tina in the back seat for the hour drive each way.

On the other hand, I think Rocky was becoming irritated with Gary, who kept on calling him "little dude." Gary seems to be a nice kid, but I think he's fallen off his snowboard one too many times. But Gary has the kind of life that most young guys would dream about – ski instructor during the winter months and surfing lessons in Hawaii in the summer and fall. With his long blond hair and perpetual tan, this guy must have more girls after him than a rock star.

Instead of remaining in Park City, Josh took us to Salt Lake City to see the sights and for dinner. On the way down the mountain, Josh pointed to an area where a road crew had been working earlier in the day repairing potholes. This is where he and another friend will soon be learning their new profession.

Before we went to the restaurant, Josh asked Rocky whether he wanted to see the University of Utah – I thought for sure that Rocky would decline, but he didn't – he was probably being polite with Josh. If I would have made the same suggestion, I think Rocky would have told me where I should stick the car keys.

We had a nice dinner, except that the main topic of the evening was where they would work next year as ski instructors. If Josh doesn't take another trip that he is considering, he said that he might end up in Northern California or Colorado, probably Aspen.

After dinner, I invited Josh and his friends for a drink (non-alcoholic for Josh since he is the designated driver) at the hotel. There, you see, yet another positive change in our kid - he is a responsible "designated driver".

While the "youngsters" were enjoying their drinks, I was still stewing – but I kept silent, despite the fact that my blood pressure was probably at a record high.

Josh then raised his glass and proposed a toast – "to the most patient Dad in the world." Tina, Josh and "Dude Gary" laughed – neither Rocky nor I knew what was happening, other than the fact that they were having a laugh at my expense. Your son is awfully sarcastic – can you imagine what would have happened if I did the same thing with my father? All hell would have broken loose. I have no idea where Josh picked up this sarcastic trait – it obviously wasn't from me. It must have been inherited from your side of the family.

It was at this point that Josh pulled out an envelope from his back pocket and handed it to me. It was a letter dated March 12 from the University of Utah and addressed to -

Mr. Josh Franklin" – the letter said:

We are pleased to advise you that your application for admission has been accepted..."

Those weren't the exact words, but you get the gist.

My spontaneous response was – "you little shit!" – which probably was not the right comment for this group, but it just flew out of my mouth.

Tina looked more than a little surprised because I think she thought I was about to slug Josh. Rocky enjoyed the reaction, but Gary was brilliant in his comment: "Dude, your father had an awesome comeback." Gary then gave me a "high five."

So "your son" played a sick joke on me for over 24 hours – he put me through torture and I'm certain he enjoyed every agonizing moment.

He even had his friends involved in the conspiracy – showing us the place where he would start working on the road and talking about his next ski adventure.

No question that "your son" was testing me to the limit to see how calm and patient I would remain as he kept prodding me. I am only surprised that he let me off the hook now– he could have had more mileage if he let me suffer another sleepless night or even worse, he could have waited until I returned to New York.

Josh said that he will start school in the summer and he has been told that most of his previous general education classes are transferable – so he will only lose one semester.

Are you ready to hear about his major? "Parks, Recreation and Tourism", with an emphasis on Natural Resources Recreation Planning and Management. Sounds pretty impressive – his goal is to work with the National Park Service.

One more thing, he has already talked to the football coach – he plans to be a non-scholarship "walk-on" player, hopefully as a safety or special teams player.

He doesn't expect to get much playing time and doesn't think he will make the traveling squad in his first year, but he doesn't care. At 6 feet, 1 inch and 185 pounds, and with his speed and experience, he will probably do reasonably well. If nothing else, he can meet some of the other guys while staying in shape.

So, that's the story about "your son."

I feel certain that you must be very proud of him, not just because he was accepted to the U of U, as he calls it, but more for the disgusting joke that he played on me in front of Rocky and his friends.

I am glad I didn't tell him that I'm fine with whatever he wants to do in his life – I was just about to throw in the towel.

Now that I think about it, I should have let you suffer with me by telling you last night about his "plans" for living in Alaska for a few years. You wouldn't have thought that he was so funny if you were in my place for the previous day.

By the way, I think that Josh finally has the brother he always wanted – he and Rocky really bonded today.

I love these two guys – they are both great kids.

One down and the more difficult one left to go – next stop, the windy city and I don't mean the atmospheric conditions in Chicago. I anticipate a very chilly reception from Maggie and even more so from my dear friend John.

Love,
Pete

I have to thank Rocky because I was close to losing my temper several times, but his presence alone gave me patience. I guess you might say he was a symbol – I can't possibly compare his medical condition with the minor problem of whether my kid attends college. If Josh doesn't attend college, it's a microscopic issue compared with what Rocky is facing.

So Rocky did it again – his involvement saved the day. If I lost my cool with Josh, he still would have attended college, but our relationship would have further deteriorated.

Thank you Rocky.

CHAPTER 32

"PARTING SHOT"

BY ROCKY

April 24, 1999 – Park City, Utah to Evanston, Illinois

Dear Dad and Laura:

I needed to talk with you tonight because I'm miserable; I really let Pete down in a big way. It is now nearly midnight in Evanston and I didn't want to wake you. Dad will probably see this e-mail while I'm on the return flight tomorrow morning, which will prepare him for my dismal mood.

Before I talk about the crappy part, let me tell you about yesterday and give you a summary of the events that led up to today's fiasco.

Yesterday morning, I thought about pretending that I was sick because I had second thoughts about agreeing to take ski lessons from Josh. He convinced me to join him and in the end, I'm glad it did. The first half of the day was miserable – I must have fallen at least 50 times.

In the last hour of the lesson, I finally became comfortable and I went down a beginner's slope without falling. But on my last run, I got cocky and went faster than I should have. As a result, I couldn't control myself and intentionally fell to slow down. I slid down the slope to a stop, but not before I barely touched a person who was taking a group lesson. He fell, causing the person below him to fall and on and on; just like dominos; one of them even brought down the instructor. I was lucky because everyone took it in good humor.

Last night, I understood what Josh meant about "jerking his dad's chain." It turns out that he is going to college after all, but he wanted Pete to suffer for a while, thinking otherwise.

We were joined at dinner by two of Josh's friends, a girl named Tina and an idiot guy who talked like an airhead. He pissed me off by calling me "little dude" and constantly rubbing my hair. At one point, I felt like shoving him out of the car.

We left Park City for the airport in Salt Lake City early this morning so we would catch our 10:15 flight to Chicago. This was the only direct morning flight so Pete wanted to make sure we arrived at the airport in time.

While we were on the plane, Pete gave me a "briefing" about his sister Maggie and her family. He told me that he gives this kind of introduction when his clients are about to meet someone for the first time. He lets them know personal information about the people they are about to meet, such as their personality type, work experience, education, family history, hobbies and their likes and dislikes.

I felt like I was one of Pete's important clients when he briefed me on Maggie.

Maggie is Pete's middle sister and he described her as the exact opposite of Amy. (Laura – I had told Dad that Amy is pretty much like a middle-aged hippie – a true free spirit who is still gets into trouble with the authorities while she is protecting mankind.)

I didn't know exactly what Pete meant by the "Amy opposite" comment until I met Maggie. Now I understand (I will explain later).

While they were growing up in Connecticut, Pete's dad was often missing from home because he spent most of his time working as a big-time lawyer for a Wall Street law firm. He kept an apartment in the city and would only see the family on weekends, but not every weekend.

Maggie always wanted to have her father's attention, but I guess he wasn't that kind of parent – a nice guy, according to Pete, but not what you would describe as a warm, affectionate person.

Unlike Pete and Amy, Maggie couldn't accept her father's emotional distance. Pete thinks this is why she has always had low self-esteem.

During her college years, Maggie met a guy named Alan. They fell in love and got married before Maggie finished college. According to Pete, the family liked Alan and he treated Maggie well. But there was a problem – Alan didn't want children.

Pete's mother thinks that Maggie could never stand to be alone, which is why she married Alan at such a young age. She also believes that Maggie may have initially agreed with Alan about not having children, but probably changed her mind a few years after they were married.

At one point during their marriage, Maggie got pregnant. This caused a major flap – Alan believed that the pregnancy wasn't a mistake. Anyway, when Alan threatened to leave her, Maggie got an abortion.

After college, Alan became a salesman for a number of different companies, which led to constant relocation, mostly in the Midwest. The more they moved around, the more difficult things became for Maggie because she is not a "joiner".

Maggie would always work wherever they moved, but she couldn't get great jobs because she didn't have a college degree. Pete felt that her reserved nature and lack of confidence also might have influenced the sort of job offers she received.

The more Alan traveled, the more insecure Maggie became.

What finally broke up their 12-year marriage were her constant accusations that Alan was playing around during his business trips. Alan denied that he was having an affair and he asked Pete to help convince Maggie. Pete regrets telling his brother-in-law that he didn't want to get involved in their domestic problems.

After Maggie separated from Alan, she returned to Connecticut and stayed with her mother for a while.

A few months after her divorce became final, a friend of Maggie's introduced her to John, a philosophy professor at a small college in Connecticut. They had a whirlwind romance and were married in less than six months – the second marriage for each.

Unlike before, with Alan, the family didn't like John – I guess he is an only child and his parents had money, so they tended to spoil him. He studied at Harvard, and in France and England. What bothered Pete the most was John's expectation that Maggie would continue to pamper him.

Maggie's marriage with John hit an immediate obstacle – which was John's mother. Pete thinks that Maggie didn't live up to the mother's high standards – either in her looks or education.

John's mother made Maggie's life hell because she constantly interfered in their marriage. The fact that she lived only a few miles away from them while John was teaching in Connecticut made matters even worse for Maggie. The situation improved for Maggie when John accepted a teaching position at Northwestern University in Evanston - Maggie was now far away from John's mother.

Maggie became pregnant with Brian shortly before she turned 37. We didn't have a chance to meet Brian because he is in a boarding school in Wisconsin. I don't know the details, but I guess Brian had problems in school and at home, especially with his father. The final blow occurred when Brian and two of his friends broke into a neighbor's home and stole stuff in order to buy drugs.

I asked Pete whether John is a good husband – his response was: "You make up your own mind after you see them together."

The thing that separated Pete and Maggie was her treatment of their mother. I guess Maggie has always taken her frustrations out on her mother and she did it again at a recent family reunion. Pete defended his mother and that was the last time that he spoke with Maggie.

I gave you this background for a reason – you'll see why as you read this note.

The flight to Chicago was fine, but Pete seemed nervous. He didn't have any drinks during our long flight from New York to San Francisco, but he had three on this shorter flight. I don't think he drinks much, but I assumed he needed to settle down before seeing Maggie.

Our plane landed at O'Hare pretty much on the dot at 2:25 in the afternoon. Pete's assistant had arranged for a car to take us to Maggie's house. However, instead of going directly to Evanston, Pete asked the driver to drive by Wrigley Field and then along Lakeshore Drive. The driver said that this would double our drive time, but Pete wanted me to see the home of the Cubs and the North Chicago area along the lake.

As I'm writing this, it occurs to me that maybe Pete was just trying to buy some time before he saw Maggie and John. I think he would have been happy if our flight was diverted away from O'Hare. You could tell he didn't want to confront his sister.

Incidentally, as you read about Maggie and John, picture a neurotic Diane Keaton as Maggie and a mean and nasty Gene Hackman as John.

Evanston seems to be a very nice little community and according to Pete, Northwestern is well respected for its academics. I guess this is another school I should consider if I ever think about college, which is doubtful. It may be a great school, but it's not Santa Barbara– on this rainy day, there were no girls riding their bikes in skimpy outfits.

Maggie greeted us when we arrived. We didn't see John immediately because he was in the basement, where he has his office.

I could immediately see why Pete said that Maggie and Amy are opposites.

Even though Maggie seems nice, she is far less animated than Amy. Maggie seemed uncomfortable with both of us; she and Pete acted like complete strangers. Amy gave us both big hugs after we entered her door, but Maggie only gave Pete a light kiss on his cheek. There was absolutely no emotion in the greeting.

After we took our bags to the guest bedroom, we joined Maggie in the dining room. It was a pretty odd scene –there were no smiles exchanged by either Pete or Maggie – it was more like a meeting between an IRS agent and a delinquent taxpayer instead of a reunion of a brother and his sister.

When she spoke, Maggie's eyes were either looking down at the table or somewhere else, but never at Pete or me. Her voice was so low at times that it was hard to hear her, even though she was just a few feet away from us.

After a while, John came up from the basement. He is a pretty large man with a graying beard – he looks like a grumpy college professor. The greeting between John and Pete was pretty damn cold and he barely noticed me. John didn't say much to either one of us – he asked Pete a "how's business" kind of thing, but that was about all he said.

While Pete was still talking, John interrupted him and asked Maggie to get him a cup of coffee. He complained that the last cup was cold by the time she brought it to his office.

After less than 10 minutes with us, John excused himself and returned to his hole. He said he was communicating with a philosophy professor at Berkeley about a topic that I can't even begin to try to repeat –it had something to do with a Greek philosopher. I really think John was trying to impress us with his knowledge of a complex subject.

Believe me – he wasn't impressive in any way; he just seemed like a total jerk. But after all of the nice people I met on this trip, my luck was bound to end. I'm glad it happened now rather than the beginning of the journey.

Maggie told Pete that when John is not at school, he spends the better part of his day in the basement, reading philosophy books, preparing for class or working on the computer. She only sees him when she serves dinner or when he calls her to the basement.

The only time I saw any emotion from Maggie was after Pete asked about Brian – she didn't say much, but she started to get weepy. She simply said that he is doing better, but that John will never allow him to return to the house.

When the coffee was ready, Maggie rushed it down to John – he said something in a loud voice which didn't sound pleasant.

It didn't take me long to answer the question I had asked Pete – John is a big bully and, unfortunately, Maggie won't defend herself against him. It's no wonder she has little self-confidence.

It was even worse at dinner – she was constantly running back and forth between the kitchen and the dining room table in an effort to make everything perfect for John, but this was an impossible task. I doubt he would have been satisfied with anything she could have done. He seemed to enjoy verbally harassing her.

When she cut the roast, he said she had overcooked it. When he drank the wine, he made a face and said she doesn't know how to select quality wine. This criticism continued non-stop through dinner.

To his credit, Pete remained calm and collected, and often said things to make Maggie feel comfortable – for example, he told her that the same wine was served to him at an important business dinner. This probably wasn't true, but he wanted to make her feel better about herself.

After dinner, we went to the family room to watch television. John sat with us for a few minutes and then went down to his office again. He asked Maggie to bring dessert and coffee to him.

*While flipping through stations, I ran across the movie "**An Affair to Remember**" with Cary Grant. Maggie sat down on the sofa and while she was staring at the television – she talked about the time she first saw the movie. It was in the late 1950's and their mother had taken Maggie to New York for the weekend as her birthday present.*

This is when the memories started to pour out and Maggie began to relax.

I guess that while they were in New York, their father was stuck with Pete and Amy in Connecticut. Pete said he has faint memories of seeing his dad trying to cook breakfast.

The ice had finally been broken – Pete and Maggie were acting like a brother and a sister who cared about each other as they reminisced about their childhood.

Maggie broke out in laughter when Pete told the story of how Amy had bleached her hair blond when she was less than 10. Their father came home for the weekend and he thought she was the girl from next door.

As the saying goes, that's when "the shit hit the fan". We could hear John yell from the basement, "where's my coffee and dessert?" I'm sure the neighbors probably heard him as well.

Maggie's expression suddenly turned from happy to complete fear.

Pete held his tongue, but he looked pissed – this bastard was pushing around his little sister.

All of a sudden, I got up, took the cup of coffee and dessert to the basement; I put both things on John's desk and said something like: "You're not disabled, so get your own food. Why don't you let your wife and her brother have some quality time together?"

I returned up the stairs and closed the door leading to the basement.

Less than a half an hour later, Pete and I were sitting on the front porch waiting for a cab to take us to a hotel near O'Hare. I tried to apologize to John, but he didn't accept. He asked us to leave his house "immediately".

While we were on the porch, I was crying like a baby - not because John yelled at me; I could care less about him since he is such a jackass. I was crying because of the stupid thing that I had just done.

My reaction will further distance Pete and Maggie and worse yet, John will make Maggie's life even more unbearable.

Pete tried to console me, but it didn't help.

It's now past midnight and I should be getting to sleep because Pete has arranged for an early morning flight back to New York. There is no need for us to stay in Chicago any longer. I actually wish we could go home right now – I just want to go in my room at home, close the door and stay there forever.

I really feel awful –I wanted to help Pete in the worst way, but I screwed things up for him and his sister.

I haven't felt this low since the day Mom passed away. I never said this to anyone before, but I always felt partially responsible for Mom's death. If she hadn't wanted another child, she wouldn't have needed surgery.

Today, there is no one to share the blame with me because I'm totally responsible for what happened at Maggie's house. I just wish I could rewind the clock and start over again, but the damage is done.

There's no way I can ever cure what I have done.

Rocky

CHAPTER 33

"SOMBER RETURN"

BY PETER

April 25, 1999 – Chicago to New York

What a miserable way to end our "trip of enlightenment".

There was nothing I could do to relieve Rocky's pain – I even told him that if he didn't say something to John, I would have. I couldn't hold back any longer, seeing my sister verbally abused by that totally insensitive and pompous prick. Maggie should leave this guy because he will never change, but I know she doesn't have the inner security to start over. As she once told me, she would be a "two-time loser" if she divorced John.

During the entire flight home, Rocky stayed in his seat – he didn't eat, read or listen to his CD player. He kept looking out the window and never took off his sunglasses.

I was relieved to see Michael at the gate when we arrived at Kennedy.

Obviously he knew about the "John incident" through Rocky – he immediately hugged Rocky, who was like a scared little boy returning from a scary incident to the comforting arms of his father.

I told Michael that since I wasn't upset, there is no reason for Rocky to be down. I can't quarrel with his actions in Evanston – he was simply trying to help Maggie and me. Despite what I said to Rocky and Michael, the ride into the city was incredibly quiet –none of us said a word.

When we arrived at Rocky's place, he gave me a long hug and thanked me for the trip of a lifetime. Rocky offered one more apology and then quietly went into the lobby of his building with Michael's arm around his shoulder.

It was a terribly sad scene. I remember feeling the same way when I let my baseball team down after making a costly error to lose a championship game. There is little that anyone can do for Rocky at this time.

When we got home, I told Kathy that Rocky seemed to have a magical ability throughout the trip when connecting with people and helping them. However, the magic didn't work in Evanston.

Kathy disagreed – she made an interesting comment. Perhaps what happened might have some benefit in convincing Maggie that she must escape her desperate situation with John.

I hope this is the case, but I have my doubts. I think that Maggie will remain with John and as a result, we will see little of each other in the future. Before making this trip, I wouldn't have cared if Maggie and I remained estranged. But now, I feel differently. After clicking with Amy and Josh, I was hoping that all of the branches of our family were finally coming together, but I guess this just isn't meant to be.

It occurred to me on the plane that if this chronicle is published, we probably should get John's consent. But in the end, I reached a different conclusion. Screw him. I have said nothing but the truth about him and if he is going to sue me for labeling him as an insensitive bastard, then he should fire his best shot. As any qualified attorney would tell him, truth is a defense in defamation litigation.

CHAPTER 34

"THANKSGIVING"

BY PETER

November 26, 2000 – Westport, Connecticut

So much has happened in the 19 months since my introspective trek with Rocky that I'm finding it hard to organize my thoughts in a logical manner.

Probably the best way to give you an update is to start with the changes that have occurred in my life and this will naturally lead to a discussion of other people whom you have met. Yes, I can't help myself – I'm still thinking about "number one" to some degree, but trust me, much less than I did in the past.

Kathy hit the target with the question she asked in one of her e-mails during the Rocky trip, namely, "How will I deal with my life after I return to the day-to-day grind at the office?"

Well, as you would probably expect, I didn't make any drastic changes in my working life and I basically maintained the same stressful pace. To be honest, while I may have been a bit more sensitive to the feeling of others, I was still a bulldog.

The only major difference, however, was that I allocated more of my free time for family matters than I had in the past. Even though I was still working long days, there were far fewer weekends at the office, barring crash projects.

The turning point for me was in June of last year after I received a call in the middle of the night from Jack Trill's wife. Jack had been rushed to the hospital after suffering a drug-related seizure.

To this day, I'm not sure whether the seizure was due to an accidental overdose or an attempted suicide. However, the combination of massive amounts of alcohol and a prescription pain medication on the very day that Jack's wife filed for divorce seemed more than a little suspect.

Since Jack and his wife were estranged at the time, I spent the better part of the following week with Jack at the hospital. Good or bad, I had plenty of time to ponder my life during those long, lonely hours at the hospital.

After Jack was released from the hospital, he was in complete despair.

Everything fell apart for him – not only the breakup of another marriage, but also his involuntary termination from the firm. This was his third strike and no one, including yours truly, could protect him any longer. To compound matters, his creditors were so relentless that he had no choice other than to file for bankruptcy protection.

Following his release from the hospital, I was concerned that Jack would try to end his life after he confided in me that there was no reason for him to continue living. He basically lost everything, including his children.

This was when Kathy offered Jack temporary refuge at the "Nest." To my surprise, he accepted, partly to get away from everybody and everything. Jack remained in seclusion at the Nest for five weeks.

I asked Rocky and Michael to join me for two weekends with Jack at the Nest. In his own way, Rocky worked his magic with Jack. I don't know what they discussed, but each morning and afternoon, they took long walks near the lake. Rocky has an uncanny ability to get close to people who are lost and help them find their true sense of direction.

As a result of the trip with Rocky and Jack's problems, I became philosophical. So, as you read this update, you may think that I've gone over the edge, which is not the case. Let's just say that my vision has been expanded. By analogy, I used to look through a high–powered telescope and only focused on one object. I have traded in the telescope for wide-angle binoculars, which enable me to view everything around me.

Here is another analogy. The trip I took to the West Coast with Rocky brought me directly in front of a six-foot block wall. My side of the wall is familiar to me, but it is stressful, noisy and everything seems to move at a fast-forward pace.

As a result of my experience with Rocky, I peeked over to the other side of the wall, which looked relatively tranquil in comparison to my side. But it is virgin territory and, therefore, scary.

What I am trying to say is that I didn't want to take the risk of climbing over the wall because once my father did so, he was immediately unhappy. I should clarify this statement – he was even less happy after going to the other side.

Although I'm not sure why, Jack's miserable situation gave me the willpower to finally climb to the top of the wall. Maybe it was the proverbial "broke the camel's back" thing, with Rocky's trip stirring much of my thoughts and emotions and the circumstances behind Jack's close brush with death being the "final straw."

In any event, this is when profound changes began to occur in my life.

After I helped Jack locate an appropriate clinic to treat his addiction, I started focusing on myself. The first thing I did was to begin an intensive therapy program during which I saw a psychiatrist three times a week. Due to my compulsive nature, I wanted an immediate fix for my problems and the prospect of one session a week for many months or perhaps even years wasn't an acceptable approach.

I "analyzed my analysis" with a personal progress report after 12 sessions. Although the psychiatrist was helping me focus, I still felt that I wasn't connecting with myself, partly because I was often defensive when I felt that he was critical of my behavior. However, the psychiatrist assisted me in two ways: by giving me a process by which to self-analyze my situation and by prescribing anti-depressants, which helped clear my head.

During a Denver business trip, I made a difficult decision; one that I appreciated would have major ramifications both at home and with the firm. I decided to take a leave of absence for the month of July. I would tell Kathy and those at work that I need to "recharge my batteries", but in actuality, I wanted the time to search for answers about my life.

While it wasn't easy explaining this decision to my partners, it was even worse with Kathy. She was understandably worried about me, probably because she thought I would follow in Jack's footsteps. It was an interesting process because the three people who comforted Kathy about my decision were Rocky, Josh and Jennie.

My next step was to decide where I would spend the month. I had a number of choices, but remaining at home in the city wasn't even an idea I considered. One option was to take a solitary road trip to points unknown, but the thought of constant driving turned me off. Another possibility was to rent a remote place in the mountains or along the coast, but this would undoubtedly involve research, and I didn't have time to waste. The answer was clear; I would seek solitude at the Nest. It seemed to help Jack focus his thoughts and I hoped it would do the same for me.

Kathy was incredibly helpful in setting me up with everything I would need. I took six books with me: two self-help books that were recommended by my psychiatrist, two biographies about people who experienced major internal struggles and two mystery novels for light reading.

However, during the first two weeks, I wasn't making any progress. I was enjoying my lengthy walks around the lake and I had finished three of the books, but I was going through work "withdrawal." I was tempted to call the office, but I somehow mustered the willpower to resist. I was actually becoming bored at the Nest because there were no momentous breakthroughs. Sadly, I even focused on how people at the firm would react when I returned to work. Would they whisper as I passed that I had a breakdown? I was beginning to regret my decision about taking a leave of absence.

While eating a pizza dinner one evening at the Nest, I glanced at a family picture taken at my parents' home during the Christmas holidays in the mid-1980's. I focused on my father in the picture; he had a slight smile, but he didn't look happy despite being surrounded by his loving family.

I tried to remember the occasions when I had seen Father truly happy. They were few and far between, but the only ones that came to mind related to some kind of achievement by one of his children. I saw delight in his face when one of us received high grades in school, we won an academic award, we were accepted to a quality college or those few times that he attended one of our performances. Beyond that, he rarely displayed happiness while we were growing up. It became even worse after we all moved away from him. He became totally absorbed in his work and spent even less time in Connecticut. When I would come home from college, it was like talking with a neighbor instead of my father.

Sadly, the only time he exhibited a fair amount of enthusiasm was shortly before his death. As I told you before, the first year after his retirement was a difficult period for Father. However, he somehow had a revival during his last year. He was excited about his volunteer work, his plans to travel with Mother, reading history books and even with his atrocious golf game. But then he went to sleep and never woke up.

These thoughts about Father led me to consider my life and recall the times when I was truly happy or at least more upbeat than I have been in recent years. Two periods in my life came to mind, the first being the summer between my junior and senior years in high school. I worked at the country club, which enabled me to play lots of golf and to see movies or Broadway shows in the evenings. That was also a great time because I was eagerly looking forward to my senior year and the prospects of applying to colleges that would train me in theatre arts. The future looked bright.

Little did I know during that magical summer that the college application process would turn out to be a nightmare because my father had already preordained where I would attend school.

The other special period in my life was shortly after our marriage and until Josh was around five. We had a wonderful time as a family, often going to the park, the zoo or weekend trips to the country. Even though I worked long hours, I still had time to enjoy Kathy and the kids. We both realized that my work schedule went hand in hand with success in my profession. But I maintained balance in my life.

The long hours and stressful pace weren't the culprits. Something led to a dramatic change in my personality that started in my late 30's and became worse as time passed. It wasn't Kathy, the kids or anything that occurred at the firm. But I developed a mindset of winning at everything I did, regardless of the cost. I also lost trust in others and didn't want to become close with anyone, until Rocky rekindled my urge to connect with family members and my few true friends, like Jack.

I'm not sure what prompted me to think back to determine why my personality changed. It might have been Rocky's daily e-mails of encouragement. In one of them, he suggested that I focus on the happy times in my life. In another one this week, Rocky urged me to think about the times when I became extremely agitated. After considering the major events that stirred me up, two immediately came to mind. This was when the lightening bolt finally hit its mark.

There were many times during my career that I felt embarrassed because I had made a mistake or more likely, when someone, whether a partner or my opposition, made me look bad. I hated that feeling and as my career blossomed, I was determined that no one would beat me. This became a compulsion the more successful I became. I felt that I had to live up to my reputation as a "take no prisoners" kind of person.

The other source of great irritation didn't relate directly to me, but instead, it was something that happened to Father. You remember that I told you about Father's last project, in which his firm opposed my client in a deal. After we finished the transaction, Father was dejected because he felt that he didn't adequately represent his client. As a result, he threw in the towel and gave up, in many ways. I remember the walk we took near his home when he told me about his decision to retire because he could not longer keep pace with younger guys like myself.

After he announced his retirement, Father was treated in a blatantly insensitive manner by the firm, even though he had devoted himself to it at the high cost of losing his family life. He was a broken man, defeated and angry, until he had his breakthrough shortly before his death.

Now I realize that this may have been the "defining moment" for me. I know that I wasn't a particularly good husband or father even before this event, but at least I had maintained my integrity. But Father's decision to retire and the resulting unhappiness was clearly a turning point.

I became so determined not to be like Father that I tried to make myself indispensable to my firm – running faster and harder than anyone else to win "the race" each time. Rather than mellowing in the twilight years of my career, I became a ruthless tyrant. Unfortunately for my family, I simply couldn't leave this attitude at work and change into the role of a gentle husband and father at home. But despite this price, I was determined to not be pushed aside rudely by my firm, as my father had been.

When I thought about my feisty attitude, it occurred to me that it not only applied in my business, but it had somehow engulfed every aspect of my day-to-day life. I felt like I was waging a fierce battle on every front, and at times, I even resorted to dirty tricks to survive the hand-to-hand combat. If it wasn't an argument with a bank teller, it was loudly complaining to an airline employee about getting a window instead of an aisle seat. My war was even waged against my business associates and family members. No one went unscathed and everyone was a logical target. There were few allies and far more enemies.

The other related point is that I was truly afraid of going to the other side of the "wall". Even though Father eventually recovered and began to enjoy his "quiet year", I didn't want to take the chance. I thought I would lose all sense of power by becoming "Joe Citizen", a demoralized man for my remaining days.

I also realized that I had effectively alienated my family and friends, so I wouldn't have emotional support when I became a man of leisure. I feared that I would become a lonely and miserable old man. Since I assumed that the decision to go to the "other side" is irreversible, I didn't have the courage to make the move because I could never return if it didn't prove to be what I considered a suitable life.

To be honest, I don't know whether all of this self-analysis really touched on the sources of my unpleasant personality and negative attitude. However, the important thing is that reaching these conclusions worked and that's all that matters. I didn't want to come to the conclusion that whatever molded me was the fault of others. That would have been too easy to fall back on. I'm a problem-solving guy and I needed definitive answers that would help me make appropriate changes. Whether these self-analytical conclusions are the right answers is frankly irrelevant.

The point is that Walden Pond helped Henry David Thoreau in "simplification" and the Nest did the same for me. I had made life far too complicated.

My return home was an interesting experience because I hadn't shaved during my time at the Nest. I looked like a derelict, but Kathy saw me in a different light. Instead of alarming her, she said that my eyes told the whole story; they finally showed signs of renewed life.

After walking around the townhouse for a while like a guy who was recovering from a massive amount of anesthetic, I fell on the couch and began to cry uncontrollably. To her credit, Kathy wasn't alarmed by this scene. She just caressed me, just like a mother would a teenage daughter who had just been dumped by her boyfriend.

That evening, I told Kathy everything that happened during my recovery at the Nest. While she was supportive, I could see that she was also dubious of my veracity. After returning from the trip with Rocky, I had promised that changes would be made, but I didn't come through. So, her cautious reaction was understandable. I must admit I was a little scared that her suspicion might be well founded. What if I'm just going through a bizarre reaction after being in solitary confinement for weeks?

Thankfully, it turned out that my revelations were real and the feeling of freeing myself from demons wasn't temporary.

The next stop was to Father's grave. I apologized for not previously understanding him or his priorities. We ended up much the same, but I was fortunate to experience intervening events that helped direct me. For him, the defining moment came too late and he was ill equipped to understand what was happening to him. In his day, a "stable" adult male would never consider seeking help for his personal problems from others.

Sadly, by the time he realized what had transpired and why he felt so low, he simply ran out of time.

Instead of leaving flowers, I left the stubs for two tickets to a 1959 Yankees game. This was the only time we attended a baseball game together. I also told Father for the first time that I loved him.

I returned to the office the first week of August, still unshaved, but at least better groomed. The fact that I was dressed casually must have raised further questions. The reaction by my partners was predictable. There is no question that many of them concluded I had fallen off the career train without a helmet. A "source" revealed to me that the Executive Committee called an emergency meeting to review my situation, although I wasn't sure what they would discuss. Typically, such a meeting would have bothered me and in the past, I might have stormed into the conference room, but I honestly didn't care what was said.

I know you will find this hard to believe, but after only one day at the office, I felt miserable. My stomach was in knots and I had a splitting headache. Even though I had a number of supporters on the Executive Committee, there were far more enemies. They might have appreciated the contributions I had made to the firm because it increased their wealth, but they couldn't stand me as a person.

I suspected that the Committee would recommend an additional leave. So, instead of waiting for my partners to decide my fate, I took a preemptive strike by asking for a two-month extension of my leave. I can't tell you how good it felt to send this memo to the Chairman of the Executive Committee.

The following month, Kathy and I followed virtually the same route as I took on the April trip with Rocky. The main differences on the second trip were: playing Spyglass Hill instead of Pebble Beach (I still didn't break 105, but I only lost nine balls!); staying two days in Las Vegas; and spending more time with Josh in Salt Lake City.

We visited Cliff and Emily in Cedar City, but we didn't stay with them. Since I last saw them, they have rescued two more dogs. Sadly, Cliff's condition has not improved and may actually be worse – although he faked it well through prompting from Emily, I don't think he remembered me.

I was pleased to hear from Emily that Rocky remained in constant contact with the Pass family, by regularly calling and sending goodies.

The most recent package arrived the day we visited Emily and Cliff – it was a dozen bagels.

By the way, Emily asked me to communicate with their son to find out if I could possibly help him. I wrote him a letter and he responded by saying that he could easily return to the U.S., but he would need to pay a small amount of back taxes.

This turned out to be another fabrication. I had a friend in Washington check on him – I found out that their son hadn't filed tax returns for at least four years. His problems were far more significant than he had described to his parents. I told Cliff and Emily that I could only help him if he is willing to cooperate. I haven't heard from their son after offering my assistance.

On the positive side, Josh completed the summer term at the University of Utah and was practicing with the football team when we visited him. Much to my surprise, his buddy Tina also entered the U of U. I didn't realize there was a romantic connection between the two of them, but Kathy quickly figured this out.

After returning to New York from our trip, Kathy and I mapped out a tentative plan for our second life together.

The first part of the plan was the most difficult. It was when I told the partners in the firm that I would be retiring on December Thirty-first. I don't want you to get the misimpression that this was a spontaneous decision. Actually, I agonized for weeks before making the announcement. The positives in favor of staying on the job were a great income stream that was improving yearly because of my status and the recognition that the partnership brought me. I would also miss a few of my long-term friends, both inside the firm and those with clients.

The negatives for staying far outweighed the positives and the most important factor was my desire to do something else in my life. There is no question that my association with Rocky was critical in arriving at this conclusion. So, even though I was about to leave a great deal of money on the table by retiring early, it didn't matter. I was tired of doing the same thing year after year and even more exhausted by the ever-present bullshit. I finally had the courage to escape it all.

Much to everyone's surprise, including mine, I met my departure schedule despite repeated requests that I stay for another month to groom my successor. I was actually tempted to extend my stay, but was convinced otherwise by my dear friend Rocky.

Actually, meeting the departure schedule was yet another one of Rocky's many challenges. Once while we were having lunch, he said he wouldn't be surprised if I extended my stay with the firm because I didn't have the guts to move on. He knew I had to prove him wrong.

The next decision was where we would live – I favored remaining in New York, but to my great surprise, Kathy preferred that we retire outside the city. I wasn't convinced about the idea until we went "community" shopping. I was hoping that she wouldn't like any of the places we would visit.

We took short "research" trips to Connecticut, New Hampshire, Massachusetts and South Carolina, where one of my former partners is enjoying retirement in a golf course community.

Kathy enjoyed this process far more than I did. She was armed with a checklist of essential and desirable community requirements, such as medical facilities, shopping, weather, crime rate, educational opportunities, nearby airports and, most of all, places that had community theatre groups. She correctly assumed that I would automatically eliminate a particular area from consideration if it didn't offer a community theatre group.

We exchanged personalities during this search – she was far more methodical and analytical while I was moved by the look and feel of a community.

After the initial search was completed, we reduced the list to five potential communities. Then we listed our preferences from top to bottom and exchanged our lists.

We only agreed on one, but fortunately it was the top choice – the winner was...Westport, Connecticut.

Westport is ideally located, just off Long Island Sound, about 50 miles from New York City, 10 miles from Bridgeport and 30 miles from New Haven. We could depart by train from Bridgeport and arrive at Penn Station in less than one and one-half hours.

The population of Westport is about 25,000, so it has all of the essentials we would need. If we can't locate something in Westport, we can find whatever we may want in either Bridgeport or New Haven.

Anyway, we sold our two places and moved to Westport in February. We used the proceeds from the sale of the Nest to start a charitable fund, which we named the "Katherine Franklin Charitable Foundation" and although it's not a huge amount of money, the Foundation keeps Kathy involved with more than enough charitable organizations. The hard part for her is to decline any worthy cause, so at the rate she's going, I don't think the fund will survive for more than five years.

After our move, I joined a local country club and a community theatre group. By the way, Dad would have been right – it's good that my livelihood never depended on my acting abilities, because frankly, I'm not nearly as good as I thought.

Kathy surprised me by participating in three of our stage productions. The truth be known, she is much better than me, but there's no way I would ever confess this to anyone, particularly to her.

I also serve as a volunteer at the Westport Playhouse, which is based in a 162-year-old red barn. Six professional summer stock productions are staged at the Playhouse for two-week runs. I find this program most beneficial because it enables me to work with professionals.

This past summer, I also became a volunteer contributing writer for a Bridgeport newspaper. I review restaurants, movies and stage productions, and plan to take a trip to New York with Kathy at least twice a year to review current Broadway shows.

As you would imagine, I'm an awfully harsh critic – I love the power of ripping the hell out of productions and restaurants that I consider below expectations. In fact, last week, I tore into a children's animated movie because I considered it far too "sweet". In other words, sometimes things don't work out and kids should be prepared for life's lessons. The letters to the editor were brutal. If I weren't a volunteer, I would have been fired.

In last week's article, I admittedly went overboard. I cruelly panned a senior citizen production of ***Hello Dolly*** – it wasn't appropriate for me to say that I was distracted because the actors were reading their lines from hand-held scripts. That was a cheap shot, which warrants an apology in this week's column.

I love the house we bought in Westport, but frankly, it's much larger than we need. Kathy convinced me that we should have extra room because our place will serve as a "safe house" for friends and relatives who need a place of refuge. It turns out she was absolutely right because we have had our share of visitors this year, many of whom we hadn't seen in years.

The house is colonial style with four bedrooms and three baths. It was built in 1978 and updated by the previous owners just three years ago. The best part is the location - it sits on two acres located on the Saugatuck River, which leads to Long Island Sound.

We also have a two-bedroom, one-bath guesthouse on the property, which has proved useful for our many visitors, starting with Jack, who frankly overstayed his welcome.

This past summer, I was approached by a friend about teaching a business class at Yale University in New Haven. I first hesitated about accepting this course because of the time commitment and since part of the course deals with "business ethics". I took, however, the challenge and even though it requires a 60-mile round trip on Tuesdays and Thursdays, I have enjoyed the class. But I doubt I will teach again because this course brings back too many unpleasant memories of my prior life.

I thought about buying a small sporty car and even had my eye on a Mustang, but in the end, I realized that a larger car is more practical in the "country". I now drive a black, four-wheel drive sports utility vehicle.

One of the best parts of my life is my ability to dress as I wish. In the winter months, I wear jeans and sweatshirts most of the time. In the spring and summer months, it's typically shorts and golf shirts.

Rocky and I speak by phone at least once a week and we usually exchange e-mails more often. He has visited us a number of times after we moved and spent the better part of July in our guesthouse.

Rocky recovered from the ghastly episode in Evanston after he received a call from Maggie. She had asked me for his number the day we returned from Chicago and at first I was reluctant to give it to her because I was afraid that she would make him feel worse, but she didn't. Maggie thanked Rocky for helping her; from what Rocky said, she was incredibly warm and thoughtful.

You may remember that Rocky briefly fell in love while we were in Beverly Hills with a Seattle beauty named Mandy. Well, Mandy joined her parents in New York during March while they attended a trade show. She met Rocky twice, the first time for a Broadway show and then for lunch.

It probably would have been better for Rocky if he had lived with his memories of Mandy because she was very different from the time they met in Beverly Hills. Rocky said that her face was caked with makeup; she smoked constantly; she was popping pills to help her relax; and all she spoke about was her new Jeep Cherokee and her weekend drinking binges with her boyfriend, a University of Washington football player.

During their lunch, Mandy told Rocky that he was way too "uptight" and she offered him some of her little pills, but Rocky turned her down.

Rocky doesn't know what set him off, but as is typical of him, he couldn't hold back his comments during their lunch.

He apparently told Mandy that while she will always be pretty, she had lost some of the qualities that made her so very attractive to him when they first met. From Rocky's standpoint, she was no longer the cute and bubbly teenager he saw in California – she had become an irresponsible adult in a very short period of time. The final comment that led her to abruptly leave the restaurant before they finished lunch was when Rocky suggested that she seek professional help to curb her addiction to drugs and alcohol.

Rocky knew that he would probably lose her friendship by making this suggestion, but it didn't matter because he couldn't live with himself if he didn't try to prevent Mandy from ending up like Jack - in an emergency hospital as a result of an overdose.

After their "separation", the enlarged picture of Mandy and Rocky lounging around the pool in Beverly Hills was permanently removed from the wall in Rocky's room.

Sometime in August, he received an e-mail from Mandy while she was recovering from a broken leg and other injuries that she suffered in an automobile accident.

It turns out that while driving under the influence – it wasn't clear to Rocky whether it was alcohol or drugs - Mandy drove her Cherokee into a ditch. The car rolled over and because her friend wasn't wearing a seat belt, she was thrown from the car. The friend suffered major injuries, but she recovered after a long stay in the hospital. Unfortunately, the head trauma resulted in the loss of her left eye.

Mandy told Rocky that as part of a plea-bargain agreement, she agreed to participate in an abuse program, although she didn't think it was necessary.

It seemed to Rocky that she was seeking his support, so he sent her daily e-mails and often called her. In September, Mandy's father told Rocky that she was in a drunken stupor the previous week. Her father advised the authorities that she had violated her probation. He made this painful decision in order to force her to enter a full-time abuse clinic.

To his credit, Rocky still contacts Mandy, who is currently residing in a clinic in Southern California. She now finally concedes that she is an addict – something she previously denied, even after her accident. Rocky calls her daily and sent her roses for her birthday.

Mandy plans to attend weekly support group meetings after she is released and intends to complete her high school education so she can attend the University of California at Santa Barbara. She recently visited the school with her parents at Rocky's suggestion.

You will also remember Rocky's "list" – well, you will be pleased to know that he fulfilled another item on the list – his opinions and points of view are published in a weekly "my turn" column for a free New York paper.

His most recent article took shots at the major Hollywood studios for the dearth of quality movies. To quote Rocky: *"Hollywood only wants the big bucks from movies full of obscene language and gratuitous violence and sex. Most of today's major studio executives only care about their fancy cars, massive houses, fat bonuses and further inflating their huge egos. These Hollywood big shots lack the backbone to produce worthwhile movies and they are totally devoid of common moral behavior."*

You have to give this to the kid, he never pulls any punches. In another article, he lashed out at industrial giants for failing to take minimal steps to protect the environment. He also brought attention to a homeless shelter that was about to close its doors due to the lack of financial support. He even called for a peaceful demonstration to show support for the shelter. As a result of media coverage, the shelter received a grant from a local foundation that will help keep it afloat for at least three years.

Last month, Rocky departed from his typical current events article by writing, **"High Road Through The Park"**, a two-part children's story, about two birds living in Central Park. The older of the two is Percy Feather and the younger is Ritchie Bird. I'm sure the similarity of their initials to the people you met in this book is sheer coincidence.

In any event, Percy is a loud and more than slightly obnoxious crow, who was once a pleasant young crow, but then started pushing other birds around in order to get more than his fair share of food. Even though Percy doesn't need all this food for himself and his family, he enjoys being a bully.

As you might expect, Ritchie was described as an "extremely intelligent and likeable" swallow, and is remarkably resourceful despite his small stature. But sadly, Ritchie was born with only one leg, and as a result of his disability, he lacks confidence about his abilities.

Ritchie has always had a desire to see other parts of the 843-acre park, but is scared to leave his secure tree house in the "Strawberry Fields" section of the park. The author tells us that "Strawberry Fields" was named after a song called *"**Strawberry Fields Forever**"*, in honor of John Lennon, a singer, who often enjoyed visiting this part of the park.

After Percy overhears Ritchie tell another swallow of his fear about traveling to other parts of the park, Percy calls Ritchie a "scared chicken". In order to prove his bravery, Ritchie reluctantly challenges Percy to take a journey with him to foreign destinations in the park. In his typical arrogant bluster, Percy claims he knows "every square inch of the park."

During their first day of flying around the park, "worldly" Percy becomes hopelessly lost and begins to panic as the sun goes down. But Ritchie saves the day by maintaining his cool and finding a safe place for them to spend the night. Over the next three days, Ritchie surprises us by becoming the leader of this trek. Throughout the journey, Percy and Ritchie help other birds with personal problems and in turn, our feathered friends benefit from these experiences.

After they finally find their way back home, Ritchie is treated like a hero, which gives him confidence to face his challenges despite his disability. Percy also benefits from his experiences and becomes more accommodating to his neighbors.

The moral of the story is: "First impressions of people and birds are often deceiving."

I told Rocky that while it was a fine piece of writing, it was pure fiction because I didn't see any parallels between our trip and the one described in the story.

His articles confirmed what I already knew - that Rocky truly has a natural gift for connecting through every mode of communication, whether oral, in his writing or simply by the way he looks at a person.

For example, you will remember Maria, the hotel housekeeper Rocky met while he was ill in Las Vegas. Rocky immediately connected with her and learned about her life and plans after only two brief encounters. He is also a good judge of character because he ended up winning both of our bets regarding Maria. First, she signed his letter and he sent her a loan in order for Maria to pay her tuition. She became a hairdresser and has been sending Rocky $200 a month to repay her debt. Every Tuesday afternoon, she gives haircuts at half her regular price to residents of a convalescent home, which was part of Rocky's deal with her – to give haircuts to those who can ill afford them.

Michael's life has also improved in several respects. First of all, he and Rocky recently moved from New York to Connecticut. Michael's company recently announced a major headcount reduction and he was one of many employees offered an enhanced early retirement package, which includes medical insurance for him and Rocky. Michael said it took him less than five minutes to accept the proposal, even though he is only 49 years old and will need part-time employment to supplement his income.

Michael bought a small home in a community near New Haven. It has everything they want, including a large backyard for Rocky's new dog, a golden retriever that Rocky rescued from a local animal shelter.

One of the reasons Michael selected the New Haven area is because of the Yale-New Haven hospital that has a dedicated unit to care for HIV and AIDS patients. The three of us visited the hospital before Michael made his move to make sure that Rocky would be comfortable with the facility and its staff.

Michael also has a new love in his life – her name is Debra. At first, I was surprised that Michael was able to meet someone in New Haven so quickly. But I later learned that Rocky was responsible for the introduction. After receiving Laura's blessing, Rocky secretly placed a "personals ad" describing Michael and the type of woman he thought would be suitable for his father.

In order to keep this project secret, Rocky arranged to have interested women respond by voice-mail, which is part of the personals process. After he reviewed the messages, he narrowed his choices to two women, whom he met privately. I learned from Michael that Rocky created a grading system, with a possible two points for each of five categories. The first woman scored only six points, primarily because of her extremely short skirt, low cut-top and attraction to "rap" music. So Rocky selected Debra as the first choice, who incidentally scored nine points.

Michael was so livid with Rocky that he initially deprived him of his computer for two days. For Rocky, this is a significant punishment. Rocky said that he had not seen his father so angry since the time he tossed water balloons from their apartment at kids who were harassing an elderly woman. While his intentions were good, his aim was poor, and one of the balloons hit the woman in the head. Rocky was, however, given a "pardon" for the matchmaker crime after Laura confessed to being his accomplice.

Since Rocky had scheduled a blind date with Debra, there was little that Michael could do other than to meet her for dinner. When Michael returned home, he told Rocky that they had nothing in common. He also instructed Rocky not to place any more personals ads.

What Rocky and Laura didn't know was that Michael continued to see Debra on a regular basis. After their relationship blossomed, Michael informed Laura and Rocky. Oddly enough, despite the passing of Evelyn many years before, Michael still felt a slight degree of guilt about his relationship with Debra. However, after he got the blessing of Laura and Rocky, he felt more comfortable.

I don't know whether this relationship will be permanent, but at least for now, it doesn't matter since Debra is a wonderful person who makes Michael and Rocky happy.

This brings you up to date. I'm writing this note at the conclusion of our Thanksgiving family reunion. Kathy and I splurged on this reunion by paying the travel costs for a number of family members, but this may be a once in a lifetime occasion.

We flew Josh and Tina in from Salt Lake City. Things are going relatively well with them, but Kathy sensed some tension because she believes that Tina wants more of a commitment from Josh.

We weren't sure that Amy could leave the inn during this busy weekend, but Frank volunteered to mind the business in her absence. It was comical to see Amy call Frank every few hours to check on things and to give him constant reminders.

Amy brought a special guest with her from California, the newest member of our family, a six-year-old boy named Erik. She recently adopted Erik, who has bounced around foster homes in the San Francisco area since he was four. Erik's natural mother was murdered by her pimp in 1998.

I doubt that Amy realizes the difficulties she will encounter, but I give her full credit for her courage to take on this responsibility. This is what she always wanted and she is helping another soul at the same time. I didn't know until this weekend that Rocky had sent Amy information about San Francisco adoption agencies, including the one that helped her with Erik.

Maggie's story is even more interesting. John was telling her the truth when he said he was constantly communicating with another philosophy professor at Berkeley. What he neglected to mention, however, was that he had been having an Internet romance for more than two years with this woman – from the time they met at an educational symposium.

After visiting Brian one weekend at his boarding school in Wisconsin, Maggie returned home to a "from John" letter. He had packed up his personal belongings and moved to California to be closer to his Internet love. He later arranged to have his mother move to California to live with him and his new wife. Good luck to all of them.

Following their divorce, Maggie took her portion from the sale of their Evanston home and relocated – guess where? Yes, also to Connecticut, close to Mother's house. I honestly think a little too close for Mother, but it's none of my business. In order to make amends for her past, Maggie has become incredibly warm to Mother, to the point that it is truly nauseating.

Maggie is now working at a local library and managing very well. I thought she would be crushed by the divorce, but she was actually quite relieved. Her new boyfriend, also a librarian, couldn't join us for Thanksgiving because he was visiting his widowed father. I feel sorry for Maggie's boyfriend because she finally found a man that she can push around, and believe me, she takes advantage at every possible opportunity.

Since her son Brian's anger was due to the way John treated Maggie, she released him from boarding school and he joined her in Connecticut. He plans to enlist in the Navy this year after he finishes high school.

As for Laura, she is still studying at Cornell, but plans to take a year off to work and tour throughout Europe. Michael told me that Laura looks very much like her mother – whenever Michael mentions Evelyn, he still feels sad, but on the other hand, I haven't seen him smile as much as he does when he is with Debra. I was pleased to see that Debra offered a special prayer for Evelyn before our Thanksgiving dinner.

Now that Josh has basically settled down, Jennie has become my nemesis.

Unfortunately, I suggested that she spend time in Santa Cruz with Amy – this was a huge mistake. She was so taken by Amy and the area that she plans to transfer to the University of California at Santa Cruz. I'm afraid that with Amy's influence, Jennie will become a pot-smoking, tree-hugging radical environmental crusader.

Jack joined us as well – with his new girlfriend. Thankfully, she worked in the rehab clinic that he attended so I hope she can keep him clean. Jack is now working on smaller deals with a partner who was asked to leave our former firm because of a sexual harassment claim. Unfortunately, despite the bankruptcy, Jack is still intoxicated by the power of money.

At one point during the trip with Rocky, we agreed that some day we would give a duet concert for friends and family members. Rocky has been living in our guesthouse since last weekend in order for us to practice our "act" with rented Karaoke equipment. Rocky and I had secretly researched the favorite songs or singers of our guests and we entertained them with an "unforgettable" duet concert after Thanksgiving dinner.

We sang the following renditions for our guests:

>   My mother – "*Smile*" by Tony Bennett
>   Kathy's mother (Nancy) – "*Nancy*" by Frank Sinatra
>   Kathy – "*What a Wonderful World*" by Louis Armstrong
>   Evelyn – "*Imagine*" by John Lennon
>   Jack – "*Jumpin' Jack Flash*" by the Rolling Stones
>   Maggie – "*Misty*" by Johnny Mathis
>   Debra – "*Can't Smile Without You*" by Barry Manilow
>   Amy – "*California Dreamin*" by the Mamas and Papas
>   Michael – "*Mack the Knife*" by Bobby Darin
>   Josh – "*Hotel California*" by the Eagles
>   Jennie – "*Music of the Night*" from *Phantom of the Opera*
>   Laura – "*Vincent*" by Don McClean
>   Brian – "*Easy Lover*" by Phil Collins
>   Jack's girlfriend – "*Hot Legs*" by Rod Stewart
>   Erik – "*Rudolf the Red-Nosed Reindeer*"

After we finished our concert, Rocky asked Josh, Jennie and Laura to join him at the front of our living room and I was "instructed" by Rocky to take a seat in the audience. Unbeknownst to me, Rocky had sent the words to the other three for my favorite song, "*As Time Goes By*." The four "kids" sang it in my honor.

For once, I didn't attempt to pretend that I had a foreign object in my eye – I couldn't have fooled anyone even if I tried. The floodgates opened and I cried like a baby.

After reading this update, you would think that by and large, life is better for all of the members of our extended family. Unfortunately, this is far from true.

I must confess that every once in a while, the old "Pete" creeps back into my life and as a result, I act like a spoiled child. But thankfully, it rarely happens, and when it does, I'm quickly reprimanded for my behavior by those near and dear to me.

Sometimes, however, I'm still my harshest critic. This happened last month after I realized that I simply couldn't continue to volunteer at a homeless shelter. After I analyzed the situation, I realized that I was having mixed emotions while serving food at the shelter; I was incredibly sad and angry. Sad about the condition of many of the recipients and angry because I feel that some could be doing something meaningful with their lives. So, I just quit, which resulted in guilt followed by personal disappointment due to my "failure".

What I am saying is that people don't suddenly change overnight; all you can ask for is improvement. For example, I know I've made small strides in my interpersonal skills because when I now enter our home, Kathy's dog no longer growls at me.

It may be paranoia, but I suspect that as you have read my accounts, you can't empathize with me. After all, I came from a privileged background and continued to prosper. I can't agree more, which sometimes made it even more difficult for me to understand my general unhappiness and need to win at all costs. While it may be difficult to understand, a high social or financial position doesn't immunize a person from carrying loads of emotional baggage. I can't say it is more than people who are less privileged, but it isn't automatically less.

So, regardless of our affluence, we all face our daily emotional issues, problems and fears. Despite a dramatic turnaround in my life, I'm no exception, particularly for things beyond my control, such as the health of my family and friends.

As an example, my mother's mental condition continues to degrade, to the point were she no longer recognizes the children. I doubt she can continue to live alone much longer and the thought of Maggie moving in with her is frightening. However, it may be the best thing for both of them given their improved relationship.

And this past week, we got a real shocker. At a routine annual exam, the doctor noticed a lump in Kathy's right breast. She insisted that we keep this confidential during this weekend. Follow-up tests are scheduled for this week. She remains calm, but I'm an absolute wreck.

Turning to Rocky, while he was with us this week, I noticed that he quickly tires and took long naps every afternoon. He also declined an invitation to join me for a daily walk in our neighborhood.

Before Rocky, Laura and Michael left our house, I took a walk with Michael. He confirmed my worst fears that Rocky was developing symptoms that show a rapid deterioration of his immune system.

Rocky didn't want any of us to know that his lymph nodes are enlarged and that his most recent blood tests show a noticeable decline of T-cells. Since I researched HIV and AIDS following my trip with Rocky, I knew this meant that his immune system's key infection fighters are being destroyed. This explained Rocky's general malaise over the past week.

In the past, Rocky had taken medication only when necessary. Now, he takes daily medication, including "inhibitors" that Michael said are intended to delay the onset of "opportunistic infections." Apparently, their doctor believes that Rocky's infection is already becoming resistant to the first class of inhibitors. The troubling part is that the side effects have been brutal for Rocky, including constant nausea, diarrhea and other gastrointestinal complications. I'm sure Rocky was suffering this week, but he never complained.

As I had expected, Rocky was not serious when he asked me to help him with his college applications. This was Rocky's way of further disguising his worsening condition.

Reality hit me when Michael mentioned that he had already contacted a local Hospice organization should the need arise. Michael made it clear that he wasn't suggesting that Hospice will be needed in the near future – he was simply covering all of the bases if Rocky's condition suddenly worsens.

When Michael and I returned to the house after our walk, Rocky and Laura were packed and ready to leave. In order to protect Michael, I pretended that I didn't know anything about Rocky's condition.

As I was saying goodbye to Laura, Rocky gave Kathy a hug and then whispered something to her. He then grabbed me and I held him for a long time. As much as I tried, I still couldn't fight the tears.

After they drove away, Kathy told me what Rocky had whispered to her, "Thanks for taking care of my best friend."

That evening, I sent this e-mail:

Dear Rocky:

There is something important that I should have discussed with you today before you left.

I have been seriously thinking about this for some time, but I hesitated to mention it previously because I wasn't entirely comfortable with the concept. After our concert this weekend, I am very confident.

I know I can rely on you to give me an objective point of view and as always, I expect you to be brutally honest with me.

You know that in Vegas, Atlantic City and in hotels throughout the country, piano players, comedians, magicians and other entertainers perform in small lounges.

Here is my idea – you and I go on the road singing duets, but in order to make the act unique, you would dress in drag and impersonate famous female vocalists. Naturally, because of my lower voice, I would take the male leads.

Again, this is just a thought and I know it may need some refinement.

What do you think? Is this a big idea or not?

You want the truth – I just wanted to give you a hard time for making me cry in front of everyone when you surprised me with my favorite song. You actually did a reasonably good job, but I still need to teach you some of my techniques for moving around on stage. You guys are way too stiff.

Now to some serious stuff.

When Jack was admitted to intensive care following his overdose, I sat in the waiting area for several days. By the third day, after reading a bunch of work-related material, newspapers and magazines and watching television soap operas, I got really bored.

I took a page from your book and wrote a list of things that I would like to do or places I would like to see before I reach my deathbed.

My list is far different than yours in two respects – first, I couldn't come up with creative adventures like you and second, I only had eight items, but as you will see, they are more than challenging given my advanced age. You are much younger and can handle 15 items.

The first thing I wrote was my most significant regret about my life – after much deliberation, I summed it up this way:

I didn't enjoy the journey."

This simply means that I'm in my mid-fifties and by most standards, I'm a "successful" person, but the ride wasn't fun. Actually, probably a *better way to say this is that I didn't enjoy myself along the way – I was always looking forward to reaching the next destination and I never took time to relish the scenery along the way. It was like our trip in the Monterey Bay – you wanted to stop the car more often to look at the sights and I was eager to get to Amy's, despite the fact that there was no rush to reach her place.*

Then came the eight things I would regret if they were not fulfilled before I lay on my deathbed –

1. *Becoming much closer to my family and friends,*
2. *Helping others who are less fortunate,*
3. *Living a quieter life with Kathy in a comfortable house near the ocean,*
4. *Doing more in the theatre and appearing in at least one Broadway play,*
5. *Teaching young people not to repeat my mistakes,*
6. *Playing with my grandchildren,*
7. *Visiting the Galapagos Islands, and*
8. *Spending many more years with my best friend Rocky.*

I have a confession to make to you. After you told me about your condition, I walked around Las Vegas that evening in a complete daze. I asked myself whether I would trade places with you if I had the opportunity to do so – my confession is that I wasn't sure I would at that time. But now, I'm certain that if transferring your disease to me would make you healthy, I would do it without any hesitation.

Even though you may not think so, you have given a little piece of yourself to so many people and if you are able to live a long and healthy life, I know you can have a positive impact on many more.

Rocky, you will never know how special you truly are to those you have touched.

You will also never know what you have done to improve my life and, consequently, the lives of those close to me.

I hope you know that you are my best friend, but I doubt you will ever know how much I love you.

Pete

I'm glad Rocky can't see my face at this moment.

CHAPTER 35

"ENCORE"

BY ROCKY

November 26, 2000 – New Haven, Connecticut

You notice I called this chapter "Encore" – I did so because I frankly had not planned to make another appearance, but I'm doing so by "popular demand" . Actually, I first thought about calling this chapter "Conclusion" or "Closing Act" , but those sound far too final, at least at this stage.

Before I make my personal comments to you, I first need to take care of a little business with Pete.

Dear Pete:

On behalf of Dad and Laura, we wish to thank you and Kathy for an outstanding Thanksgiving weekend. It couldn't have been any better – the best part was seeing our families closer together. On second thought – one thing would have made it more pleasant – I missed our dear friend John. Actually, I hope his mother and new wife are making him a raving lunatic because it couldn't happen to a more fitting person.

I was happy to see that Maggie didn't hold a lasting grudge against me about what happened last year at Evanston. Actually, she was very "sweet" to me, Dad and especially Laura. I can't believe this is the same lady – she is a completely different person. She even looked years younger that she did on our aborted visit. If fact, Laura said that she wasn't anything like I had described.

I wish that Frank and Mr. and Mrs. Pass could have joined us – that would have made the group complete.

By the way, I wasn't sure whether Jack's girlfriend appreciated the "Hot Legs" song in her honor – but at least Jack enjoyed it. After seeing her, I know what you mean – the song title is quite appropriate.

Now, about your proposal to take our act on the road - I like the idea, but with one minor variation. The people in the lounges are typically older types so they would more likely appreciate songs and singers of their vintage.

Here is the twist on your proposal – you'll be the one in drag. With your large hips and full breasts, you have a much better build for the woman's role and your voice can easily go much higher than mine.

I figure we would open the act with a solo rendition by you of **"There's No Business Like Show Business"** featuring you as Ethel Merman. It would bring the house down.

Think about it.

As far as your list is concerned, I'm not at all surprised that you could only come up with eight items. What little creativity you once had was lost many years ago – probably after you completed your first merger.

By the way, speaking of your creative talents, I have to be honest with you about something. How should I say this in a delicate manner? I guess I should just come out with it - your last performance in the community theatre sucked. Don't ever take a role in which you are asked to use a foreign dialect. I know you were supposed to be a French detective, but some of your words sounded like you just arrived from Bombay and at other times, you were using a Spanish accent. Stick to American roles in the future. You should also know that objectively speaking, I think that Kathy is actually more talented than you on stage.

This is probably more than you wanted to hear – so, over and out for now.

Rocky

I have to keep things light with him because I suspect that he had a hard time writing the last part of his e-mail. Judging from his look when we left their house, he obviously knows that my condition is getting worse.

To be honest with you, I expected this time would come, but secretly, I always had a slight hope that I would be an exception – a kind of "miracle" kid who would remain untouched by this disease. But no such luck.

Whether this disease takes me in months or years, I will remain as upbeat as possible, not for myself, but for Dad, Laura, Pete, Kathy, Josh, Jennie and the remainder of my extended family.

Dad thinks that I got our dog (" *Cliff* ") for myself – it's really for him. He will need a companion after I leave.

I don't want you to think that I'm a courageous guy who will be able to bravely confront what I will soon face with AIDS. Actually, as I told you before, the end doesn't bother me very much – it's what will happen between now and then that literally scares the crap out of me. But for the good of those around me, I can't show sadness or fear.

Before I sent the e-mail to Pete, I looked at my "Regret List" and after reading it over one last time, I deleted the list from my computer's memory. Sure, I can always retype the list, but I know this won't be necessary.

The most important thing for me is that Dad, Laura and Pete have all moved on to improve their lives.

In one of the early chapters, I essentially said that my death would end up as a meaningless event. People would be sad, but life moves on and I would be quickly forgotten. I no longer have this belief. I don't want my friends and relatives to dwell on my death, but maybe my early exit will have a beneficial affect for them. When times get tough for them, I hope they will remember me by asking for my advice. I just have the feeling that long after I'm gone, I will continue to help my family and friends.

Last month, I shredded the plans for my funeral service. Instead, I left a note for Dad in a sealed envelope asking him to play an audio tape. The first part of the service would be devoted to six of my favorite songs that are on the tape. There is nothing morbid or solemn, but not heavy rock either. After a moment of silence, the tape continues with my voice saying:

Don't be sad for me or yourselves. Thank you for being my family and for always supporting me. Whenever you need help or guidance, think of me. I will do whatever I can to direct you, just like Mom helped me. I love you all. Please know that because of you, I had no regrets when I went to sleep."

The truth be known, I didn't mind the fact that I was going to die at a young age before the trip with Pete. Now, after that experience, I wish I could live to a ripe old age.

POSTSCRIPT

BY PETER

June 5, 2001 – Westport, Connecticut

   Much has happened since my Thanksgiving report. Here is a summary of important events.

Maggie got married to the meek librarian and continues to live in Connecticut. Her ex, John, called before her marriage in an effort to reconcile after his relationship with the California professor fizzled. Maggie enjoyed telling him to get stuffed up his mother's ass.

Brian decided against enlisting and has enrolled in a community college to study graphic arts. It seems that he has turned his life around after meeting a college bound girl in his senior year of high school.

Josh is still in Utah, but he and Tina severed their relationship. Kathy was correct in her observation that Tina expected a commitment from Josh, but he isn't ready to do so. He continued to work as a part-time ski instructor this past semester and plans to go out for the football team again at the University of Utah.

Amy adopted another child – this time a nine-year old Hispanic girl who has been in foster homes for four years. As a result of her new responsibilities as a mother of two, she no longer participates in demonstrations. Instead, she now expresses her points of view through a rabid letter-writing campaign to elected officials.

As a result of Frank's health problems, his daughter moved with her two sons to Santa Cruz. She has formed a partnership with Amy for the seniors' home project. They have now added a second location, a few doors away from the original house.

Jennie plans to take a sabbatical next year to "find herself." Thank you Amy for contributing to Jennie's "awakening".

Laura is in France, where she is working at the Paris office of a U.S. software company. She has fallen in love with a cook at a local bistro and plans to extend her stay in France for another year.

Maria repaid Rocky the entire amount of the loan. She and her sister opened a beauty shop in Los Angeles. Maria still cuts hair once a week at half the going rate for residents of a neighboring convalescent center.

Cliff died a month ago from a heart attack. Emily plans to remain in Cedar City with her church friends and her pack of dogs. Their son is still a tax fugitive in Mexico, but he has remarried and plans to open his second real estate office servicing Americans seeking a home along the Baja coast.

Jack was lucky enough to participate as one of three investment bankers in a large deal. He then closed his office, took his fee and opened a business called "The Refuge" in Sedona, Arizona. Jack and his wife renovated a large home with three adjoining guesthouses and cater to well-heeled people, mostly from the California entertainment business, seeking a peaceful getaway. You might ask how they could make a living at such an operation. Well, according to Jack, they charge $300 per day, for a five-day minimum, and they are fully booked for the next few months. Jack now sports a beard and long hair and is considered a "guru" for lost souls searching for meaning in their lives. Jack will always be the consummate salesperson.

Michael and Debra are still together and according to Rocky, they have talked about marriage. Michael works part-time at a local accounting firm.

My mother is doing well, but her memory is fading. She also has a "significant other" – a retired real estate person who lost his wife three years ago.

Kathy had surgery to remove a lump in her breast. The bad news was that it was malignant, but fortunately, the disease didn't spread. As a precaution, she underwent radiation therapy and we are hopeful that this is the end of this nightmare. As a result of her experience, Kathy has become active with a breast cancer awareness program.

As for yours truly, I removed myself from the community drama group because of "artistic differences" . Kathy claims that I was actually kicked out, but I disagree because I resigned before I received the kiss-off letter. I now teach a drama class at a local high school and we will stage two major performances this year.

The star of the show, Rocky, is "hanging in" , but he is constantly weakening. The "cocktails" he takes have indeed arrested the spread of the disease, but the side effects have proved to be brutal. He was relatively thin when we took our trip, but he has lost more than 10 pounds since. But he continues to be my hero – he will soon publish a children's book that expands on his story about the crow and sparrow in Central Park.

I often think back to the foundation dinner – it's ironic that the simple act of raising my hand to volunteer for the trip with Rocky changed the course of my life. I was saved by a fortuitous event, and more importantly, by Rocky. Since that night, I have come to the conclusion that someone raised my hand for me – it was my father.

SECOND POSTSCRIPT

August 1, 2001 – Santa Cruz

Amy and Frank stood together at the beach as the sun was setting. It was another dazzling show as the sky turned bright orange.

Then they each released a blue helium-filled balloon.

Frank gazed at the disappearing sun and said, "Goodnight Rocky."

AUTHOR'S NOTE

We have all heard the expression that a particular project is a "labor of love." Writing this book was truly so for me for a variety of reasons.

Since the two main characters in this book gave you personal backgrounds, it would only be appropriate for me to do the same, but in an abbreviated version since my life is not nearly as exciting as Pete's or Rocky's.

I am the youngest of three boys of a first generation family in the United States. My parents immigrated to the United States by way of ship in 1956, when I was seven years old.

While it may sound like a cliché, the reason my parents immigrated was to provide a better life for my brothers and myself. Specifically, they had a desire to raise their sons in a stable political environment and to have the resources for a solid education and a better way of life.

Their dreams were more than fulfilled.

I thank them for sacrificing everything for their sons.

Following a lengthy and successful career at Mattel, I was blessed to have the opportunity to retire early. After traveling, during my working years, an average of one trip each month for over twenty years with many of my journeys outside the U.S., I finally had the opportunity to spend more time with wife, Dianne and son, Ryan.

People speak about defining moments and they often seem trivial at the time, such as Pete's decision to raise his hand at the foundation dinner. In my case, it happened in 1968 when I saw a lovely girl shopping at the drug store where I worked part time. After a while, I got the courage to ask her to the movies. The morning of our date, while playing golf, a close friend urged me to join him at a party that night instead of going on my date. I was literally in the phone booth dialing my date's number when I hung up - I decided not to cancel the date.

That girl was Dianne, who was 16 at the time and I was 20.

The two most important days of my life were the day I married Dianne and the day Ryan was born. All other events pale in comparison. They have always been incredibly loving and supportive, far more than I ever deserved at times. During the writing of this book,

Dianne gave me insight that dramatically improved the quality of this story, and she never let me give up despite the obstacles I encountered.

Shortly after my retirement, I experienced a tragedy that led me to write this book. A close family friend named Joe McKay was diagnosed with terminal colon cancer. Joe was one of those special individuals who are liked by everyone they encounter. He was also a rare breed as an executive in the corporate world – Joe had an enormous heart and always thought of his fellow employees before himself.

Since Joe lived alone, Dianne and I, along with other close friends, became Joe's lifeline during his last year. After spending time with Joe virtually every day during his illness, we became like brothers.

At one time, while we were waiting for one of his radiology treatment, I asked Joe whether he had any regrets about his life. His response will remain confidential. However, this discussion with Joe was the genesis for the story about Rocky and Pete. It is not only speaks of past regrets, but more importantly, about changing or fine-tuning our lives to prevent deathbed regrets. This book is dedicated to Joe.

Thanks to all those who supported this book, including my good friends Rick Dellacquila, Ann-Marie Hennessey, Tony Wainwright and members of my family; Bill, Mike, Anne, Janet, Nick, Chris, Pat and Amelia. My special thanks to my editor Kathleen Marusak for her patience and invaluable comments.

When I wrote this story, I assumed it would never be published. I decided, however, that if I got lucky and it is published, all of my royalties would be divided equally by the following worthy recipients:

> The Hospice Foundation, Torrance, California
>
> Children Affected by AIDS Foundation (" CAAF"), Los Angeles, California

I chose The Hospice Foundation because they were truly angels when Joe was suffering at the end of his life. My donation will be directed to their TrinityKids program, which will treat terminally ill children and as well as helping their families.

The CAAF organization was selected in part because of its founder, Joe Cristina, who is a current Mattel executive and close family friend.

This organization has done wonders in helping children whose lives are somehow impacted by this dreaded disease.

Ned Mansour

P.S. – If case you are wondering, I'm not Pete and my friend Joe is not Rocky. In fact, none of the characters in this story portray anyone I know, although I suspect that subconsciously, the personalities of many people contributed to those of the characters. As far as their travels are concerned, I have never played any golf courses in the Monterey Bay area, but this is one of the items on my "list" . Even though I have traveled to New York City dozens of times in my career, I have never had the opportunity to see Connecticut. This is also on my "list" .

GOD BLESS AMERICA

Thank you for adopting me and my family.

Printed in the United States
24940LVS00004B/316-369